Methadonia

Methadonia

Henry Everingham

Published by Tablo

For Rosie and Victoria

Folly

"Nnnnggghhhh unnnnggggghhhh nnnggghhh. Uuuurrrrgggghhh."

Zac Watts gripped his head, trying to push his fingers and thumbs through his cranium in the desperate hope he could stop the pain. This fucking pain. Christ. If he could just apply specific pressure to his brain, maybe, just maybe, the brutal combination of white noise and screaming agony in his temples and jaw would ease.

Please, he thought. Any minuscule relief.

Zac was familiar with the occasional migraine but this was purely evil. Somewhere from deep inside the cacophony of what sounded like twisting metal came a vaguely lucid thought. What is with the jaw?

He kept gripping and squeezing, emitting groans of the tortured and doomed. What in God's name had happened?

With a modicum of focus he could see the world was on its side. Well, this little corner of the world. From his peculiar perspective, Zac was looking at dozens of geometric grey lines criss-crossing a mottled plain of off-white tiles. They ended at a dank, carmine-coloured wall, with all manner of grease oozing down it.

Closer to home he noticed droplets of blood, probably his. Strangely enough, this neither surprised nor worried him. What did worry him was the jaw. This fucking jaw…

Half a metre away was a tatty black running shoe emerging from a navy blue pants leg. Zac slightly loosened the grip on his head, drawing a long, deep breath through his nose, half expecting the iron-like tang of blood. Instead, the odour of rancid urine and some other horrendous stench forced him to retch up a mouthful of bile, which rolled from the side of his mouth and pooled between the rank floor and his throbbing cheek.

"What do you say? A TKO?"

Zac's world filled with a raucous laugh and, as he looked up at the blue trouser, he noticed three other legs. Peering down at him were two paramedics. One a wiry, hard-faced redhead with her hair tied back so tight it made her look like a test pilot in a centrifuge. The other was a shorter, portly male with a beard so formidable Zac wondered if the guitarist from some long-forgotten southern rock band was moonlighting.

He gently released his throbbing head, levered up off the floor and propped himself up on a cold steel lavatory. He didn't dare look inside; a thick aroma told him exactly what lay in there.

Crouching before Zac, the woman began dabbing his forehead with a gauze. The antiseptic briefly overwhelmed the lingering stench but sadly did nothing for his pain.

"Hey, ahh. What happened to my jaw?"

"Your jaw's the least of your worries, champ," said the beard. "When are you shitheads going to figure out that locking the door is more fucking stupid than the reason you come in here?"

Zac saw that the stall's door was now only two hinges with some splintered remnants. He recalled that when he entered he had to lock it with a coin because the latch handle was missing. At the time something inside him said this was not very clever, but then again any reasoned thinking had taken a back seat long ago.

As he cringed at the tell-tale sign of his ever-so-elegant Zegna belt loosely wound around his left forearm, the woman carefully picked up two disposable plastic syringes, some wrappers with 'naloxone' printed across them in bright red letters, and Zac's much-treasured glass syringe. It was apparent they were all going into a small, yellow sharps container.

"Don't throw that out. It was my late grandfather's. He was a…"

The devices rattled into the emptiness of the plastic.

"… a dental surgeon. It's the only thing of his…" His voice tapered off into a pathetic mumble.

The beard laughed again.

"Hey T, that's better than that kid who said her mother needed them to brandy apricots."

T gave a half-hearted smirk, then fixed her gaze on Zac. He wasn't sure what was coming, but through the agony of whatever was going on with his mandible, he felt an overwhelming sense of guilt and shame. Yes, his grandfather had been a dental surgeon. And yes, it was a remnant of his surgical implements. But Zac also understood the last thing Pop would have ever dreamt of was his only grandchild using it to self-administer heroin.

"How much do you use?"

He couldn't look at her now. She asked him in a way that was devoid of any blame or judgment, but he remained silent. Not because he was dishonest. Or stupid. Simply because he didn't know. It wasn't like he was prescribing measured amounts to himself at specific intervals. His life had become some carnival express train of crazy, and drugs were now more incidental than foremost. Or so he kept telling himself. Confusion had become a big part of Zac's life.

The paramedic took a business card from her shirt pocket, suspending it between the two of them, slightly beyond his reach.

"I don't know what your story is," she said. "But going by your clothes, that watch, your fancy briefcase, well…" She looked around the graffiti- and shit-stained cubicle. "I get the feeling this isn't what you want to be. But believe me, you will become who you don't want to be." She gave him a knowing look and, for a second, Zac felt a strange affinity with her.

"Make an appointment."

He expected her to drop it in front of him in a gesture of disdain, but she lowered the card into his limp hand and patted his shoulder before gathering the yellow box and the paramedic's kit bag from behind him.

"You know he'll be dead by Christmas," the beard grunted.

"Fuck you," she muttered back.

A MONTH later Zac tentatively pushed open the door of Paradise Palms. For all the grandiosity of its name, Paradise Palms was neither a seaside resort nor nursery. In fact it was one of the furthest places from paradise imaginable. After the paramedic had given Zac the card, he stuffed it into his coat pocket and promptly forgot about it. It wasn't until he was dropping off some clothes at the dry cleaners that he found it. On the front was the business name, a phone number and address. On the back it said 'Heroin problem? We can help you.'

Zac knew he had a problem - a $250-a-day problem that wasn't going away. He called Paradise Palms to discover it was a methadone clinic. He then spent a few days researching the drug to work out whether he actually needed it. This included a home clinical trial in which his heroin withdrawals started becoming unbearable after 16 hours and which spurred him on to arrange an assessment.

Zac sat in the waiting room of the clinic, nervously listening for his name to be called. The words on the back of the card had played on his conscience for over a week. People in secure, well-paid jobs don't go on methadone, he told himself. But, then again, those same people probably don't have drug overdoses in public toilets.

The walls in the clinic were splashed with posters promoting sexual health services, hepatitis C treatments and 'morning after' medications to help stave off HIV transmission. A muted television was broadcasting a daytime chat show where three almost identical blondes were reverently passing around a gaudy glass pitcher. Their accentuated facial expressions were in total contrast to the stoned, bored looks on the couple sitting opposite Zac. And his, for that matter. He flipped through a pile of tattered old supermarket tabloids, hoping there'd be a publication of some substance. The dull withdrawal cramps in his thighs were taunting him to get up and leave just as his name was called.

Zac had been expecting Dr Vanessa Asher to look like, well, a doctor - lab coat, stethoscope draped around her neck, horn-rimmed glasses. Instead, her purple jeans and T-shirt with a cartoon of a cowgirl straddling a syringe - the slogan 'Fuck safe Shoot clean' emblazoned above it - reminded him that stereotypes were for fools. As she ushered him into her office, Zac began to make obsequious pleasantries.

"Why have you come here?" she interrupted before he'd even sat down.

He struggled to conjure a reply he thought she might want to hear, so simply said, "to get off heroin".

Despite his tailored appearance and polite demeanour, Dr Asher could see he was already in narcotic withdrawal. Zac fidgeted with his attaché case handle, his face had a waxy sheen and his pupils were dilated.

"When was your last shot, Zac?"

"A tenth of a gram late last night. Before bed."

She reiterated what she'd told him over the phone the previous day; how methadone blocks the receptors and diminishes the effect of heroin.

"When can I come off it?" he asked.

This was probably the most asked question she heard from new patients. No matter how long they'd spent using narcotics there was always an urgency for them to turn their lives around as fast as possible.

"How much do you use each day?"

"Three $50 shots," he lied coyly.

She tapped away at her computer, then looked at a laminated list.

"Let's start you on 40mg a day, and we can reassess that in a few weeks."

Zac had done some internet research around the effects of opioid substitution treatment, and was chuffed at the prospect of being off methadone within a month. What he missed was that, in all likelihood, it would be at least a year.

Winter

FOR THE sixth time that day, Zac picked up the phone and punched in the number. Somewhat aggressively, too. Bored rigid, he leant on his elbow with the handset pushed against his ear, waiting for the now-too-familiar 'I can't take your call at the moment, but if you care to…' blah blah. He wondered how a wealthy celebrity lawyer-turned-politician on a ridiculous six-figure wage could sound so dull. Listening to the message yet again Zac contemplated the significance of an old candy wrapper hidden in among the newspaper cuttings, photos, badges, stickers, cartoons and postcards pinned to his desk's partition. Then it came to him. Years before he'd interviewed a famous rock singer. He remembered how enamoured of her he was, not just because she was a true star but because the chemistry between them was palpable, and at the completion of their 30-minute professional encounter she touched the back of his hand and suggested…

"David Chambers," snapped an unexpected voice.

"Ahh, yes, Mr Chambers. Hi there. My name is Zac Watts. I'm a journalist with…"

"I know who you are, and I highly doubt I have anything to either say or discuss with you."

"Mr Chambers," said Zac quickly. "I respect and understand you must be under a lot of pressure at the moment, but if I could just…"

"You don't understand or respect shit. Because if you did, you and your colleagues at that rag would stop to think about the ruin you visit upon innocent people, for what? To prop up your failing circulation? Give yourselves some pathetic semblance of… of…. of relevance? Just out of curiosity, Mr Watts, why did you choose to become an asshole?"

"Sir, your son has been charged with the embezzlement of $3 million from a leukemia charity and…"

The line went dead.

Zac returned the handset into its cradle, stared at the wrinkled waxed candy wrapper and grinned impishly.

"I think I'll frame you."

ZACHARY WATTS was born to be a precocious brat. Not that he had any choice in this; he was indulged from the get-go. By deliberate design, he was conceived the night after his mother and father spent a day wandering around The Louvre. Throughout his gestation they referred to him as both l'entrecôte and Lafite; the former in honour of the delectable meal they'd had that evening in a romantic bistro on Rue Daguerre, the latter as a reminder of the two exquisite 1959 bottles of Chateau Rothschild they reverently consumed in both the restaurant and their suite - one in which Dali had reputedly lived. While Ruth Watts was "with child" (as her husband Ian so pompously referred to her pregnancy) they would only play Debussy and the occasional Italian opera.

Instead of classic children's books his parents were reading him Shakespeare when he was in preschool. On the rare occasions he was allowed to watch television, it was either esoteric Czech claymations or long and slow documentaries on architecture and composers. By the time he started school - at Ian Watts' exclusive alma mater, of course - they were vetting his friends, based primarily on their parents' professions. In year five he formed a particularly strong bond with a boy called Charlie. They had a similar level of social awkwardness, even looked alike, and for the first time in his life Zachary felt truly connected to someone else. He and Charlie would excitedly while away the time talking about their three favourite topics - steam ships, Zeppelins and medieval Japan. Their fervent imaginations fostered a dream in which they would one day time travel and observe the first Mongol invasion of Kyushu from the safety of their personal dirigible. They embodied innocence and joy, so neither boy fully comprehended why they were ridiculed, punched and ostracised when they would occasionally walk around holding hands. When word of this got back to his parents, Zac was forbidden from associating with his "sick friend" again.

As Zac continued to withdraw, his already exceptional grades began to improve even more. He retreated into his own world of reading and studying, which suited his parents just fine. They wanted him to always be under their watchful eyes, kept away from an imagined world they feared would corrupt and hinder the academic growth of their wunderkind.

All this changed in year 11 when, after a music lesson one of the older students pulled out an LP - its cover graced with a decrepit, yellow-tinted man in a large dog collar. The boy put the record on and an avalanche of electric guitars confirmed the disdain for rock music Zac's parents had instilled in him. But they'd also taught him to suffer in silence so he fought to ignore the glissando dexterity of the guitarists and went about cleaning, retuning and stowing his cello. By the time he'd put his music folio in order and disassembled the music stand, the record had segued into a soft, simple ballad, carried along by a monotonous male vocal. By now Zac's attention was pricked and he listened intently to the lyrics.

"Who's this?" he asked.

Zac's rapport with René had solely been around their music classes with Miss Kozlowski. Like all his academic pursuits Zac was comfortable operating in his own world, and teachers and students alike had long given up trying to engage him in any conversation of note.

"Lou, of course," René replied.

He kept listening, entranced by the poetry of the lyrics. Suddenly it burst into a loud, tempered rock riff which hit Zac in his gut. The melody and sustains flowed into his soul, then returned to the song's placid beginning.

"Lou who?"

René stopped waxing his viola and turned to the dorky cellist.

"Why, do you like it?" he asked, handing Zac the LP cover.

Zac opened the gatefold and read the six lines of lyrics in the top left-hand corner.

"Yeah, it's good. Hey René, can I ask you a question? What's smack?"

René took the album off the platter, carefully put it in its plastic sleeve and handed it to Zac.

"It's all yours, my friend."

By the time Zac had played that particular song half a dozen times that evening, he knew two things. What smack was. And whatever it was, he wanted it.

IT WAS possibly Zac's favourite row of shops in the world. Or, to be more precise, his neighbourhood. Travel was something he craved but could never do. Not by design of course; mere circumstance. There's a good reason why methadone is known as liquid handcuffs.

He stood on the opposite side of the street and pondered the vista - his own postcard of weird. There was the candle shop Wax'N'Ollies, emitting a zephyr of seductive scents that battled the lingering smell of hops from the local brewery. The proprietor was an avid skater so the walls were adorned with dozens of skateboards. Or rollerboards, as she preferred to call them. Due to the proximity of a nearby theatre, it wasn't uncommon for touring musicians to pop in and purchase candles to counter the funk of the venue's dressing rooms. Not long after opening her store Matika cheekily asked Beastie Boy Adam Yauch to sign one of the decks, thus beginning a trend. The walls were now an internationally famous autograph book.

To the right was Fat Doris's brothel. Whether or not the proprietor was named Doris, or even corpulent, Zac didn't know. The joint was actually called The Candy Store, but for decades locals had called it by its sobriquet. It was probably owned by someone called Thug. Or Brick.

Zac was on a first-name basis with at least six of the women who currently worked there and au fait with dozens of previous employees yet he'd never set foot inside. No, he'd made their acquaintances in Paradise Palms, the anonymous establishment next door. While The Candy Store announced itself with an illuminated box hanging from the awning, a flashing neon one in its window and a hand-painted sign on the entrance, the Palms was a wall of blackened glass, with a discreet street number on the door and a carpet of cigarette butts before it.

Here was Zac's Mecca. For the past 10 years he'd made his pilgrimage twice a week at 7am and queued with the rest of the faithful. When the previous devotee had moved on, he'd approach the counter and make wonderfully polite banter with Alan, an impeccably maintained gentleman whose immaculate hair and beard, and careful application of foundation and lipstick, made it impossible to determine his age. He always said he was 48, but going by his taste in movie stars and music, Zac had pegged him for late 60s - if not more. Their discussions were usually around any tidbits of celebrity gossip Zac had picked up in the newsroom, or Zac feigning interest in what was happening at the local repertory theatre where Alan's 'real' job was - "as the wardrobe mistress, darling". He would pay Alan $56 on Mondays to cover the cost of his weekly prescription then take six steps to a window sporting a piece of high-tech gadgetry which not only 'read' Zac's irises to confirm he was one of the clinic's clients, but also made sure he would receive the correct dose of methadone. He'd stare into this small plastic box and wait until an electronically generated voice ordered him to "Please centre your eyes". This done, the machine on the other side of the glass would automatically dispense 8mls of bright pink syrup into a small plastic cup, which Zac would dutifully drink. On Thursdays the woman overseeing this would give Zac three small brown bottles containing his weekend takeaway doses. Lucy liked Zac for two simple reasons; he was one of the few who didn't utter "bottoms up" as he threw the medication back, and he always thanked her.

HE HADN'T even logged on to his computer when Carol Sanchez, the paper's chief of staff, called out across the newsroom.

"Watts, don't get too comfortable. The boss wants us."

The two of them paraded across the floor and into the boss's office. Sue Molloy, The Register's editor in chief, had started out as a cadet reporter with an eye to writing about popular culture and fashion. After a stint on the industrial relations round she had developed a fierce interest in politics and law - to the extent that she did a law degree at night. By the time she was the paper's political editor, politicians from all camps both loathed and feared her. No-one had a clue what her own political leanings were and, for that, Zac had nothing but respect for her.

"Let me guess," he said sinking into the leather Chesterfield sofa opposite her desk. "That moron David Chambers has been threatening lawyers and lynching parties."

"You wish." She peered across the top of her spectacles. "Let's deal with him after you've actually filed the story."

As Sue looked out at the impressive midtown view Zac wondered why he was in there. He'd written a number of good articles recently, and both Carol and Sue had showered him with accolades for these efforts. At best, there must have been some disgruntled reader taking umbrage at one of his reports.

"How long have you been on methadone, Zac?"

Her directness shocked him. He felt confused. Was he about to be sacked?

"I, uh… about a decade."

He looked to Carol, disappointed and betrayed. She was the only person he had confided in, and there was no way Sue could have seen him going into the clinic because that area was way off her radar. Carol just mouthed "it's okay".

Finally, the editor turned around and shook her head.

"You're one dark horse, Zac. I can't imagine what got you on to that. Obviously you and heroin became very familiar with each other at some point. Tell me, and please be honest, do you still use it? Heroin?"

"Er, no. Not at all. No."

Sue sat down, examining him across the desk.

"Truthfully, the last time you used it?"

"Well over 10 years ago," he said.

"What other drugs do you do?"

"None," he confessed, heart pounding. "I can't even remember the last time I got drunk. Honestly Sue, I went on to methadone and just never bothered to get off it. Why has this suddenly become a problem?"

"Oh shit, you're not in trouble. Jesus, sorry, Zac. You're okay. No, it's Wanda Faragher. She's finished her three years in the Washington bureau and wants out. I want you to replace her."

This was the last thing he expected. Zac looked from Sue to Carol and back again, trying to figure out what to say but he was, quite literally, speechless.

WHETHER it was due to his particularly brutal upbringing, Olaf Shapiro could never be sure, but somewhere along the line he'd developed an extraordinary aptness for diplomacy. Holding court at The Hague might have been ambitious but he rarely failed at helping two people work their way toward a resolution in whatever paltry dispute they were feuding about.

Of course, Olaf was neither a human rights lawyer nor a mediator; he was simply a counsellor at In The Light, a rehabilitation house for people wanting to come off methadone.

ITL was the brainchild of Aisha Daniels, an over-qualified academic who woke one day wishing there was more to life than writing staid government health policy. The same morning that had brought a distressing phone call from her oldest friend, telling her that her only son had died from a heroin overdose after abruptly ceasing a three-year methadone regime. It was a tragedy that got Aisha's mental cogs turning: why are people on methadone marginalised? What do they do when they want to get off it? A few phone calls to doctors and health industry honchos got her the answers: they're modern day lepers, and rarely do they stop taking it.

Within six months she had duchessed philanthropists, donors, medical professionals and other luminaries to help her acquire the run-down two-storey mansion which she converted into a residential rehab for what she so affectionately called "methadonians".

Aisha never failed to smile at the memory of when she used the term at the organisation's first board meeting, and her lawyer and dear friend Jean-Pierre raised his eyes from behind his bifocals and innocently asked, "And are they at war with the Heroinites?"

Her two greatest assets, however, were Dylan Dunaway and Olaf Shapiro. Dylan had worked as a drug counsellor in rehabs all over the globe, from basic hospital units in Glasgow to gated Zuma Beach retreats catering to Hollywood A-listers. Olaf was an erudite junkie for whom Dylan had developed a deep affection while nursing him through a heroin detox/rehab in northern Thailand. After he 'graduated' Olaf decided he wanted to be like his new hero and mentor and got himself a counselling degree. Neither of them really expected Olaf to go anywhere with it, but he did. Quietly and humbly.

When Dylan got word about Aisha's rehab proposal, Olaf was the first person he nominated. And as they learned to adapt to each others' styles - and Aisha's expectations - they became a formidable trio.

OLAF LEARNT early on that the best way to resolve conflict was to allow both parties time and space. While his fellow counsellor Emma Hawkins would hurriedly control and direct the individuals into a perfunctory handshake and apology ("otherwise you'll be here all fucking night") Olaf was more interested in studying the dynamics of the two and dissecting their loathing. Emma's method, Olaf soon realised, only delayed the inevitable - and one of the other staff would end up dealing with a far bigger drama within 24 hours.

One of his first ITL conflict resolution sessions (or "love ins", as the clients sarcastically called them) was between two young men who were on the brink of violence one afternoon. With Olaf acting as referee, the two men took a 'support buddy' into the chill-out room and got down to business.

Olaf brought his own support buddy - a green rubber drinks coaster. This was an idea he'd picked up in the one session of relationship counselling he'd ever done. At his then girlfriend's insistence they went to see a therapist who told them that while one was holding the foam ball she issued, the other could not interrupt. Which was great, except the therapist spent the whole 50-minute session calling Olaf 'Craig'. This amused him no end, but drove the Goddess Of Doom into such a frenzy that she had an utter conniption at the end of the session and refused to pay.

Two things came of that encounter - one of the wildest afternoons of rage-fuelled sex they ever had, and the introduction of the 'I'm talking' prop. On the few occasions they argued, Bori the green rubber drink coaster was employed, and most effectively, too. When their relationship ended, Olaf took custody of Bori.

The basis of the current conflict between the two rehab residents was from when they had been in prison together. With the aid of Bori, Olaf learned that it came down to an incident when Knucklehead One was slipped some contraband during a family visit and refused to give Knucklehead Two some of the drugs he'd not so subtly inserted into his anus during the visit. For 10 minutes they argued over something that Knucklehead One could clearly not remember. Other prisoner's names were invoked, but all that did was confuse the issue more.

"Dave was there. He'd remember."

"Yeah right. That cunt."

Or, Olaf's favourite part of the discourse.

"Just ask Animal."

"Which Animal?"

"You know, Animal with all the ink."

This went on for nearly half an hour. The support buddies occasionally waded in with well-intentioned but misguided observations. It was going nowhere. Until…

"You ask anyone who was in Long Bay nick that year," Two said.

One curled his lip, looking back at him incredulously, and Olaf could tell he was he was perplexed about something deeper.

"I've never been to the Bay," he said.

"Nah, you were there. Trust me."

Olaf had to use every ounce of self control not to laugh.

"I've only ever done one laggin'. Three years in Parklea. Only time I left there was on release."

"Bullshit. You were in the Bay."

"I swear on my kid's eyes, I have never been anywhere except fuckin' Parklea!"

"So your missus never slipped you a bag of crystal at the Bay?"

"Ice?! Fuck off. I've never even touched that shit."

After it was established that they had, indeed, never encountered each other, Olaf invited them to shake hands, and told them they had to give the other a heartfelt compliment in morning group for the next five days. Within a minute the atmosphere went from an undercurrent of tension to an almost convivial air of silliness.

From that day on, any love-ins Olaf presided over began with him asking if both parties were referring to the other, and not someone else. However, nothing could have prepared him for Jesse and Simon.

Simon was admitted on a Wednesday afternoon. He was expected on the Tuesday morning, but in a series of flustered phone calls throughout that day Simon explained how he had to check in with his parole officer, pick up jewellery from a pawnbroker, say goodbye to his mother, sell an exhaust system to some bikers, buy cigarettes and gum - and lots more. Dylan, who took the calls, relayed this comical tale of woe to Aisha.

"Well, he's certainly coming to the right place," she said. "Tell him to be here first thing in the morning."

First thing in the morning for Simon turned out to be mid-afternoon, at roughly the same time Jesse was due. Jesse was the antithesis of Simon; he epitomised institutionalisation. Due at the rehab at 2pm, he arrived 20 minutes early and lurked down the block. His morning had been spent emptying his fridge, getting a very neat buzzcut, buying socks and underwear, and having his utilities disconnected until further notice. He checked his watch at 1.57pm, wandered up the street and pushed the doorbell exactly on the hour.

When Dylan opened the door, Jesse called him "chief", for the first and last time. He walked in with one large black duffel bag and a copy of the day's tabloid. In doing so, he ignored the people gawking at him as he moved through the building; this was a dynamic with which he was all too familiar, and he knew they had all the time in the world to get acquainted.

Dylan loved clients like Jesse. They were invariably accustomed to prolonged admission processes, offering little resistance to the prying questions, and not at all interested in discussing minutiae. Jesse knew it was all pro-forma nonsense that would have little, if any, bearing on his sojourn.

"Been to prison, Jesse?"

"Eight times."

"Last release?"

"Seven months ago."

"Length of that sentence?"

"Twenty nine months."

"On parole?"

"Five months left."

Et cetera. No embellishments. No justifications or explanations. It was Jesse's way of preserving some dignity. Regardless of his crimes, he wasn't proud of having been imprisoned. Besides, Dylan wasn't the slightest bit interested in his tawdry past.

As they waded through the formalities, it was Olaf who went to answer the second doorbell. Soon, the hall resonated with a voice which sounded like it was trying to conduct a frenetic conversation with a dozen people at once. Jesse and Dylan glanced at each other with the same look; their shared moment of zen was about to end.

"So, this is your office is it Olaf?" Simon queried at 100 decibels. "Hey, isn't that a picture of what's his name? The Beatles guy?"

He lurched towards the two men staring at a computer screen and began to ingratiate himself but Dylan cut him off.

"Hi, you must be Simon. We spoke yesterday."

Unlike Jesse's stoic entrance, Simon's arrival had all the mania of a rodeo clown on crack. He was about to launch into more raving when Dylan raised one hand in a 'stop' manner, and put his index finger in front of his lips.

"Simon, we are very busy here, and I need you to sit down and wait calmly for Olaf to get you into our system. Can you do that for me?"

Simon, taken aback, simply nodded.

"Thanks buddy," Dylan said, knowing fully well this wedge of calm would not last long.

Dylan continued his interrogation of Jesse while Olaf rifled through various documents and prepared Simon's profile. Simon continued to fidget, jiggling his leg up and down at such a rapid rate that it shook the whole floor.

Jesse turned to Simon, glared at his pumping knee, then up to his morose, unshaven face, back to the knee, and up to his face again. Simon squirmed and his beady eyes darted around nervously.

"What?"

Jesse met his stare with the unblinking technique he'd perfected in various jail yards over two decades. Simon gulped and, eventually, the leg steadied.

"Thanks," said Jesse, and turned back to Dylan's computer.

He sat calmly watching the cursor dart around Dylan's screen while Olaf double-checked the details of a fax of Simon's methadone script. But then...

"Does that passive-aggressive crap work for you? Is that how you move through the world, is it? Threatening people with your suppressed violence. Well let me tell you something, champion..."

"Hey. Hey. Hey. Simon. It's okay, I need you to breathe," said Olaf calmly.

But Simon kept ranting at Jesse, who didn't react in the slightest. While Olaf continued the futile coaxing, Dylan diplomatically invited Jesse to join him outside for a smoke.

Sweat was now pouring down Simon's brow and his leg had resumed its incessant jiggling. He was desperate to engage Olaf in the perceived drama but the counsellor sensed there was something bigger at play.

"When did you have your last dose of methadone, Simon?"

The new client twisted at the sleeve of his soiled white satin jacket, a memento of some Malaysian motorbike race from years before, and gasped for air.

"It's okay Simon. You're here now, and we're not about to throw you out. When did you last dose?"

Simon grabbed the jerking knee with one hand, and pushed the fingers of his other hand hard against his protruding cheek bone, as though he had some phantom toothache.

"A few days ago. I can't remember," he stammered.

"Good, thanks for that Simon. Now, tell me. Have you slept since then?"

"Why are you asking me that? What are you saying?"

Again, without breaking the orchestrated calm of his own delivery, Olaf continued.

"Simon, you look like you've been doing it really hard. And I'm concerned for you. Now, as I said, you've got a bed here. But you've been on a meth bender - and that's okay; you've just been doing what you normally do. But I need to know exactly what and how much you've been using so we can get you settled in here. Can you tell me that?"

Olaf was careful not to inflame the situation. From his years of working with drug users, he could tell if someone was even slightly intoxicated or withdrawing. What was very apparent here though was that Simon was in major withdrawal - from two drugs.

"I booted all my takeaways after I got them, and I dunno. I guess I've been in a shooting gallery since."

Olaf checked the fax the clinic had sent of Simon's last dose details. He wanted to scream when he saw that six days beforehand Simon had been issued with five 15ml bottles of methadone. All up that was 375mg of the opioid, more than enough for a fatal overdose. He knew that ITL's doctor would have requested Simon be given no more than one day's supply, but he was also used to administrative fuck ups like this. Then there was the fact that some clinics were more than happy to see the backs of their more challenging clients, a category into which Simon clearly fitted.

"Tell me about your last few days, Simon."

"I really need a cigarette, ah… what's your name again?"

"Olaf. Just wait a second."

He surreptitiously sent Dylan a text message. "He wants a smoke."

The response was immediate. "Take him out the back door."

The two of them sat outside for half an hour, during which time Simon worked his way through four cigarettes and a litany of debauchery. After he received his takeaway doses, he vaguely remembered he and his girlfriend going home, injecting a bottle each, then heading to a local bar to score 'xannies' - a benzodiazepine which, when misused, fast tracks the consumer into a blackout. Not surprisingly, time wasn't a major factor after that. Simon dimly recalled dealing with some bikers and seeing his mother, and became quite animated while regaling Olaf with the sordid details of a non-stop orgy at the shooting gallery. Olaf was by no means a prude, but Simon's overly descriptive recollections involving slings, belts, dildos, fisting, gang banging and every other facet of chemsex were thoroughly pornographic. Olaf remembered a film critic once saying "other people's drug experiences are a bit like other people's sex lives - boring", and wondered how he would have reviewed Simon's get-together. Doubly boring?

The worrying aspect, though, was that Simon hadn't had his methadone for a couple of days, and as soon as that morning's benzos and antipsychotics began to wear off, he would slide into an unforgiving withdrawal.

Olaf made a call to Eugenio Prato, ITL's doctor. Known simply as Dr Gene, loquacious didn't begin to describe him; Aisha called him Pratchat. He was frighteningly intelligent, unbelievably engaging and never boring.

"Young Olaf," he answered in a theatrically camp baritone. "To what do I owe this pleasure?"

Knowing that the good doctor had a propensity for interrupting himself to recall some fantastic and dubious escapade, Olaf got straight to the point.

"Gene, I have a guy here who is on 75mg a day, hasn't dosed for a few days but thinks he might have had a couple of street doses, and is at the tail end of a methamphetamine bender. Oh, and he's been eating benzos and antipsychotics like candy."

"The silly boy," bellowed the doctor. "Well, he'll certainly be feeling a bit ordinary by cocktail hour."

Olaf could hear the doctor tapping away at a keyboard.

"Here he is, the poor dear."

More tapping ensued.

"Aaaand, here's his script transfer. Why don't I make some calls, you get him over to the pharmacy in an hour and we'll sort the old darling out."

"I can't thank you enough, Gene. You're worth your weight in treasury bonds."

The doctor roared with laughter.

"Oh, young Olaf. Either gold is fucked, or my girth is. Listen, have you perchance encountered that fabulous med school intern we have working here? She's into that hideous noise you assail yourself with, has tattoos galore and a mind like a laser beam. I foresee a beautiful future with you two having extraordinary adventures and vile offspring."

Olaf smiled, and looked across at Simon while Dr Prato continued his cupidesque rant. There were no smiles on Simon, though. Slumped, beaten and looking like death, the effects of the pills were visibly wearing off. Welcome to the world of consequences.

IT TOOK Olaf fewer than five minutes to get from his front door to the rehab. On foot. The back of his property abutted the alley behind ITL. There were exactly 58 steps between their respective rear entrances, but he never went anywhere near the lane, for fear that the residents would discover where he lived. As much as he enjoyed working with his clients, he had no desire to have them darken his doorway. Or, more probably, his bathroom window - with a brick. That's why whenever he finished his shift he always walked toward the local train station then back-tracked down a parallel street.

The convenience of living so absurdly close to work was twofold. First, he could set his alarm quite late, and second, in the event of an emergency, he could be there before Aisha or Dylan. In spite of the clientele and their dysfunctional lifestyles, real emergencies were few and far between. When any occurred they were usually limited to day-to-day events like people slicing themselves while dish washing, minor sprains and the odd scald from boiling water.

The one that went down in ITL lore was when young Jack overdosed. This was in the days before naloxone was kept on site, so when a client found Jack unconscious in the bathroom it was hysteria plus. Dylan rushed in and commenced CPR on Jack's undernourished body - to no avail. He was violently pumping Jack's sternum and heart almost halfway into his body cavity when Gene Prato walked in.

"How long has he been gone?" he asked Aisha, who stood looking on, teary and paralyzed with disbelief and shock.

"Eight minutes," she replied.

Jack was on his sixth tour of duty in four years; testament to the tenacity of drug users seeking respite, but also to Aisha's boundless compassion and her inability to say no to them. Also, Jack was one of the special ones - he could be cheeky, youthful, manipulative, defiant, scared and disrespectful, all before breakfast. And still he was adored. Maybe too much, to his detriment. What was apparent in the bathroom, though, was there would be no more rehab stints for Jack.

"You can stop, Dylan. I'm declaring him dead," said the doctor.

Dylan continued his furious pumping, urging "come on" every now and then. Gene assumed he hadn't been heard. He softly touched Dylan's shoulder and repeated that he was declaring the young man dead.

"Do what you fucking want," Dylan barked. "I'm not giving up on the little cunt now."

The doctor stepped back and gently ushered Aisha away. She threw her arms around him and let out an anguished howl. It was a noise he'd heard far too many times, and one he would never become accustomed to. He embraced Aisha and soothed her while she fell apart. Even a veteran medico like Gene was affected by death sometimes, and he could feel her agony. Dylan's too. Her immediate process was grief while his was rage. Dealing with the undealable, he thought.

Jack was, in his urchin ways, like one of their own. He'd been bounced from foster homes to youth detention centres and back since he was three, so hitting a drug rehab at 16 was inevitable. Aisha had negotiated a forest of red tape to get the youth in there, and now... part of her was dying with him. Jack had been a special kid to her and, as she watched his lifeless body being pumped by Dylan, grief overwhelmed her and she began to sink to the floor. At that moment, a violent guttural sound exploded from the bathroom. At first, Gene thought Dylan had hit critical emotional mass and lost it - he certainly wasn't prepared for what he saw. The counsellor was rolling Jack's now very alive and flailing body to stop him choking on his own vomit. The young man was heaving and gasping. Gene raced back in, yelling for an ambulance to be called.

Jack was sitting upright, propped up from behind in Dylan's arms. His face was a ghastly grey - offset by a splat of vomit on his right cheek and shoulder. The scene looked like a study for a modern La Pieta. The near lifeless manchild and the beatific apostle in a check flannel shirt.

"What the fuck?" Jack asked no-one in particular.

"Our thoughts exactly, Jack," said Gene, checking the pulse in the boy's wrist. "Who's the prime minister?"

Jack continued his blank stare while taking short breaths.

"Hey Doc," Dylan said. "You'd be better off asking him his favourite musician."

As Gene started to rephrase the question, Jack broke into a wide, happy stoned grin, tilting his head back toward his saviour.

"Fuckin' Tupac. All day, dude."

OLAF'S SLUMBER was broken by the raucous duelling guitars of his ringtone, well before the alarm was expected. He blindly slid a finger across its facade and mumbled.

"Sorry to wake you," said a frantic voice. "It's Sarah. I think the two new guys are gonna kill each other."

Sarah was one of the overnight staff at the rehab. Their job was to basically finish any paperwork and filing, make themselves available to the clients, dispense bedtime medications and make sure lights were out by 11.30pm.

As he rolled to the edge of his bed, peering up through a tree at the dawning light, he could hear Simon's hysterical bellowing from up the alley.

"Right," Olaf said. "Grab Ronnie and Luke, tell Simon to get into the shower, and tell Jesse to be cool and hang around in his room. And tell them that the neighbours just called and they're going to call the cops if they don't shut up."

"Really, did they call you?"

Olaf looked at the phone, rolling his eyes.

"Forget the neighbours stuff. Just try to separate them."

He cut the call and looked at the time. 6:07. Those uncivilized brutes. His gut reaction was to throw on some clothes and race over there, but that didn't seem right. After all, had one of the clients reacted in a similar situation they'd have been castigated for going into 'rescue' mode. Instead, he fired up a pot of coffee, put on his current favourite alt-country playlist and lost himself in the shower for the duration of Gillian Welch's *I Dream a Highway*.

Olaf wandered into the office an hour later to find Sarah tapping away at her keyboard and looking very pleased with herself.

"I've already written some case notes on what I believe happened, and I've sent everyone an email about it."

"Fabulous," said Olaf. "But let's go through that later. And a hot tip, kiddo. Never write what you believe. Just stick with the facts, Max."

Much to the frustration of his colleagues, Olaf had a policy of not opening emails for the first two hours of a shift. He'd read a study that said work-related communiques too often contained some belittling crap from management, and was not a good way to start a work day. Nowhere had this been more evident than in his previous career - the poisonous, shallow world of commercial radio. Not that Aisha ever sent such an email. In fact, one would be hard pressed coming up with a time she was even slightly mean. Still, old habits die hard; Sarah's emailed report would just have to wait.

"I'm going to drag these two palookas into a conflict resolution now. You're more than welcome to sit in on it, or..." he paused, knowingly. "Or you can head off and have an early breakfast with Mr Sarah."

She beamed. Sarah was still in the giddy throes of her recent nuptials, so the opportunity to split from work early would likely be a godsend.

"Wow. You're kidding! I'd love to watch a conflict reso."

As is often the case, the love-in was unpredictable. Maybe Jesse and Simon got all their *sturm und drang* crap out at sunrise. Or maybe the worst was yet to come. Regardless, both were unnervingly civil to each other during the course of the mediation. Simon's emotions became a bit elevated a few times, but Olaf would have been more worried had they not. Jesse was the interesting one. At one point, while Simon was trumpeting his pansexuality, Jesse just sat nodding in agreement. Not missing an opportunity to wind his adversary up, Simon proposed that everyone ("including you Jesse") might be bisexual. Jesse just shrugged and shook his head.

"No, Simon. I don't think so. But it's an interesting theory."

The two of them worked through their differences and, as is so often the case, the source of their frustrations with the other was what they disliked within themselves. Whether they'd ever sort those differences out was another story. At the end of the encounter, Olaf invited their two support peers and Sarah to offer some input. The first two gave the obligatory "just move through it and seek support from us when you need it", which was code for "can we just get the fuck out of this bullshit and have a coffee and smoke". Sarah was the wild card. She looked both excited and anxious, clasped her hands, bit her bottom lip and gave her opinion.

"Well, it's funny because - and I don't want to upset you two or anything - but you guys are so much alike. You both are so used to being you, you don't know how to be anything else. Simon, it's like you long to be able to filter your emotions and behaviours the way Jesse does, but you struggle with it. And Jesse, why do I get the feeling that you would love to be able to be not so pent up? Don't get me wrong, I'm not saying you're pent up pent up..."

Jesse interrupted her.

"I get what you're saying, Sarah, and it's true."

He looked across at Simon.

"She's right," he said. "I hate that I see a bit of me in you. I'll be honest. I judge you for who you are. But I don't want to. Who am I to tell you how to live? But you know what? I came here to change. And if change means accepting some hard truths about myself, and, and others, well... I'm prepared to give it a go."

Either Jesse was a consummate actor, or he meant what he said. Olaf was banking on the latter. The two men looked at each, neither showing a hint of animosity or aggression.

"Me too," Simon said in a measured voice that didn't seem to belong to him. "You're the kind of guy I'd like to be, but I just can't ever slow down enough."

They both smirked before Jesse broke into a wider grin and shook his head. When they rose to their feet Simon opened his arms but Jesse balked and offered a handshake.

"Let's not get too far ahead of ourselves, you crazy galoot."

GENE PRATO was slumped on the red sofa shuffling through some medical documents and faxes. For the next two minutes Aisha, Dylan and Olaf sat motionless while he read through the paperwork. As autonomous as she was, Aisha rarely gave a client the go ahead to come into rehab without consulting her three associates.

"Are you sure you want him to come in?" he asked.

"Why not? He was here four years ago and did really well," she replied.

A sceptical look crept across Dylan's face.

"Come on doc. Spill the beans. What do you know that we don't?"

"He's got court coming up," Gene said.

"They've all got court coming up," Olaf said. "Half of them think getting a bed here is some kind of get-out-of-jail-free card."

"That they do, my dear Olaf. But not many of them are going before the judge on arson charges."

Criminal behaviour did not preclude anyone from being admitted to ITL, except when it was for arson or sexual assault. There was simply far too much risk involved. Olaf, when he started working there, naively challenged Aisha on the legitimacy of this unwritten policy, suggesting it stigmatised prospective clients and robbed them of hope.

Her frank reply - "people don't come here to be raped and barbequed" - made it clear this was something not open to debate.

Gene peered over his spectacles at them all. Aisha nodded, and the firebug's paperwork was fed into the shredder.

"Next is Jane Tulles," the doctor continued. "A fairly straightforward application. 31; been on methadone for four years; current dose is 30 mg a day; hasn't used heroin in over eight months; smokes a bit of the green and glorious here and there. Jane will be transitioning to being a woman over the next year and all of her psychological and psychiatric profiles are in order."

"So, Jane is technically still a male?" Dylan asked.

"She is, but we've always known her as Jane. And she prefers to be called that. Her birth name is on all her identification and medical paperwork, but she is Jane."

"Will her transitioning present any blocks?" Aisha asked.

"No. She's been seeing psychiatrists since she was nine years old. Her decision to transition was made five years ago and, as you'll see from the report, both her shrinks fully endorse her need to change gender. Believe me, she's in no hurry. She's doing it all according to Hoyle."

"Let's get her in then," Olaf said. "Just one question. Ask her if she prefers to do her urine samples with female or male staff."

"I can tell you right now. Male. She is incredibly mindful of that. Oh, and one other thing. She hates being referred to as either them or they."

Dylan took Jane's history and started making up a file.

"And finally, young Jason Button. Though he's not so young anymore, everyone calls him The Kid."

"We'll call him Jason then," Dylan said.

"Good luck with that. Now The Kid is a fascinating specimen. At 17 he took up surfing. By 20 he had won millions in prize money, owned a to-die-for house on Maui and was rolling in product endorsements. Got smashed to smithereens on a reef in Tahiti. Broken back, punctured lung, clavicle replacement, the whole shebang. Took a shine to oxycodone hydrochloride, discovered the joys of heroin and, well eight years later, wants to get off methadone. He's in arrears to the clinic for $340. I think you'll like him."

"Is he ready for us?" Aisha asked.

"Probably not, but let's start sowing some seeds now. Besides, you'll have him for a while. He's on 140mg."

Dylan let out a whistle of astonishment.

"Christ, what did he do to get himself up to *that* amount?"

"Arch recidivist, old darling. Arch recidivist."

Spring

THE TAXI pulled up in front of an impressively large two-storey mansion. It was rundown, twice the size of neighbouring properties, had a faded, peeling sky-blue paint job and a brick fence in disrepair. A vine creeping up the side wall looked more structural than ornamental. The 'garden' was a deep stretch of overgrown grass with a slightly listing palm tree toward the front and a magnificent magnolia half way down. Zac craned his head to see if he had the right address. The surrounding houses were all immaculate Edwardian-style manses, but none had a sign indicating it was a rehabilitation centre. Despite his desire for something more salubrious, he knew this was the place.

He was quaking with nervousness. And the closer he got to the door, dragging his wheeled suitcase across the uneven, broken pathway, the more he wondered what exactly he was doing. Wouldn't it be just easier to get his methadone dose transferred to DC? Surely that's been done before? Of course, that was never going to happen. At least not for Zac Watts.

After he had gone through the formalities of Molloy offering him the Washington posting, she suggested that although he hadn't been using illicit drugs for all those years, maybe there was something going on for him at a deeper level which kept him on methadone. In the interim, he saw his therapist Dr Rosigio four times in 11 days. She had established that Zac was harbouring deep feelings of insecurity, manifested by his long-term methadone dependence, and her personal association with Aisha helped fast track him into the rehab.

Zac squeezed his thumbs against the sides of his index fingers, and massaged his sweaty palms with his other fingertips. His heart was racing. Strange, since he'd drunk 12ml of methadone only 30 minutes beforehand.

Just as he was about to press the doorbell – which he suspected would not work – the security screen door sprung open, and at the end of the flinging arm was a tall, lank, sparkly-eyed man in his early 60s wearing a grey pork pie hat and a similarly coloured Jason Isbell tour T-shirt.

"You must be Zac. Come aboard."

Zac wrestled his suitcase and backpack through the narrow doorway, half expecting to be given a hand.

"I'm Dylan. Just park those in that room and follow me."

They wandered down a long corridor filled with all sorts of framed certificates and photographs. Zac scanned them in the half light then did a double take; one photo was of one of the country's most conservative political leaders shaking hands with the guy he'd just met, both surrounded by a dozen or so motley looking people. All had beaming smiles, and all looked terribly pleased with themselves. What threw Zac was that this politician had always been particularly inflexible with his views around illicit drug use and its milieu.

Dylan punched in a code on a garish orange door into what Zac rightfully assumed was an office and began a boisterous conversation with an unseen male. He waited until Dylan stuck his cheerful head back out the door.

"Come in. We won't bite. Well, Olaf might. But he responds well to oysters."

Huh? Zac, timid, stepped inside, where another man was waiting.

"I'm Olaf, Zac," he said. "Glad you made it."

Olaf was as tall as Dylan and dressed in mauve suede boots, blue jeans and a black T-shirt advertising 6th Street Cycles NYC. He wondered if Olaf was a client or staff, and tried to shake hands with him.

"Whoa, not with me, baby," Olaf declared as he threw his hands back up in a surrender gesture. He then placed his hands together and tipped his bowed forehead with them. "Ohayo, motherfucker."

Definitely a client, thought Zac.

"Olaf's going to be your counsellor, Zac. So what we'll do is get you seated here, and the two of you can start going through all the admission bullshit."

Bullshit? Motherfucker? Oysters? Zac parked himself next to Olaf.

"I'm sorry about the handshake. I'm old school."

"Cool," said Olaf. "And I'm just plain old neurotic. I don't do bodily contact stuff, unless of course ... you'll get used to me."

With that, Olaf started tapping away at his keyboard. The computer screen sprang to life with a garish logo spelling out In The Light, accompanied by four suspended, ascending electronic notes from a song Zac could not quite place. He watched Olaf log on and saw that his surname was Shapiro. He wondered whether he might be related to his colleague Inez, but after his last assumption he thought the better of saying anything.

"Hey, ah, Olaf," Zac said. "You don't know what those four notes that just played are, do you?"

Dylan let out an exasperated groan from the other side of the office. Olaf turned, smiling weirdly, baring his teeth and raising an eyebrow.

"96 Saint Marks Place," he grinned.

Dylan spun in his chair, leant toward Zac with his arms straight, gripping his knees.

"You. Stop torturing the new client. And Zac, don't ask him questions about music. You'll get more sense from the Sphinx."

Olaf snorted like a horse and Dylan gave Zac a big, conspiratorial wink. Zac, naturally, wanted to ask them questions - that was his job after all - but he also knew there was serious administrative stuff to be completed. And, besides, he was probably going to be here for a while. Well, at least long enough to figure out these two nut jobs.

Olaf and Dylan were both looking at him. They were smiling. Not cultish, dopey, we-smoked-too-much-weed smiles, but calm, welcoming smiles. Zac thought how he'd usually be uncomfortable in this situation, but instead just sat there. Feeling okay.

Dylan picked up a coffee mug with WORLD'S GREATEST MUM on it, and strolled toward an ante room. Still grinning, he raised the empty mug in a quasi-salutation and winked again.

"You've made the right choice, buddy."

For some reason, Zac knew he had too.

The next hour was spent going through page after page of questions. Much of it was mundane stuff like next-of-kin details, religious and cultural needs, people who you want to let know you are here, privacy contract, rules and regulations contract, agreement to treatment contract, etc. And then there was meatier stuff. Criminal history (no to all those questions), drug use history (a few beers every now and then, but nothing else in the past decade). Zac was particularly fascinated by a psychological profile with 20 questions pertaining to experienced emotions, each one answerable with either always, sometimes, not often or never. Olaf barrelled through this part quickly, not allowing Zac the time to contemplate each response. At the end he tapped a key and the number 43 came up in a dialogue box. Zac jokingly asked Olaf how he went. Without looking up from the screen, Olaf said "You did well. Are you on any mental health medications?"

Zac took umbrage at this question.

"No I am not."

Olaf nodded. It was then Zac saw the prompt under the box. *Scores of 36 and above are to be referred to the doctor.*

THE BEDROOM was befitting of the rest of the building - slightly shabby, in need of repainting, the carpet somewhat worn. Despite that, it was surprisingly cosy. A reassuring warmth emanated from the radiator near the door.

There was a wardrobe as old as the building and two single beds pushed sideways against the opposite end walls. Each had a chest of drawers next to it. The one with a can of spray deodorant and framed photo of a child on top told Zac he would be in the bed next to the wardrobe.

Standing sentry-like out in the hall was a stoic-looking man with absurdly muscled arms folded across his chest.

"Zac, meet your roommate Warren. Your primary goal while you are here is to be like Warren. You know why?"

Zac glanced at Warren, who gave him a wink and a wry grin. Warren's pristine white singlet top matched his equally pristine white runners. Separating these two items of sartorial glamour was a very small pair of bottle-green training shorts and the most heavily tattooed skin Zac had ever seen. Warren looked as big and as immovable as an automatic teller machine. He had an air of being as dangerous and as bad and as fucking scary as he probably was. Zac could not begin to imagine why he needed to be like Warren.

"I'll tell you why," Olaf continued. "Warren came in here five months ago on a bucket of methadone. Warren's been clean for four weeks and will be heading home soon. Warren might well be your spirit animal."

Warren didn't respond to Olaf's ringing endorsement, and Zac sensed he didn't particularly like the counsellor. He looked at the picture of the child.

"Is that your daughter, Warren?" Zac asked.

"Yeah, me little princess Chloe. You might meet her when they pick me up on Saturday."

Most men that look like Warren tend to have deep, gravelly, threatening voices like B grade movie gangsters. Not Warren. He had a disarmingly high voice, as though he'd never hit puberty. Not that Zac was going to ask if he had. They obviously came from different social circles, so he knew he would probably have his work cut out simply sharing a room.

Olaf was searching through Zac's bags, "looking for contraband". By which he meant drugs, weapons or porn.

"Many people try to sneak that stuff in?"

"Young Warren brought a trailer of that shit in."

Warren let out a squeaky laugh.

"I'm not kidding," deadpanned Olaf.

Zac wasn't sure if Olaf was taking the mickey out of Warren, or they were trying to make him feel uncomfortable. Either way, he wasn't appreciating their routine.

"You can take your dildos home Warren," said Olaf, "but the .38 stays with me."

This provocative statement made Zac nervous. Warren didn't look amused in the slightest, and shot a withering look at Zac. Then he grinned.

"Come on, O. You know you'll be ringing me a week later begging to trade."

REHABS ALWAYS look like high-end furniture display centres, with sparkling chrome-and-leather seating, immaculate bookshelves brimming with new hardbacks, and stylishly framed art prints of Van Goghs or Cézannes. The denizens are inevitably healthy looking people in their 20s, with a token 40-something geriatric thrown in for balance. Well, the ones on television do, but not this joint.

The common room was deceptively large, with room for an air hockey table and a pool table. There were four well-worn couches draped with crocheted travelling rugs, and three aging armchairs. A far wall was covered with hastily built track-and-plank shelving, full of yellowing books and old magazines. A few tattered posters of Beyonce, Wu Tang Clan and Taylor Swift adorned the walls, along with a large and detailed framed map of Indigenous Australia, but there were certainly no European masters.

A dozen or so grey plastic and tube steel chairs were stacked in piles in a far corner next to a large whiteboard. On the right hand side of the board was the day's timetable, incorporating morning, harm minimisation and discussion groups, meal times, dosing, meditation, walks and down time. Any ideas Zac may have had of idly sitting around throwing playing cards into a hat were pretty well nixed. The board also indicated which staff members were facilitating what groups, and doubling as that day's first aid officer and fire warden. In the middle of the board was a section called Today's Goal. Under this was a hastily scrawled "I will honour my emotions, using the knowledge I gain today to survive my feelings." Somewhat twee, Zac thought, but you know… when in Rome.

He looked across at the board on the opposite wall, which listed the names of the residents, their methadone dose and a comment. Next to Warren's name was a tick, indicating he was no longer dosing, and a neatly written note. It said: 'As you prepare to return home, be mindful of your new skills like listening respectfully.'

Jane was on 30mg/6ml, and 'your peers would like to hear you challenge yourself more. Let us know what concerns you have - especially around being drug free.'

Zac flinched when he saw Zachary at the bottom of the table. He'd never been comfortable with his name, so always introduced himself as Zac. When people asked if it was short for Zachary, he'd reply, "No. It's short for Zac." Yes, I am on 60mg/12ml. 'Welcome to ITL. Now is the time to let go of fear. Take emotional risks. Reach out to your peers.' Zac pondered this and decided that his biggest fear was psychobabble like 'reach out'.

He was looking through the disparate collection of dog-eared paperbacks when Dylan came and guided him toward the other residents. He cleared his throat exaggeratedly and three of the seven people lounging around rolled their eyes toward him. The others just kept staring blankly at a TV commercial for incontinence pads.

"Hey guys, this is Zac. He's joined us this afternoon, so please make him feel welcome. Marty, could you just turn the television off for a few minutes, please."

A lanky, ginger-bearded young man in a tartan kilt and hideously loud yellow shirt seemingly stretched his arm way beyond its reach, grabbed a remote, and zapped the pleased-with-herself, bladder-challenged actor into the void.

"So if you'd all like to introduce yourselves to Zac, tell him a bit about who you are, and we can begin to make him feel at home.

Suddenly, Zac felt like some alien interloper as the group eyed him up. Given he was dressed in a white linen shirt, navy blazer, tan chinos and black brogues, this was not surprising. Zac thought that half of them looked like they had dressed in a charity clothing bin. At 4am. Three days ago. Drunk.

"Persephone, would you like to start?"

Persephone? Zac certainly wasn't expecting to be acquainting himself with anyone named in honour of the Greek goddess of vegetation. A serpentine woman untwisted her legs, rose and nodded politely.

"Welcome to our little rehab," she said in a clipped, elegant voice,

Zac was about to engage in some basic social niceties when, in an almost robotic delivery, Persephone continued.

"I'm Persephone. I'm here to get off methadone. Again. Been on it for God knows how long. Done more rehabs than you've had hot..."

She accentuated and suspended the last word long enough for Zac to decide that he wasn't there to engage in double-entendre nonsense with crazies.

"Yeah, yeah," he said. "But I am rather partial to a Sunday roast. Thanks Persephone."

She did a double-take, her chin sinking back and the coquettish peer turning into wide-eyed surprise. Zac assumed she wasn't used to this kind of response, and suddenly worried he may have got off on the wrong foot.

"By the way,' he said. "I'm not being facetious. I just get awkward with, well... awkward silences."

"Vunderbar. That makes two of us."

Zac was all set to banter with Persephone when the rather gangly Marty went to shake his hand and unwittingly proffered him the TV remote. He shuffled it toward his other hand, dropped it onto the crossed ankles of the woman next to him, and went into a muttering chant as he stooped to retrieve it.

"You can usually find me on channel 13," Zac said to the back of Marty's head. Marty sprung back up - sans remote - then drove his hand into Zac's stomach.

"Oh shit, my glasses fell off."

And with that he returned to the floor to continue his search.

Crossed ankles let out an exasperated huff and gave Zac a very obvious once over.

"Y'ain't from 'round here, are ya?" she queried in a faux-Texan drawl. "But ah sure like ya style, cowboy."

"The pleasure's all mine, ma'am," he replied, falling into the cheesy routine. "But my stirrups fell off on the way into town."

"Pity. Anyway, I'm Jane."

"And why are you here, Jane?"

Jane looked at him incredulously.

"Umm, get off the 'done, get my shitful life in order, prepare for my transition, kill a few ghosts, become absolutely fabulous. You know, same reasons you are."

Sometimes being a journalist could be a real hindrance for Zac, especially in non-work situations. He was so preoccupied with gathering information that he often forgot that he didn't always have to start questioning everything, looking for the story even if it wasn't there. Why had he started to engage in repartee with a group of people he was just meeting? It wasn't like he was in a bar. Christ, you fucking imbecile, he thought. You've just admitted yourself to a long-term rehab because your life has spiralled into some woeful morass and groundhog day. Yet here you are trying to point score and win people over because you are so pathetically insecure. Zac could feel his psyche giving way and crumbling like an Antarctic ice cliff. What bothered him most was he was terrified the others could see it, too.

He looked across at Dylan, who was smiling at him. Zac felt his heart stuttering, and there was a low tone of white noise vibrating from ... where? His head? He felt incredibly nervous, and looked around the room for... what? Salvation? Sympathy? Understanding? He didn't feel like he was breathing. An Elvis Presley wall clock with pendulum legs loudly ticked away the seconds, but time was slowing. He remembered a favourite novel where a kid learned to stop time by playing with a pencil. Zac felt he, too, had stopped time, and as soon as everyone - and Elvis - froze, he could slip away from the house and start his life anew.

"Hey buddy, let's get you seated."

Zac's upper arms were being held from behind by Dylan. Tattooed across the counsellor's fingers was the word love, in black ink, but with a red valentine heart replacing the O.

Jane and Marty moved away, and Zac felt himself being gently lowered into the deep, enveloping couch. His heart was still racing, the ringing still present. But in this maelstrom of emotions he felt secure. Trust wasn't something Zac moved through life with, but it was present now. He noticed his mouth was dry and, just as he was about to ask for some water, Warren's heavyweight division paw handed him a promotional mug celebrating the movie Spider-Man: Far From Home. The irony was not lost on him.

"I, ahh, I don't... I don't... I think I had..."

Zac felt totally discombobulated. He wondered if he'd been slipped a Mickey Finn.

"Zac, just sip on the water, buddy."

Dylan looked benevolently down at him. Despite their brief interaction, Zac felt comfortable with this guy. He could feel tears welling in his eyes and was mortified that he might cry in front of these strangers. He tried to contain them by not blinking but all this managed to do was make his breathing shallow and labored.

He slurped at the water.

"Hey Zac," Dylan said in his lilting Kiwi accent. "You're safe."

With that the trunk of Zac's body convulsed and he was unable to stop his jaw shuddering or the cascade of tears flowing. His lower lip trembled uncontrollably as he gripped the mug of water, battling the combined waves of grief, fear, loneliness ... you name it. He felt a hand softly grip his right shoulder. He wondered if it was Persephone's.

"Why don't we allow him to feel this, eh?" suggested Dylan.

The hand went, and so did Zac. He gave the mug to... someone, and began to weep. He folded into a foetal position and let out a howl. As confronting and embarrassing and humiliating as everything felt, he kept remembering Dylan's reassurance - you're safe.

And he knew it.

For the next few minutes Zac spiralled into his breakdown with combined feelings of embarrassment and relief. As he began to regain his composure, he unfolded himself and looked around the room. Everyone had left, except Dylan, Olaf and Warren.

"I'm really sorry. I, ah, I..."

"There's no need to apologise, buddy. You just had what we call a feeling."

Zac wondered if Dylan was being a smart ass or just patronising. Of course he'd had a feeling. He had just lost his emotional shit in front of a roomful of people he didn't know and he was worried what they thought of him for being so childish and weak.

"I don't know what happened."

Olaf grinned. It wasn't like Dylan's; Olaf's grin did scream smart ass.

"How are you feeling?"

"I, um, a little bit embarrassed, I guess."

He and Olaf looked at each other. After about 10 seconds Olaf nodded slightly, raised his index finger, tapped his forehead, then dropped it to his sternum.

"Not up there. How are you feeling in here?"

Silence embraced the room. Zac waited for someone, anyone, to say something. But it was apparent the floor was his. He thought about his heart, which was now beating regularly, but he knew Olaf wasn't asking for a medical diagnosis.

"Sad."

It came out softly, and Zac wondered what sad really meant. It was as if he'd never understood its true definition. It suspended itself in the room, like a surrealist cloud. He thought about the construct of the word, what it looked like, and why it was so prevalent to him at this moment.

"Define sad to me," said Olaf. "And spare me any OED bullshit. You're not a Civil War surgeon, and this ain't Bedlam. Yet."

This snapped Zac out of his funk and he looked at Olaf quizzically, trying to comprehend the man's gibberish while also defining a common and simple word.

Dylan cocked his head toward the door and nudged Warren towards it.

"I'm going to leave you two fellas to talk. One question, Zac. Will you be staying for dinner?"

"Of course he is," said Olaf. "Aren't you due back at the sober gents' quarters by sunset?"

Dylan laughed, walked back to Olaf, and embraced him. With their noses barely an inch apart, they smiled then kissed each other's cheek. Dylan looked down at Zac.

"Remind me to sack him tomorrow."

OLAF AND Zac sat on the couch for an hour, having, for Zac, a particularly confronting conversation. It started with the continuation of the meaning of sad but Olaf wasn't so much interested in what it meant to Zac as to why he felt it. Sadness turned out to be a fairly easy distraction but the more they talked, the more Zac understood his sadness was merely a veneer hiding a far deeper pain - the pain of being Zac.

Occasionally his mind would drift back to conversations he'd had with Dr Rosigio, and all the psychoanalysis around his relationship with his parents. As interesting as it always was, Zac would often leave her rooms wondering what exactly he was getting out of it, and what bearing it really had, if any at all. He told Olaf this, and was shocked by the response.

"Fuck on that shit, baby. Have you consciously ever wanted to jam it to your mother?"

"Er, well no. Of course not."

"Cool, then let's look at why a nice kid like you started jamming needles full of dope into your arms before you could vote."

From there the discussion took off. Zac would say something innocuous like how he felt different to other children, and Olaf would goad him into exploring what the feelings were behind those memories. What was most disconcerting for him was that Olaf would not interrupt him. If he stopped what he was saying mid-sentence, they'd just fall into a protracted silence. Not once did Olaf lead him in any way, nor even suggest a single word. At one point Zac found himself ruminating on how he never really wanted to go to the expensive private school he attended, and promptly lost his train of thought because he was trying to figure Olaf out. Here is this guy who comes across as some unfocussed rock-and-roll burnout, yet seems to have a concise understanding of the human condition. Savant or dilettante? After he'd repeated that half a dozen times in his head, and contemplated its place in a haiku, he caught himself.

"Sorry Olaf. I got distracted."

A few seconds passed.

"By what?"

Zac squirmed. He began to concoct a lie strapped to the back of his school experiences when, without a warning, he decided on honesty.

"I was determining whether you're savant or dilettante, and feeling pleased with its rhyme, and whether it would work in a haiku."

Olaf smiled and studied the silver-and-turquoise ring on his middle right finger.

"Savant. Or. Dilettante," Olaf half sang to a familiar refrain, still looking at the jewellery. "You'd be pushing it making that t and e into a syllable, Basho san."

This was the moment Zac felt he had done the right thing in coming to the rehab. He wasn't contemplating the hell journey of reduction and withdrawal that lay before him; he knew exactly what he was in for on that level. Nor was he particularly fussed about the other clients. Although he had only met a few of them, he could sense his arrogant preconceptions were going to do him no favours were they to run wild in this environment, so best to quietly liberate those suckers later. No, he thought, if all I walk away with is the ability to call myself out on my own bullshit as effectively as this kook does, then I might be okay.

DINNER WAS at a communal table in a separate structure at the rear of the property. Downstairs housed the dining area, laundry, kitchen and walk-in pantry, while upstairs were three 'chill out spaces' for when one wasn't in the mood for television or loud music in the lounge. Zac figured he'd be getting well acquainted with those particular rooms.

The table seated 12 but there were only nine places set. Zac knew he was one of nine residents, but noticed there were only eight of them there.

"Is someone missing?" he asked no one in particular.

"Yeah, Leon," said Jane, who was intently studying the tines of her fork. "He's gone to spend the evening with his mother. She'll be dead soon."

Zac was surprised at her callousness, but no-one else seemed to notice. Or care.

At one end of the table sat Warren, of course. Zac suspected his roommate had been the alpha baby in the maternity ward within minutes of being born - a position he would grip till his last breath. Next to him was Jesse who was also covered in prison tattoos and seemed quite happy to converse out of the corner of his mouth with Warren, and only Warren. Perched at the opposite end of the table was the stunningly elegant Aisha.

Dressed in a fire-engine red, full-length ruffled dress, huge gold hoop earrings and a red, white, green and orange head scarf, out of place didn't even begin to sum her up. She looked like she should be singing Carmen's Seguedille at the Lincoln Center rather than lording over a table of end-of-the-line dope fiends.

Sitting to Aisha's right was one of the clients, Claudia. She, too, was a picture of style in an out-of-place double-breasted pants suit, but any of the verve so apparent in Aisha looked like it had left Claudia years ago. Zac pondered whether they sat next to each other as an act of sisterly solidarity or to merely emphasise the homogeneity of the rest of the table. He was deciding 'both' when Aisha caught him looking at them.

"Am I wearing something of yours, honey?"

"Yes. My evening gown. And I want it back."

After the laughter subsided, Aisha cheekily introduced herself as the night staff and welcomed Zac to "our table." In truth, Aisha had the admiration and respect of so many influential high flyers she could dine with whomever she chose on any given evening, but she actually preferred the company of her charges.

"We spoke at length when we did your phone assessment," she told him.

"And the pleasure is mine," Zac charmingly replied.

Marty sidled up to Zac and coyly asked if he was vegan or vegetarian. Told he was neither, Marty presented him with a plate of lasagna.

"This looks scrumptious," Zac said as Marty headed back to the servery.

Jane glared across the table. The look on her face said everything he knew was about to come out of her mouth. Five, four, three...

"So you're quite okay with murdering sentient creatures to tear their mortal remains apart with your teeth?"

An uncomfortable hush fell over the room. Zac was deliberating what to do or say when Aisha spoke up.

"Jane, my support for you is to remember the terms of your contract."

Jane looked across at Zac, her sneer dissipating.

"I'm sorry for attacking you like that, Zac. It was out of line, and I didn't mean to offend you."

Zac was confused, unsure what was going on but also feeling Jane had a right to stick by her principles.

"I'm not offended, Jane. You have as much right..."

"Zac," Aisha interrupted. "And I'll support you to hear Jane, and practice some acceptance and respect for her apology. Let's all consider this a reflection."

The room returned to the previous convivial atmosphere but Zac was nonplussed. He wanted to hear what Jane had to say but also knew there was some unwritten code at play.

"You look confused," Warren said. "Don't worry about it for the moment. Enjoy your meal, and I'll take you through it afterwards."

Warren and Jesse resumed their conspiratorial mumbling and Zac realised that he was the only one at the table affected by what had happened. Jane went straight into a lively rant about lipsticks with Claudia and Aisha, Marty and Persephone doled out everyone's meals - including vegetarian lasagna for Jane and Warren. All helped themselves to the large Japanese and Greek salads in the middle of the table. Interspersed along the table were cans of Coke, bottles of fruit juices and mineral water.

Persephone, ferreting around in the fridge, asked if anyone wanted ice. While most declined, Zac chimed in and asked if there was any beer in there.

Yet again, the room went silent. Jesus, now what, he thought.

Aisha smiled.

"You haven't been to rehab before, have you Zac?"

He shook his head sheepishly and looked to Warren, who winked. Jane beamed at him.

"Dude, you and I are gonna be besties for sure."

For the rest of the meal Zac decided the old adage about still tongues and wise heads had a lot of bearing. Without appearing withdrawn, he contributed little to the conversations but listened intently. He had been privy to some incredible discussions with some extraordinary dining companions over the years, but this was truly fascinating. Everyone at the table seemed devoid of pretentiousness. The topics weaved between life, sport, music, spirituality, prison, dreams and cars. He noticed Claudia, Jesse and Warren were fairly reserved and wondered if the boys' general reticence was some prison-related condition. Jane would go off on unrelated tangents as her excitement levels rose at light speed. Zac didn't know much about the Diagnostic and Statistical Manual of Mental Disorders, or mental health in general, but he was fairly sure Jane was textbook crazy.

He couldn't quite put his finger on Persephone. She spoke a lot about law and finance, and in a way that showed she knew what she was talking about.

But it was Marty who gripped Zac's curiosity the most. He had a gentle nature, totally at odds with the bumbling tv-remote-and-spectacles routine he'd turned on for Zac's arrival. Marty's voice was measured and caring, his actions graceful. Even when the conversations got rowdy, Marty would laugh gently and only raise his voice as an indicator of incredulity, as in "Oh, you're kidding". And while 'fucks' and 'cunts' flew around the table like paper darts, not once did Zac hear Marty swear. On that front they were fellow travellers. When Jane started to get elevated it was Marty who came in with a relaxing "hey Jane" before engaging her in a chat about something less provocative.

All through the meal Zac kept dreaming of a pinot noir which he knew would have complemented Marty's lasagna. Rather than minced beef, he had used shredded duck meat. Zac could make out hints of ginger and chilli, but there was no visible sign of either. He asked Marty, expecting the usual "if I told you I'd have to kill you" schtick. Instead, Marty's face lit up, and he explained how he finely sliced the ginger and chillies, then virtually dissolved them in heated olive oil. Any remnants were removed with a pair of tweezers, and the oil used to sear the duck meat.

The absence of alcohol remained confusing. Zac had never been a big drinker but he couldn't fathom the correlation between methadone and merlot. On the other hand, everyone was being polite and respectful; there was no overly loud yelling, and they all seemed to be genuinely interested in what each other had to say.

After the meal, Zac took himself outside to a wooden bench, looking wistfully at the night sky. It wasn't a romantic gesture - he was more curious about why he'd had such a daunting panic attack that afternoon.

Why did it happen when it did? Was it some kind of celestial test courtesy of Zeus and the gang? Or just the gravity of his lot that day? He tried finding some astronomical bearings, with what little knowledge he had of the heavens, by determining true south.

"I wonder if we'll see one explode tonight?"

Claudia joined him on the bench and looked toward the same diamond-flecked patch of black.

"Sorry, I don't understand," Zac said. "You mean one of our cohorts?"

"No. The stars. I wonder if we'll see one become a supernova."

"Well, my understanding is we need to look at Betelgeuse for that, but we still have a bit of a wait."

Claudia kept star gazing.

"Oxygen, hydrogen, carbon and nitrogen. The building blocks of our universe," she said. "It just all ties in so perfectly."

Zac couldn't decide whether she was demonstrating a rudimentary knowledge of chemistry, or starting some hippie rant about the cosmos.

"That's what they're made of," she continued, pointing toward the zenith. "And that's what we are. I heard this brilliant NASA scientist explain how we are fused from supernova remnants. She described us as dead stars looking back at dead stars. Don't you find that the most incredibly beautiful observation?"

As Zac ruminated on this Claudia took a pouch of tobacco from her jacket. "I'd offer you one," she said. "But, you know. Rules and shit."

Zac didn't know. He had an inkling about some basic guidelines but was yet to read the large manifesto issued to him.

"What would they be?"

"Oh, don't worry. Your buddy Warren will take you through them - that is, if he can read."

Zac let out a faux-humoured grunt, wondering why she disliked Warren.

"Fuck, I'm sorry," she continued. "That was so judgemental. Pretend you didn't hear it."

She struck a match and took a long drag on the hand-rolled cigarette.

"You're forgiven. I promise not to say a word. And anyway, I don't smoke."

They kept looking toward the stars, now fogged by the bluish cloud coming from Claudia.

"So," Zac said, dragging the vowel out. "What's the story with Claudia? If you don't mind me asking?"

"Well, it all depends if you want the whole shooting match, or the safe-for-kiddies edited version."

"Fire at will."

Claudia regaled him with a life story that most Hollywood script writers would die to conjure up. She told him how she came from a wealthy family who'd made their fortune building a national supermarket chain, how she was the product of a private education, ran away with a bad-boy junkie at 17, became a heroin addict, went on to high-end sex work for touring rock stars, found an even badder boy who killed a pharmacist in a robbery they did together, went to prison for 10 years and, while inside, got a doctorate in addiction studies…

"…and here I am."

Zac returned the favour and gave her a rundown of his far less exciting background. As much as he wanted to embellish his existence, the truth was anyone's story would pale next to Claudia's. As he spoke about how awkward he felt as a 13 year old he remembered his therapist's observation that drug users tend to be so self-absorbed that they're not interested in anything but themselves. At the time he found this a callous and arrogant observation but now, every time Claudia cut him off with some snippet about herself, he realised that the good doctor was right. He willingly allowed her to wallop him with her one-upmanship.

Zac played down his professional life, telling her most of his work involved making sure other people's grammar and syntax were in order. He caught Claudia trying to stifle a yawn, which satisfied him; this probably meant she would - for her sake - avoid prying into his life and opening that gate of excruciating boredom ever again.

What did bug him, however, was remembering that one of his colleagues had written a feature about Claudia soon after she was released from prison, because the childhood Zac had just heard about didn't gel with what was published. Was she, indeed, the product of privilege as she said, or the wrong-side-of-the-tracks victim he'd read about? Either way, Zac wasn't lost on the irony of feeling perturbed that she may have been less than honest with him.

ZAC WOKE at some ungodly hour to hear Warren doing sit-ups. He'd been in the midst of a convoluted dream involving his cousin and a giraffe safari, so to come around in a strange setting with a sweaty, tattooed muscle man whispering "483, 484" was unsettling. Warren finished at what Zac assumed was the requisite 500, gulped down a bottle of water, sprung to his feet, then rolled his neck till there was a progression of disconcertingly loud cracking sounds.

"You're awake. Good. Let's hit the showers and we'll go through the day."

As they went about their morning ablutions, Warren gave a running commentary from the next stall.

"First group of the day is where we all check-in as to how we're going, call each other on any bullshit behaviours we've picked up on, talk a bit about what we are expecting to get out of the day. After that we go to the clinic to get our dose, then it's lunch, then group work. What day is it? Thursday. Then we go to the park and have a long walk, then back for more group work."

"What does group work entail exactly?"

"All sorts of shit. I can't remember. If you get stuck, just ask me. But don't ask me stupid questions. You seem bright enough, so try to figure it out for yourself."

Watching the suds drain away between his feet, Zac wondered if Warren didn't like him or if he was simply uncouth. He reached for his towel and wrapped it around his waist as he stepped out of the shower. He was confronted by Warren standing there naked.

"I'm gonna level with you, Zac. I'm here to avoid a laggin'. I'm not interested in all their life skills, harm reduction, acceptance therapy bullshit. I'm my own man, and I don't need no fucking know-all fuckwit like that Olaf cunt telling me how to live my life. Get what I'm saying?"

Zac didn't have a clue. The message he felt Warren was delivering was 'stay out of my face', but then why was he so kind to him yesterday? Why did he talk so openly with Zac the night before about the joy of having a young daughter, and being allowed back into her life? What was the crime that had him incarcerated? Why doesn't he cover his goddamned prick?

"Loud and clear, Warren."

Day two was going to be a long one.

"GOOD MORNING group," announced Persephone in a sing-song tone.

"Good morning Persephone," they choused in return.

Zac looked around the circle of people, remembering everyone's name. The only exception was a thin man, dressed in the dandiest of attire, that Zac hadn't seen before.

All eyes were on Persephone as she rifled through a folder. Olaf, sitting next to her, whispered something. Zac was half hoping he'd told her to use a lot less of her overpowering perfume.

"Oh yeah, icebreaker. Um, Marty. You wanna start it?"

Marty peered back through his round spectacles, looking like a stunned owl in need of more coffee.

"Sure." He looked around the room, fixed his eyes on Olaf's boots, then said in his gentle, lilting voice, "What's your favourite colour and why? Mine's green because it reminds me of nature."

Jane, sitting to his left, thought for a second.

"Mine's black, because I want a little black cocktail dress."

A few people chortled, but Zac noticed Claudia visibly clench her jaw and shoot Jane a quick glare.

Warren, with his characteristic arm fold, grunted "red".

Just as Zac was about to speak, Olaf interrupted.

"Sorry Zac. Why's red your favourite colour, Warren?"

Warren stirred, pushed the heels of his hands into the seat of his chair, straightened his back.

"I don't know. It's one of my football team's colours."

"Thank you, Warren."

Zac waited, expecting Olaf to remonstrate with Warren about his gracelessness. Instead, he felt Warren's thumb jab his thigh.

"Your turn."

In a goofy bid for acceptance and to prove there was more to him than anxiety attacks and his new-kid-in-town nervousness, Zac revealed that it was deep mustard, "because it reminds me of one of my favourite Rothko paintings".

It was Persephone's turn. She broke into a huge grin.

"Yellow, because only Marty could rock such a hideous coloured shirt."

The room cracked up, and Zac started to get the purpose of the exercise. Persephone then turned to Olaf.

"So, are you gonna play nice?'

Olaf looked at her with a deadpan expression, stared around the room, fixed his eyes on Jane and said in a monotone, "chrome".

Again, more laughter. Olaf remained poker-faced.

Mister dandy attire, fiddling with the heel of the boot propped atop his knee, tilted his head to the side, staring directly at Zac.

"Purple, because it's both the colour of regality and Prince, rest his eternal soul, man." With that, he kissed the side of his index finger and raised it toward the ceiling fan, like some rock-and-roll high priest.

Claudia stared ahead blankly. Zac was finding the quiet a little disconcerting when Claudia snapped out of her mini trance.

"Red, black and green," she said. "Because they're the colours of the pan-African flag."

After a round of applause, Persephone consulted her folder then asked who was "up for an emotional check-in".

"What's an emotional check-in?" Zac asked Warren from the corner of his mouth, as half the group raised their hands.

"Relax, mate," Warren replied. "As I said, you'll pick it up."

Persephone scribbled away for a minute.

"Right, I have Sleeve, Claudia and Warren. Warren, you want to start?"

Warren wriggled in his chair, rubbed his left calf with his right foot and scratched his earlobe. Zac thought he looked almost vulnerable.

"Well, as you all know, I'm going home on the weekend. It's been a month since I had my last dose and I feel I have got about as much as I can out of this place. You're the best crew I've ever done rehab with, and fuck knows I've done a few." He shifted in his seat, leant his elbows on his thighs, and fixed the dandy one with a long stare.

"Sleeve and me had a talk the other night, and I respect your concern, bro. But trust me, I know what I'm doing. The missus told me she's thrown all my drug shit out, and you all know I deleted all my drug-using contacts in my phone. So really, Sleeve, don't you go worrying that pretty head of yours. I'll look after number one, and you..."

Olaf, who appeared to have been studying Sleeve's face, snapped around at Warren.

"Come on Warren. Don't undo all your hard work with resentment. You're above that. And you know it."

Had Warren launched himself at Olaf, it wouldn't have surprised Zac in the slightest. After being in his waking company for only 10 hours, Zac already knew that Warren was a time bomb. He was obviously someone who didn't take directions from anyone.

"Now continue," said Olaf. "We're interested in what you're saying."

Warren's body language changed immediately. He sat up and his arms relaxed into his lap.

"Sorry, Sleeve. You know I don't cope with criticism too well. Shit. Sorry. I mean reflections. See? I still struggle with the way I'm supposed to talk even now. And I dunno what's gonna happen when I leave here.

The wife says she sees a huge change in me, but I dunno. I feel like I'm a fucking fraud or something. I've been on drugs for 20 years, spent half of that in nick, and now I've moved all that shit out of my path I'm worried that I'll ... I just want to get home to my two girls and make it right for them."

He tilted his head back, drew in a huge breath, held it for a bit, then noisily exhaled. It was surprising to see Warren with tears in his eyes. No-one did anything. The room was deathly silent, as though his previous breath robbed it of life.

Olaf stared at the hard man.

"That's beautiful, Warren. But what are you going to do to make it right for you?"

As Warren began to quietly sob, Persephone slid a box of tissues across the floor to him. He yanked a few out, wiped at his eyes, then looked back at Olaf.

"Maybe I should stay another week."

"I was thinking a year, but hey - it's not my call. I'll talk to Aisha."

Sleeve moved angularly in his chair, whether out of discomfort or restlessness Zac couldn't figure out, but either way he was a fascinating individual. He looked to be in his mid-50s, with a mane of heavily dyed black/blue hair. The taut facial features certainly screamed drug user; he was dangerously thin, his face heavily lined and sunken, and he had kohl caked around his eyes. A big, gold earring in his left ear had done its 40 years of duty and was on the verge of breaking through the last piece of skin holding it in. The shirt was a threadbare paisley affair, covering a T-shirt promoting some long-forgotten rock festival. Two silk scarves with what appeared to be horse motifs adorned his neck and shoulders. Zac figured Sleeve's jeans were probably a size 26, and loose at that. He wore a few silver rings, the centrepiece being a large burnished skull. His wrists were adorned with a variety of silver bracelets, leather thonging and coloured string. These ended a heavily tattooed left arm. Unlike the brightness and sharpness of Warren's detailed artwork, Sleeve's was an inky wash of fading green and crimson - an ageing and damaged palimpsest. His upper left incisor was gold capped. Sleeve would have been the result had Janis Joplin and Henry Morgan bred, thought Zac, and stifled a giggle at his own wit.

"Check-in, Sleeve?" Persephone prompted him.

"Yeah, ah thanks babe."

Olaf cut in.

"How about you show Persephone some respect and address her by her name?"

"Oh yeah. Sorry, Percy," he half hissed with more than a hint of sarcasm. She and Olaf were seated between Zac and Sleeve, and Zac noticed that while Persephone grinned cheekily at his nonchalance, Olaf just looked bored. What appeared new and exciting for Zac was obviously plain hackneyed for the counsellor.

"Let's see. As you all know, I just had two days of leave which, I've gotta say, was a challenge. As I told Olaf before the group, I went back to my apartment and I wasn't exactly honest with you cats."

Sleeve's voice was an indistinguishable transatlantic tone, carried by an occasional wheeze - no doubt attributable to the brownish stains around his manicured finger tips. Out of nowhere, Zac was again struck by the pungent scent of Persephone's perfume. Except it wasn't hers - it was wafting off Sleeve.

"I went back home and knew there was dope in the house, and there was lots of works. But it's okay man. I didn't use."

Claudia looked at him incredulously.

"No, really Claude. I know you were concerned about me, darlin', but honest."

"Oh, fucking spare me, will you? I mean, was that a fucking set-up or what?" she snapped.

Olaf raised an open hand and asked them both to wait.

"Claudia, we were all concerned about Sleeve's leave. But he has a voice, and now this is his space to use it in."

"I thank you for your concern, Claudia. Truly. And I deeply appreciate it."

Zac wondered if Sleeve was being sarcastic or sincere.

"As I said, there was shit in the apartment. And I knew when I left here the other day it was there. But what I did was ring one of my old friends who quit using years ago, and he met me there, and we cleaned the place out. Flushed the dope, and he took all my gimmicks and shit and threw them out somewhere. I don't know where. Doesn't matter."

He looked around the room for some kind of approval or acknowledgement, but it was apparent there was none coming. The penny started to drop with Zac that silence was an effective treatment tool in here, and his own default mode to jump in and keep the conversation rolling was not going to fly.

"And the hardest part," Sleeve murmured, "was that after my friend left, it was just me sitting in my apartment. Alone. Like I had nothing left in the world."

His voice started to tremble.

"And man, I felt scared."

For God knows how long, the silence roared.

"So. Fucking. Scared."

Zac now knew Sleeve was sincere. Painfully so. He didn't even know the guy, but he just wanted to go over and give him a hug. He noticed Sleeve's bottom lip was quivering but there were no tears rolling from his eyes. This wasn't about loss or regret, it was about terror. Pure, evil terror. The variety that would occasionally visit Zac at the mere thought of heroin.

"Anyway," Sleeve announced with a cheerier demeanour. "I spent the next few hours cranking LPs and cleaning the place up. If there's one thing I've got from you guys, it's that cleanliness is next to godliness."

He half sung the quote and then chuckled.

"Jesus, why do I always deflect with fucking humour? Man, it's so pathetic. I never cleaned a thing in my life before I came here, and I go home, feel house proud and clean it up, and then I just shit on my actions. Fuck. The sense of achievement I had the other night after I flushed my dope and cleaned the place thoroughly. Man, it felt so good."

He stared down at his hands, and twisted the skull ring under the knuckle.

"Why did it feel so good?" asked Olaf.

Sleeve's jaw clenched and his elbows squeezed into his sides.

"Because having a clean house feels good, I guess."

"Don't guess, Sleeve. Why did it feel so good?"

Sleeve's heels rose; he was obviously trying to push the balls of his feet right through the carpet and floor underneath. The lip started quivering again, and an impossible sadness fell over his face.

"Because I deserve it."

"SO, WHY journalism?"

The eight clients wandered through the neighbourhood, en route for their morning dose. Olaf's question came out of the blue.

"Why not?" said Zac.

"Well, it's a fairly thankless career. Most of society rates you somewhere between used car salesmen and rat catchers. You work in a cutthroat environment where the single biggest act of folly is leaving your contacts book lying around, you proudly file your copy so a sub-editor can remind you you're borderline illiterate, and the only time the editor speaks to you is when they've had the company lawyers flay them with a defamation claim."

"So, you were a journalist in a previous life?"

Olaf smiled smugly.

"Worse. My parents were. And my grandmother."

They laughed at the absurdity of the situation. Zac was always prepared for the usual cynicism his profession invoked, but hadn't been prepared for this.

"So why didn't you become one?"

"Intellectual incompetence. I had neither the desire nor motivation to use my brain properly and figured a life submerged in the seedy pits of rock and roll would suffice. How wrong I was."

"You're a musician?" Zac asked.

"I'm robbing this coach, pal. Why journalism?"

Zac hesitated, contemplating a fitting response.

"Hey Zac, I'm interested in why you chose your profession. I respect what you do. Your exposé of that mountain tunnel rort was a riveting read. Did you always want to be a reporter?"

"No. I was hellbent on being an architect but my grades weren't quite high enough to get me into that at university. So I opted for law, and midway through second year I applied for an internship at The Register and the rest, as they say."

"How did you end up on methadone?"

Good question, thought Zac, and why has it taken so long to ask it? He'd spent over an hour on the phone to Aisha doing his intake assessment but she hadn't asked about his drug history apart from how much he'd been using in the previous month.

"Dabbled with heroin in high school, got a habit by uni. I had a bad OD and a paramedic suggested I go on the 'done, so I did."

"And how's your heroin use been over the past decade?"

"Non existent. The last time I used it was that time I dropped. It scared the shit out of me."

It took Olaf a second.

"So let me get this straight. You overdosed, went on to methadone a decade ago, never touched heroin again, and yet they kept you on it all that time?"

Zac grinned.

"Hey they're not bad people. Every few months the doctors asked if I wanted to reduce but I was worried. I did my research, spoke to other clients at the clinic. The idea of withdrawal was too scary and, frankly, I knew as long as I was on it my inclination to use smack would be lessened."

"And in all that time they never suggested detox or rehab?"

"Nup." Zac paused You seem pissed off."

"Seem?" Olaf replied. "I'm ropeable. Sometimes the health system can be truly fucked."

IN THE five weeks Zac had been in rehab he was surprised at how quickly he had acclimatised. Not so much the place, but the routine. He lay in bed that Saturday morning listening to a squall wallop the roof and trees. Rain pattered the window, and an incoming plane's jets screamed and decelerated through the pandemonium, kickstarting a mild bout of anxiety. Zac had never been a big fan of mechanised flight and was now convinced that should one of those unnaturally airborne tubes start to come down near the 'hab it would inevitably take out both him and his newfound friends. Hearing the turbulence vortex trail behind it didn't help either. He waited for its hideous pitch to fade before breathing again.

Indecipherable conversation was carried up to his room on a plume of rank cigarette smoke. Smoking was an indulgence he never quite got the knack for, even when he was on heroin. Having a cigarette burn down to its butt and singe a hole in your clothes was pretty much a rite of passage for most junkies, but for Zac it was always a putrid antisocial act conducted with neither thought or respect for anyone.

He remembered one particular dinner table conversation where his father had regaled them with a graphic report of someone getting a heart/lung transplant, while also having a tract of their mouth and jaw removed. At the end of this horrific story Ian Watts raised his glass of wine and declared a toast "to Sir Walter Raleigh, for the gifts which we continue to receive". Master Zac assumed Sir Walter was some pompous old tenured professor until he did an online search after dessert and decided that self-induced cancer was something he would avoid. Well, Dad, you've certainly done your work with me, he thought. Yet he was now finding the prospect of the occasional cigarette appealing. He looked up at the flaking ceiling, imagining smoke rings rising from his lips.

"What happens here on weekends?" The Kid asked.

In the mental orgy of crashing planes and invasive surgery Zac had forgotten he had a new roommate. His eyes widened at The Kid's question, grateful he wasn't attending to his early morning priapus and wondering when he'd become the rehab's go-to guy.

"Modified program. Morning group, dosing - then we go out for the afternoon."

He rolled onto his side and looked across at The Kid.

"What time is it? I thought you'd be up and out there onto your second smoke by now."

The Kid grinned, and pushed his front tooth out on its dental plate, knowing fully well it even unhinged the unhingeable.

"Six thirty. Already had three smokes and two coffees. Too fucking cold out there."

Zac rolled back and resumed his study of the ceiling.

"You do that nonsense with your tooth for effect or attention?"

The Kid laughed.

"So what are we gonna do today, man? This place fucking sucks."

Zac couldn't argue with this but he also felt a tinge of sadness and concern for The Kid. In comparison, Zac's life had been positively bland, but in the five days he'd been there Zac had already grown quite fond of him. Sure, he was probably a conniving little turd with the survival skills of a rat in a battle zone, but above all that he was a charming and engaging young man. Statistically, though, he was not likely to 'get it'.

"Well, Kid, the local high school has invited us over to watch the football."

"Fuuuuuck. Off," he drawled. "Why would you go and watch TV in a school?"

The Kid bounced off his bed and rustled around in the wardrobe.

"No, we go and watch their team play another school."

Zac watched The Kid struggle into a hoodie - on top of the one he was already wearing.

"Nah, fuck that for a joke. No way dude."

The idea of watching 30 adolescent boys smash the bejesus out of each other in a rugby match didn't exactly appeal to Zac, either. He'd spent endless cold weekend afternoons sporting a jersey on the sodden clods of sportsgrounds during his own adolescence and, despite his prowess on the field, never really enjoyed it. He sat on the edge of the bed looking at his roommate. Although Zac was only a few years older than The Kid, he reminded himself of George Bernard Shaw's dictum about youth being wasted on the young.

The Kid returned his look with a crazed grin, extending his front tooth.

"I'm gonna stay here and enjoy my dose."

"WHOA, IT'S the double whammy. Big guns city."

The Kid winked at Dylan and Olaf, who were already seated beside each other in the group circle. He was hastily beelining for a chair in the sunlight while the others filed in slowly, making general chit-chat and bringing their fetid tobacco-breath cloud with them.

"And why do you think we'd both be here, Jason?" Dylan asked.

The Kid shrugged. He'd been there a bit over a week and was still trying to figure out how the place ran. Neither of the counsellors appeared to be in their usual jovial mood.

"Oh, you're not going to bust me for eating all the ice-cream last night?"

Dylan and Olaf shook their heads as a collective laugh came up from the others.

"And this morning, community," Olaf announced. "Jason will be giving a demonstration on how to drop one's self right in it!"

The group settled and began with the usual roll call and icebreaker. Three chairs remained empty. Claudia, assuming they were at a doctor's appointment, asked if she should mark the missing clients off as 'medical'.

"So, who knows what happened with Marty, Jane and Persephone?" Dylan asked. Everyone but Karen looked surprised. Since arriving at In The Light a few days before, she'd kept to herself. A few of them had tried to engage her in conversation, but she was very shut down, her primary topic of conversation centering on her child in foster care. She had developed some trust with Persephone and had told her that her sole purpose for getting off drugs was to regain custody.

A murmur travelled the room before Olaf held his hand up in the universal 'stop' sign. Thanks to the years of their covert drug behaviours on the streets Olaf and Dylan could read the room just through the furtive glances between their charges. Today, however, there were none. Only Karen looked morose, staring down at her folded arms.

"What did they tell you, Karen?" Dylan asked.

She shifted uncomfortably and jiggled a leg anxiously.

"Oh fuck. I don't want to snitch but when we went for a walk last night we ran into some guy that used to be here. Warren? He was high, but it's not like he was fucked-up or anything. Anyhow he said, like, three words to Marty, and Jesse said we all had to come home and then Warren gave Jesse stink-eye and walked off. Honestly, I didn't say anything to him."

The counsellors nodded.

"That's great, gang. Well done. And thank you, Jesse, for being principled and keeping your peers safe," Olaf said. "Now back to Dylan's original question. What happened with Persephone and Marty and Jane?"

Karen's leg jiggled even more but she looked resigned to telling her story.

"On the way home Marty told me how that Warren dude slipped him his number and said he was holding some really good gear. Honestly, I told him to lose the number and bring it to the morning group. He said yeah and threw the number in the street."

"Why do you think the piece of paper he got rid of was the one with the phone number on it?" asked Dylan.

Karen just shook her head despondently.

"Hey Karen," Dylan said. "You're not a dog or a snitch or any other stupid street term. You did the right thing, and I commend you for that. You are not responsible for what those three did, only your own actions. If they made a decision to take off in the middle of the night to use heroin with Warren, well, they're the ones who will have to deal with the consequences of that. You chose to stand in your integrity. That's how we grow."

There was a solemn mood within the room, not surprising considering a third of their group had left overnight.

"I just want to explain to you the process around absconding," Dylan said. "This place is not a drop-in centre. All of you jumped through hoops of fire to get a bed in here. Now, I can guarantee that at least one of the three who left last night will be regretting it now. I'd be surprised if one in particular hasn't already called in. Now, if you do leave without telling anyone, theoretically you can't return for three months. But we..." Dylan paused to jerk his thumb at Olaf, "also take things on a case-by-case basis. We factor in where the individual was in their reduction, attendant risk factors and various other circumstances."

Zac raised his hand.

"What can we do to help them?"

"Good question," Olaf answered. "Zip. Nada. Fuck all. If any of them do call the resident's phone, put them straight through to staff. I know you guys think you'd be doing them a great service by having a little chat and seeing how they are and everything, but you don't know what level of crisis they might be in. They could be calling simply to manipulate one of you into joining them because they're broke. Hostage-taking time. And if you are contemplating going on a rescue mission, ask yourself what your motives for doing so are. Any more questions?"

They talked a little more, concerned for their friends' safety, wellbeing and major fear of overdose. Jesse asked why they just couldn't come back in and say they're sorry.

"Because sadly," Olaf said, "when junkies and drunks say they are sorry, it usually means they're about to do whatever they're sorry for again."

The group returned to its format with both counsellors remaining in it. It was the first Wednesday of the month - Suggestions Day, when the staff would listen to any of their ideas and requirements. Jesse asked if he would he be allowed to watch TV during the night when his dose got low ("yes, but you still have to participate in groups the next day"). Zac's suggestion everyone be allowed to go home on weekends was met with a categorical "no" – and not just from the staff.

Dylan rolled the sleeves of his red-and-black plaid shirt up, exposing a blue/greenish tattoo of a clipper ship with RNZN - Homeward Bound inscribed beneath it.

"Were you a sailor?" Claudia asked.

Dylan looked down at the faded ink, feigning surprise.

"Good God. Where did that come from?"

"Come on, Dyl. I bet you've got some wild stories."

"Not really. It was all rum, bum and gramophone records."

Olaf shook his head in mock disdain and was about to conclude the group when Sleeve raised his hand.

"Ten years ago I went to NA for a while, and it was really good. Why don't we go to NA meetings here?"

The counsellors turned to each other - one with a knowing smirk, the other with pursed lips. Sleeve had apparently touched on something.

"Am I right to assume one will be supporting the proposal and the other opposing?" Zac asked.

"Yo, O-man! What's NA?" The Kid chimed in.

"Narcotics Anonymous," began Dylan just as Olaf spoke up.

"Hey, he was asking me, Daddio. You can give him your Captain Freemason sales pitch when he starts wearing cardigans."

Dylan patted Olaf's thigh and smiled. Unbeknownst to the clients, Dylan was a member of NA, but fiercely protective of his anonymity. Most Monday nights he would attend an invitation-only meeting, held in the rear of a closed cafe in a midtown arcade. All of its secrecy was for the simple reason most of the attendees were cops, doctors and other health and legal professionals, who might not appreciate running into their charges under such circumstances.

"Wee Olaf here struggles with this arcane theory called openmindedness, so we might let him go first."

"Oh no, you go first. Age before beauty and all that."

"I believe your mate Ms Parker had it right. Oink oink."

The group looked bemused both at the banter and by the fact that the two men rarely worked side by side in groups. Olaf's schtick was based around being 'loose', but this Algonquin Round Table routine, along with his naval life quip, gave them a peak into Dylan's not-so-earnest side. Of course both men were all too aware of the deep impact three people absconding would be having on the clients so their little dog-and-pony show was a way of smoothing out a lot of unspoken fear and concern around their AWOL cohorts.

"In answer to your question, Sleeve," Dylan began. "Is that NA doesn't really complement the recovery model we're offering you guys. And I'll qualify this by saying NA is a wonderful organisation, but it doesn't fit in with ITL's mission statement. Now you lot are incredible, and I truly mean that. I think for any drug-using individual to take control of their life and address things like, well, drug use is an extraordinarily brave thing to do. Take you, for instance. When you came in here buddy, you were a mess. Just remind us how you were."

"Ohh," Sleeve groaned. "Using smack like crazy, lots of pills. Abscesses everywhere. Cops raiding my place. Um, getting drunk every night."

"Great, living the dream! And what was it that brought you here."

"Methadone."

"Yes, methadone. So here you are now. No smack or cops and all the rest of your dramas. Just methadone. And how are you getting off that?"

"Very, very slowly," Sleeve replied very, very slowly.

"Exactly, because we want you to get off it and stay off it. Not much point in us bringing you down like you're all on a roller coaster, because that'll just have you running out the door to get loaded again. Now, 12-step groups believe in total abstinence. That itself is a debatable topic, and I'll leave that for my learned associate here to discuss. But NA does ask that you refrain from talking at their groups if you have used drugs that day. And whether you like it or not, methadone is a drug. Now, I don't look around this circle and see a group of people and think 'They're all smashed on dope'. I see incredible determination and commitment. But when we did try an experiment a few years back and take you guys to a nearby meeting for a while, we were eventually asked if we could take you to another meeting because your presence was triggering some of the NA people. And we weren't prepared to find out if we were welcome or not at other meetings. So that's why you don't go. I do hear some groups are acknowledging people on methadone but wiser heads around here feel it's still not appropriate. Now Olaf and I joke about how we don't see eye to eye regarding 12-step recovery programs, but I think I can safely say that we do agree that any program that helps you guys move away from addiction is to be applauded. So with that, I give you the opposition. Olaf..."

Olaf leant across and whacked Dylan on the thigh.

"I, too, went to NA many years ago, Sleeve, and to be honest, I thought it was the most delusional crap I'd ever heard. As an atheist, all that higher power slash God stuff gave me a migraine. And they abhor any intellectual discourse that challenges it. From my understanding people have been trying for years to do basic stuff like change NA's God to a non-specific gender. I mean, what century are this lot operating in? I grew up in a household where both my lapsed-Jewish grandmother told me religion is for closed-minded morons, and she qualified it intellectually. Then I go to NA and get told atheism is for closed-minded morons, and if I don't find God I'll start using gear again. Now, you could say I have taken a fairly simplistic approach to their model, and maybe I have. I have close friends who go to 12-step meetings and we occasionally get into robust discussions on this. And a couple of them agree that they should rewrite their book and spend more time on the powerless-over-drugs section and less on all the Kumbaya nonsense. But as for that "we want to hear from the person, not the drug" crap. Really? That tells me you guys aren't worthy of a voice. That's some bullshit power imbalance right there. Say someone goes there for a few years, doesn't touch a single drug in that whole time, goes on a date and has a couple of glasses of wine with dinner, you know what NA does? Relegates them straight back into 'active addiction' – whatever the fuck that means – and classifies the individual as a failure. It's like snakes and ladders. Or in their case, snakes and steps. Sorry Sleeve, but any organisation that will happily write-off so much hard work because of a drink or a joint or a bump or whatever is, in my opinion, weird."

"Is that what happened to you?" Zac asked.

"Funnily enough, no. I went to NA when I went through detox and I actually didn't mind it. But I tired very quickly of its heteronormative, white suburban middle-class dreck. I remember they had some little prayer book-type thing with these daily musings they'd read out at meetings, and some of them were just the most errant nonsense I'd ever heard."

He paused, looking around the circle at each of them.

"Disclosure time, kids. The last time I used any illicit drugs was the night before I hit that detox. The one thing I did take from NA was their 'don't use one day at a time' line. I do that because there's no mystery left in dope for me. I used skag the same way you did Sleeve. In fact, all of you. And frankly, I got bored. I don't miss it one little bit."

At that, The Kid looked up and sang, "I'm the chairman of the bored".

"No, Jason," Dylan said. "I believe you're the pilferer of iced confections. So let's see what we can do to help you overcome this antisocial propensity of yours."

AISHA WAS up to her ears in paperwork. On her desk were three stacks of client files, about 40 in all. She'd take one, look at the name on it, tap away at her computer then either relegate it into a document shredding bin, put it on another pile or write a large D in red texta on the front and consign it to a cardboard box. Dylan picked a file up from the box.

"Oh, no," he sighed. "Not Josie?"

"Yep. About 10 months ago. Didn't you hear? She went onto a hep C treatment then developed Cushing's disease and a bunch of other complications. The coroner determined her OD was self administered and intentional."

Dylan carefully replaced the file. Whether due to disease, overdose or the plain unexpected, the death of former clients always weighed heavily on the staff. Not that they felt any responsibility; it's just that when people left rehab it really was a lottery of who would find stability and who would re-embrace the chaos. Far too often it was the latter.

The penetrating ringtone from the office landline broke the gloomy mood. Aisha answered it in her usual manner.

"Guten tag. In The Light rehab."

She looked at Dylan with her eyes widened.

"Of course I remember you, Charlotte Anne. How have you been?"

Both of them knew exactly how Charlotte Anne had been. She'd been plastered all over the evening news a week before, accused of being involved in a low-level drug dealing network. Charlotte Anne was skitty and paranoid at the best of times, so Aisha took the phone outside for some added quiet. When prospective clients are in crisis, the best tactic is to get them into rehab as quickly as possible.

Dylan picked up a misshapen rubber toy - probably left behind after a family day.

"Yo, antichrist. Think quick."

He lobbed it across the office at Olaf, who didn't think quick. It bounced off the back of his colleague's head and hit a framed, autographed photo of Robert Fripp. Olaf raised his index fingers above his temples, extended his tongue and let out a devilish growling noise.

"You want to take them through overdose training, or go collect the stores?" Dylan asked.

Wednesday was also stores day. Each week Aisha, Olaf or Dylan would take a client and drive 30 kilometres to a charity food bank where the van would be loaded with all manner of groceries and staples. Gratis. It was run by a nun and a philanthropist friend of hers, primarily to feed the city's homeless. Thanks to their extraordinary resourcing abilities they were also able to provide food for a handful of community services which didn't get much funding. ITL's partnership came about one evening at a charity event when Sister Columba and Aisha bonded over a shared love of the dispossessed and Bach's St Matthew Passion.

"Hmmmm, pumping a plastic dummy's chest while singing Stayin' Alive or warping the druggy buggy out along the freeway? See you mañana."

Olaf grabbed the van keys and called out the back door.

"Hey Zac. Come with me. We're off to fraternise with the great unwashed."

TRIPS TO the food co-op were uneventful affairs. The residents would invariably ask if the radio could be tuned to a station neither Olaf or Dylan particularly cared for, with the volume turned way up. Olaf was hoping Zac would be different, purely because he knew he was capable of holding an intelligent conversation. As the engine kicked over, some light classical music came on. This was usually met with something along the lines of "what's this shit?" as the passenger punched the buttons in search of something far more primal.

Olaf steered the van out of the street, wondering why Zac was so quiet.

"Vivaldi?"

"Huh?" Olaf grunted.

"Is this Vivaldi?"

"To be honest, I don't know. I just remember his Four Seasons became the soundtrack for toilet paper and wine commercials years ago, and that did it for me."

"Relegated to piss and shit," Zac said. "How humiliating."

He turned the radio off.

"Speaking of which. That discussion we had in group this morning. Don't you *ever* have a glass of beer or wine?"

Olaf was hoping they'd be discussing something more cerebral than drinking, but this was what he was getting paid for.

"No, as I said, I haven't had any mood- or mind-altering chemicals in years."

"But you strike me as a fairly social creature, Olaf. What happens when you go out to dinner, like on a date? Or there's some celebration involving a toast? Do you pretend to drink it? Or spit it out? Or is drinking it allowed? What if a friend buys you a beer at a concert?"

Olaf laughed.

"Oh, you journos. One question at a time, okay? I drink water, tea, coffee, the occasional can of Coke and, my primary indulgence, sparkling Italian mineral water. No ice, and a slice of lime, garçon. If I'm at something like a wedding - and believe me, I avoid those motherfuckers like the plague - I will toast whoever with mineral water. Look, I'll be honest; it was difficult at first, for all involved. But society has changed a lot. Believe it or not there are people who have never had a problem with booze or drugs who wake up one day and decide no more. Maybe they don't like hangovers, whatever. Does sobriety worry you?"

Zac looked out the window, nodding.

"It does actually," he said. "I keep thinking how will I negotiate this with my colleagues? What will I say? I mean, as you know, no-one drinks like journalists."

Olaf checked the speedo and made a last-second dash through an orange traffic signal.

"News flash, Zac. Journalists think they have the market on debauchery cornered, but after a decade of working in this game I've come to realise everyone believes their profession parties harder than anyone else. Journalists, labourers, nurses, CPAs, Sunday school teachers. Doesn't matter. Every subgroup of society has this idea that their work is so challenging or whatever that they have to make beasts of themselves when really, it's just the human condition; we simply love to get out of it."

"Okay, I'll take your word for it, but tell me this; why, if the rehab doesn't send us to AA or whatever, do you guys peddle that total abstinence line? Isn't there an element of hypocrisy in that?"

Checkmate, Olaf thought.

"It is, but, and I'm loath to say this, you are an anachronism. Most people who come to ITL are chronic drug users. Their lives are riven with chaos and drama on an unparalleled scale. Control is anathema to them. But you are like some paragon of responsibility and diligence. Mind you, you also chose to stay on methadone for all those years."

Zac bristled.

"So are you saying I'm just another junkie?"

"Not at all. But do you wonder why you chose to stay on it for so long?"

"I explained that in group. I was scared."

"Exactly, and that's okay," Olaf reassured him. "But the fact you have been so successful at your job, that you stopped using heroin, that you came to rehab to get off methadone tells me you desire change. Believe it or not, we know how to help you lot change, hence the 'not even booze and weed' party line. You need to be on your toes at this stage, not letting your defences down."

"Do you subscribe to the idea that addiction is a disease?"

Now it was Olaf's turn to bristle. Over the years he'd heard all sorts of theories and explanations about why people use drugs in perilous ways. Initially he had dismissed the disease concept as the rantings of uninformed adherents of 12-step programs, but soon realised there was a phalanx of medical professionals and academics who endorsed it - Gene Prato being one of them.

"Not really," he said. "At a pinch I refer to it as an affliction, but I'm even moving away from that now. I tend to view addiction as the result of trauma, alienation, societal pressure - you name it. That whole disease thing is just a little too convenient. It really only suits one particular recovery model and, hey, if that's working for some people, God speed. But addiction is so fucking complex it can't be put in a neat little box and labelled a universal cure-all. Where do you stand on it?"

"Honestly?" Zac replied. "I'm not too sure. In relapse group the other day Dylan was talking about it and I remembered my friend Terry. He suffered a horribly long death from HIV/AIDS and I would have given anything for him to have been able to utter some platitude and, as they say, arrest his disease. Frankly, I find it a bit offensive."

They drove on without talking, rolling through the encroaching expanse of suburbia. Olaf understood Zac's quandary, but he also knew it would be better for him to ruminate on their discussion. Zac didn't have a clue what was going on for him at this stage, and it wasn't Olaf's place to foist his opinions on him.

A clutch of nondescript office blocks loomed in the distance.

"There you go, Frank Gehry," Olaf said. "Any of those float your boat?"

Zac chuckled, sunk back into his seat and peered ahead.

"Those eyesores are the reason we have demolition companies."

By the time they arrived at the food co-op their conversation had meandered through shared interests that included American politics and European cinema. As Zac noted at one point, it was like a date. He was surprised at Olaf's visceral loathing for TV, which came about after Zac revealed he held a non-partisan view of politics - much to Olaf's horror.

While they loaded the pre-packed boxes of groceries into the van, Sister Columba wandered over. Olaf was intending to introduce his offsider as "Zac, one of our residents" when Zac extended his hand and announced "Zac Watts, reporter with The Register".

The sister's face lit up as she shook his hand with both of hers.

"Have you come to write an article about us?" she asked.

"Precisely. Why have I not heard of you and your extraordinary work until today?"

As the reporter and the nun began talking, Olaf returned to the van - not so much to give them privacy as to metaphorically kick himself. You idiot, he thought. Sure, he's a great person and everything but he's only here to help schlep food back to the rehab. When's he going to get the chance to sit down and interview her? He's not on some fucking busman's holiday; he's in rehab for chrissakes. But hey, Einstein, you enabled this behaviour by playing favourites. Careful, Ollie boy.

AS THEY drove out of the warehouse, Olaf readied himself to remonstrate with Zac.

"What a fascinating woman," Zac said. "Have you spoken to her much?"

Maybe later, Olaf thought.

"Not really. Us practitioners of the dark arts have unwritten agreements to not annoy each other."

"So that's how you view your place in the world? A practitioner of dark arts?"

"You know what I mean. Believe me, she and I have nothing in common."

Zac guffawed and slapped the dash.

"You have got to be kidding. You're not going to pull that us-and-them card because she's a nun, are you? Seriously, Olaf. You need to take a long, hard look at yourself."

Olaf wanted to tell Zac to shut up but his curiosity got the better of him.

"Go on. I'm all ears," he said.

"Look, I get your whole evangelical atheist routine. It's very amusing but it also serves a purpose. The other night we were all talking about spirituality and God and stuff, and Leon was saying how great it was that you work there because it gives some balance to the status quo in which most people have some kind of faith, and Marty said that you're one of the most spiritual people he's ever encountered…"

Olaf cleared his throat and was about to get defensive, but Zac continued.

"… hang on. Just let me finish. The work you do, the way you treat others, the grace by which you go through your life is really not much different to what Sister Columba does. She advertises it with a habit and rosary, you with your wit and cynicism. But really, Olaf, Marty was right. And if you're half as clever as you think you are, you'll agree. It's irrefutable."

Olaf fumbled for a water bottle in the centre console, deftly unscrewing the cap with one hand. Part of him knew Zac was right but he just couldn't cope with compliments. Especially ones that went to the heart of his values.

"I've had this theory for years," Olaf said. "Anyone who says they're cool, enigmatic or spiritual, isn't. So I can't get behind your vote of confidence."

The traffic was starting to back up. It was well into rush hour and Zac knew the journey back was going to be a trudge.

"No-one's asking you to say you are. I just wonder why you have this block to accepting who you truly are. Like when we go to get dosed. I've watched assholes cross the street to avoid some funky homeless guy near the clinic, yet you'll give him a hug like it's a favourite aunt. Spare me your faux humility. I mean really, what's worse, some self-obsessed nose bleed saying they're spiritual, or some genuinely spiritual individual trying to be fatally cool."

"It's fatally hip, terminally cool," Olaf said.

"Yeah, whatever, Mr Cool."

A midnight black V8 - with hip hop thumping so loudly it caused the water in Olaf's bottle to vibrate - started edging in. Its equally dark window rolled down and a heavily tattooed arm waved its attendant gold and diamond jewellery to get into the lane. Olaf parped his horn to allow the muscle car to slide in.

"See," said Zac. "I was sitting here thinking this clown can wait. Yet you let him in. Why?"

"Well for a start, we're in a damned carpark at the moment. So it's not like the very fabric of society is going to unravel because I let him in. But going on that horn blast I just copped for letting him in, there's some moron behind us who wants to open both mine and Mr Muscle's head with a baseball bat because he's lost two metres of his incredibly important commute. So his rich and wonderful life will now miss out on seeing some TV commercial for a pizza, and for that, there will have to be reparations. So, did I let Muscleman in because I'm a good guy or a deadshit?"

Zac shook his head.

"I take it all back. You're just a nutter."

He turned the radio on and a mournful cello-and-piano dirge crawled out of the speakers. He hit the buttons and settled on an overproduced wall of guitars riding a wave of subtle feedback. On cue Olaf joined the vocals.

Zac turned it down.

"I'm not sure what's bugging me out the most. You being a U2 fan, or the idea of snogging Bono in the garden."

Olaf turned it back up loud, grooving to the guitar solo and joining in the vocals again.

When the song finally resolved itself, Olaf turned the radio off.

"I thought a good Catholic boy like you would be right into that song," he said.

"Well, for a start, I'm agnostic. But what's that song got to do with Catholicism?"

"Everything. Guilt, betrayal, love," Olaf replied.

"Hmmmm, might be drawing a long bow there, maybe?"

"Possibly," Olaf said. "But then it is about Judas and Jesus, so…"

"I'll take your word for it."

They watched the black muscle car continue its diagonal journey across four lanes.

"She spent two years in Sudan," Zac said, apropos of nothing.

"Yeah, I know. She's an exceptional person. So, what's your magnum opus on her going to be about?"

Zac took out a piece of copier paper covered in notes. He flipped the paper over and back.

"I'm not sure. I initially thought about a thousand words. You know, nun feeds the homeless. But after only five minutes chatting, you get the feeling there's a book waiting to be written."

The traffic continued its crawl. As they edged past a church with a large blue neon crucifix on top of it, Zac pointed up to it.

"You think that might be a sign?" he asked with a wink.

"Ahhh, the church of the holy bug zapper!" Olaf said. "Welcome to my parish, your holiness."

Olaf was about to reiterate that Zac's sole purpose in coming to rehab was to get his life in order, and that outside distractions were discouraged, when Zac blindsided him.

"Hey Olaf, do you ever pray? Or meditate?"

"For a start, it's ridiculous for an atheist to pray, but I once spent a long weekend at an ashram in total silence and, although it was an experience I don't want to repeat, the stilling of the mind can be a beneficial discipline. So yeah, I meditate occasionally. In fact, every four weeks or so I head south purely to spend a good part of the day out on the astral plane, communing with whatever."

"Do you go to one of those mountain retreats or something?"

"Something," Olaf qualified. "I go to a particular place by the ocean where I revel in the thalassotherapy of the sea air, get my dose of solitude, recharge my brain and, if the water is cold enough, reboot my limbic system with a body bash in the surf."

"Where is it?"

Olaf had been going to this spot for years but he'd kept it a secret. When friends asked where he'd been he'd just say "out of town", but for some reason he felt he owed it to Zac to tell him.

"A beautiful headland called Shappo's. It's a few hours down the coast."

"How did you find it?"

"You won't die wondering, will you? But then ... reporter. Alright, this stays here."

Zac nodded.

"I stopped at a cafe in a nearby town one day. I was having lunch, and I got talking to this woman. We were the only ones at the communal table. Outside. Bliss. Anyway, she was a single mother with a teenage kid. Interesting to talk to. Very intelligent and knowledgeable. We ended up chatting for a couple of hours. So I make noises that I should be going when she suggests we go back to her place and make love. Straight out of the blue. Junior was away with his father, so we did. I stayed the night, and the next day she took me out to this headland. We sat there for hours, just taking it all in. Sea, sun, view, the occasional whale, silence. And it became a thing where I'd go visit her every month or two, and we'd just revel in each other's company for a few days."

"What was her name?"

"It doesn't matter," Olaf said softly. "Not now, anyway."

"Did she die?"

"No, she didn't die. We died. She stopped caring. I left one day as I always did - mid afternoon. We'd had a really beautiful time. A week later I get a text message. 'I'm old, ugly and lonely. Please leave me be.' I tried to call, but she'd blocked my number. I sent some flowers to her house soon after, but the florist called to say she'd moved."

"You know her name. It would be easy to track her down."

Olaf waved his hand.

"It's hard to explain. I drove past her house once, and it was obvious she no longer lived there. That was three years ago. All I can do now is honour her request."

They were moving along at a fair clip now. Olaf opened the windows to let the cool air disperse his melancholy.

"Anita," he said. "Her name was Anita."

ZAC FOUND he was becoming drawn to Olaf. Not in a romantic sense, but in the way he thought; the way he communicated; the way he interacted with others. Occasionally the counsellor would make obscure references to literature and art in the groups - an act that could easily be deemed intellectual arrogance given his charges. But Olaf a had a great rapport with them.

The first time Zac noticed it was when Olaf dropped 'perspicacious' into a group discussion. Straight away Leon chimed in with "here he goes with one of his six cylinder words again. What was that one?"

Olaf turned to the whiteboard and scrawled it up.

"It pretty well means insightful or observant. For example, when Olaf used one of his wanky big words, Leon's perspicacity had him challenge Olaf's motive for using such a word."

As a few of them wrote it down Zac figured this wasn't the first time this situation had arisen. Had he tried it, he would have been derided for being a patronising smart ass and, remembering a jail expression he'd learnt from Warren, 'been put on the professor'. In Olaf, however, they saw an equal.

Later in that same group he was encouraging them to think about the consequences of using drugs for that first time after a period of abstinence. After a discussion about the shit show that would inevitably happen, Jesse chimed in.

"It's not rocket science, eh?"

"No, indeed it ain't, Jesse. And neither is rocket science."

Most of them, including Zac, looked perplexed.

"Rocketry isn't science, gang. It's engineering. Once you've built your rocket, then you can move into science. Physics. Newton's third law of motion, to be exact. Google it; fascinating shit. So the next time some clown uses that expression to put you down Jesse, dazzle them with that fact. Then tell 'em to go take a fucking walk down a short pier."

The room filled with whoops and high-fives, leaving Jesse looking particularly pleased with himself. That's what I want, Zac thought. That ability to connect with others so candidly.

"But this ain't about Newtonian physics, unless you throw all your drugs out of a fast moving car. And something tells me you lot *aren't* quite ready to do that."

"SO WERE you a teacher in some past life?" Zac asked Olaf as they filed out of the meeting room.

"Why? You in need of some tutoring?"

It was apparent Zac craved his attention, so Olaf humoured him by making a cup of coffee and joining him in the garden. Olaf had enjoyed their outing to Sister Columba's the previous afternoon but he knew he had to maintain personal boundaries. As inquisitive as Zac was, Olaf was guarded about how much he gave away of himself. Zac was different in that he was exceptionally bright and not a typical ITL client but, underneath all that, he'd still ended up there.

Olaf told him he'd been working in drug treatment for a decade after a career in radio production but, after some disjointed chit-chat about media ownership, he also made it obvious he was not about to go into some game of 'you probably know so-and-so'. Zac got the hint. They sipped their drinks while discussing whether the nadir of modern civilization was instant coffee.

"Favourite architect? And building?"

"Philip Johnson. Lipstick building," Zac shot back.

"Oooh, gabba gabba hey indeed."

Zac looked quizzically at Olaf.

"What the hell are you talking about?"

Olaf started singing something about green berets as Zac shook his head.

"What is it with your obsession for referencing obscure song lyrics?"

Olaf, miffed, shut up.

Zac feigned interest in a blue winged butterfly fluttering among the pink and white petals of the magnolia tree and Olaf studied the undercarriage of a departing 787, marvelling at how its two jets would keep it aloft for a further 14 hours. Funny, Olaf thought. Zac's life trajectory is like that of the plane, yet mine is as random as the butterfly's.

"I apologise Zac. That was idiotic of me." He paused for a bit. "So, what is it about that particular building that appeals to you?"

"The main thing I guess is the use of stainless steel and the earthy red granite. That combination appears so optically magnetic. I can't wait for the day when I wander down the street and actually see it for the first time."

Olaf nodded.

"That's exactly how I came across it, but I didn't know it was there. I'll never forget it. I'd been wandering around the base of the Seagram Building, surprised at how the once dominant skyscraper was now dwarfed by the surrounding buildings. So I continue down 53rd Street, gawking up at that crazy pitched roof on the Citigroup building. What I didn't realise was how incredible the base of that building was."

"Hold on," Zac interrupted. "Are they near each other?"

"Yeah, but wait. You know the base of the Citigroup?"

"Only from studying tons of photos. Isn't there some crazy church under it, too?"

"Exactly. Oh man, it will blow your mind. So I spend ages taking all that in, then head down the block toward the subway. And there's the Lipstick! I'd never even heard of it. But it was just like you imagined. And it reflects this gorgeous soft light all around."

"So you mean to say those three buildings are all in walking distance of each other?"

"One on each block. It's incredible."

They continued their discussion with Zac displaying an almost academic knowledge of the topic, where Olaf stuck to the "I know what I like" approach.

"So that was you who put the Guggenheim museum book in our, uh, library," Zac said.

"Nup. Which Guggenheim? Bilbao or New York?"

"New York. It's a damn good read. You should have a look at it. But I would be right to assume quite a few of those books are from your place."

"Maybe. Why? Have you been improving your mind with some?" Olaf asked.

"Well, I was torn between all those penny dreadfuls written by gangsters and earless thugs, or Barzun's history of Western culture. And I just knew the true crime crap was originally yours."

"You know what your problem is? You're too clever by half!"

"I mean, really Olaf, who around here is going to wade through a complex doorstopper like that?"

"Well, you for a start, you pompous wanker."

At that moment Karen came up to them with an electric lime-coloured clipboard.

"Two feelings, Zac," she droned.

The feelings review was an integral part of the clients' day. It gave them the opportunity to reflect on what they were experiencing at that moment and develop a recognition of how their emotions move in and out of each other. The correct procedure was for the person to ask the question without an audience then briefly discuss it with them. Olaf wanted to call her on her indifference but, given that she was relatively new to the community and still blaming herself over the three clients absconding, Olaf let it slide.

"Um, happy that I had another drop in my dose today and grateful that Jesse and I had an in depth conversation about our lives last night."

Cheekily, Karen also asked the counsellor. He shot her a stern look.

"Hopeful that the two wonderful people before me will continue to stand in their integrity and accomplish what they came here to do. And blessed that I have a job which I wouldn't swap for all the tea in China."

"You meant that, didn't you?" Zac asked after Karen left.

"Ooh yeah. All day, amigo."

"I want to ask you. Do you see many clients whose predicament belies their upbringing?"

"Too much. We had this one woman a few years ago. Perfect upbringing. No abuse growing up, stable loving family. Graduated from Parsons in design and technology. Just a wonderful human being. Not into drinking or drugging in any major way. A similar story to yours in fact. Experimented with skag and, long story short, ended up here. Finished our program, went home and hanged herself that same night. No indication, no goodbye letter. Nothing."

Olaf looked pensive.

"Addiction is the logical extension of trauma, but sometimes…" his voice trailed off.

"Sometimes what?" Zac asked.

"I don't know. Bad luck overrides curiosity and fun? Who knows?"

"That must be the worst part of your job. Having such high expectations of the clients yet seeing them fail. Repeatedly. I mean, Sleeve has done, what? Fifteen rehabs over the years? Surely there's a point where you say there's nothing more we can do."

The counsellor felt his hackles rise, not so much at Zac's presumption, but his insensitivity.

"There's an old saying, Zaccy boy. Where there's life, there's hope. And many of you guys entered rehab that first time thinking you'd have this thing licked from the start. Maybe even Leon did. Our hope is everyone gets it first time. But our responsibility is to never refuse a client another opportunity. As the Japanese say - nana korobi ya oki. It means fall down seven times, get up eight. We be the fucking weightlifters, grasshopper."

"Shit," Zac said. "That came out all wrong. What I meant was ..."

"Forget about it. Seeing you guys roll up here for another go warms my heart. And none of us judge you for it. If someone left here last time like a some nuclear fart from hell, so what? That was then. They might have improved. Or got worse. Doesn't matter. The point is they're still backing up. No, the worst part of this gig is that grey filing cabinet next to Dylan's desk. In it are about 40 client files, each with a big red D written on the cover. Deceased. I'm never ready for that particular shock."

Zac stared at Olaf's profile. He tried not to go into reporter mode but, couldn't help himself.

"Do you see sudden change happening in your clients, or does it take a while?"

Olaf appeared lost in the memory of the dead files, but nodded at the question.

"Yes, but not the way you expect. In the days just before you guys arrive here, you're invariably on the phone begging for help. Always in utter crisis and at your most desperate and hopeless. It's as though your drug use has wiped all memory of any previous treatment. I love it. The blank canvas brigade. Then within three days of landing here, you're all carrying on as though you wrote the fucking program and built the joint. But I hear what you're getting at. Change has to be slow, Zac. Real slow, otherwise ..." Olaf suddenly clapped his hands together so hard a noisy miner feeding in a nearby grevillea took off.

"And that's why your dose is lowered with all the pace of a glacier."

He nodded toward the clients who'd looked up to see what the commotion was.

"So what changes are you seeing in yourself, Zac?"

"Um, none yet. But I guess they'll come. Why, are you seeing any?"

Olaf shook his head.

"Gimme a break. Are you fishing for compliments? You tell me what changes have started."

Zac looked toward a Virginia creeper devouring the paling fence. He was at a loss as to what he thought he should say.

"Well, normally if I'd been asked such a question I'd construct some bullshit response and dazzle you with lies. But the truth is no-one ever asks me those sorts of questions. At this moment I actually feel quite inadequate, and I'm ashamed that I do, but I also trust you and feel I can be honest with you. Does that answer count?"

"Sounds like change to me," Olaf replied. "But don't just trust me. Trust the process. There is absolutely no reason you cannot express yourself so honestly with anyone." He looked across to Sleeve and Jane, puffing away madly and engaged in what appeared to be one serious discussion.

"Take him," he continued. "On paper you two are cheese and chalk. But in actual fact you are very similar. So what I want you to do is, at some point by tonight, open up to Sleeve. Have a chat with him about your insecurities and trepidation around being here. Find out how he wrestled with the same fears when he did his first rehab rodeo. And then - and this is the part you're going to love - tell your peers all about it in tomorrow's group."

With that, Olaf scooped up the coffee mug and headed back inside. Zac looked across at the deconstructed rock god. The man had more gold records than he could count and had written some of the most enduring pop hits ever. He had had his last dose three days after Zac arrived at ITL, but on those two days they shared the walk to the clinic, at least a dozen people stopped him to say how much they loved his music, and he was polite and respectful to each of them. Sleeve was devoid of pretense and ego. Zac relaxed. Damn, there actually is a part of him in me.

"Okay. Trust the process."

DYLAN WAS midway through the admission assessment of one Ms Sylvia Indigo when Olaf wandered into the office, glued to his phone screen. He nudged a bag aside with his foot and dumped himself at his desk. Sylvia was about to apologise for crowding the room with her luggage when he blurted "you know what the ratio of fucking wage theft is to standard crime?"

"Oh, about three to one," she said.

Olaf spun around in surprise. He hadn't noticed her and was embarrassed at his momentary lack of awareness. She sat with her legs crossed, wearing a long cotton dress, fringed brown boots and a peach-coloured cardigan. A large bottle-green hat was angled back on her head, forming a felt halo. Sylvia was a picture of health and his initial thought was 'what's she doing here'. Part of him wanted her not to be a client but the bags and Dylan's raised eyebrow gave it away.

"Well, hellooooo," he said in a manner he'd appropriated from a 1950s British comedy.

Sylvia batted her eyelids, mimicked his greeting and extended a drooped hand.

"And who might you be?" she enquired.

This proved too much for Dylan.

"Neither of you two are here for playing silly buggers."

He looked sternly at Sylvia then transferred the glare to his colleague.

"Olaf. Get everyone into a CBT group. Sylvia, why don't we focus on what we're doing here. Okay?"

Olaf got up, caught his foot in one of the bag's straps and tripped, tumbling headlong into a bank of filing cabinets. From his position on the floor he could see she was trying not to laugh.

"Do you often have this effect on people?" he asked. She had, he thought, the most incredibly beautiful hazel eyes, blending from brown out to green, much like a jaguar's, with a small, dark red freckle on the outside white of her left eye.

"First time," she said. "Oh-luff."

AFTER HE slammed the office door behind him Dylan grabbed the phone and rang through to the front desk.

"Unless it's a matter of life and death, don't call for the next 20 minutes."

Olaf was engrossed in an online report on rational emotive behaviour therapy, but sensed something was wrong.

"Everything okay?"

Dylan rolled his chair out opposite his colleague.

"You tell me. What exactly was all that bullshit about this morning?"

Olaf's immediate reaction was to go on the defensive, but he'd been trained by the best and the best was now his interrogator.

"I know, it was fucked."

Dylan, relieved Olaf hadn't gone into some lame litany of justification and excuses, parked his anger.

"Look, Sylvia is an attractive woman. There's no disputing that. But, tell me what you know about her."

Olaf didn't know shit about her, except that she was now, undoubtedly, waiting to see Dr Prato to get her dosing script sorted out.

"She's on methadone," he said. "Most likely in crisis if she's come to us. Probably has a horrific history of drug addiction, which brings with it all manner of emotional, psychological and maybe physical abuse. Going on her interaction with me, there's probably also some PTSD manifesting itself in a desperate need for acceptance."

Olaf suddenly felt ashamed at his callous disregard for her. Like most of their clients, Sylvia was from central casting; people didn't end up in there because they were well.

"In one, buddy," said Dylan. "She's one very damaged individual. So, what's going on?"

Olaf looked around the office, ruminating on his emotions that morning.

"Well, we've established she's attractive but, you know, I asked that question about wage theft and shit, not even knowing she was in here, and she came up with the right answer. Beauty and brains. That shit appeals to me."

"It's not about her, you clunk," Dylan said. "What's. Going. On. For. You?"

"Fucking Xanthe. I just miss her so much, and I know she's never coming back."

"Okay. Now let's unpack that in relation to your bullshit with Sylvia."

He's good, Olaf thought. OK.

"I go on those fucking online dates, and it's either 'I just want a friend' or 'I just want a fuck buddy'. The available ones are always morons and the commitment-phobes are Mensa candidates. I just can't win."

Dylan watched Olaf move an air conditioning remote around the table top, waiting for him to go further.

"Xanthe was great. She ticked a whole lot of boxes, and all she wanted was to settle down. But anytime we got near that discussion, I'd buckle. She'd joke about us talking about feelings and dreams, and I never knew if it was real or not. She never actually said to me 'let's move in together'. It was always hinted at - veiled references to marriage and crap. Spending time together. Renovating my house. Jesus, she was even talking about getting a fucking puppy."

"That's all well and good, but Xanthe isn't the problem here. She's cool. We all love her. It's you buddy. What is going on for you?"

Olaf gritted his teeth and rolled his eyes. When he first met Dylan all those years ago he was in awe of his ability to cut through the clients' obfuscation and dishonesty. Now, though, he was feeling extremely uncomfortable. His own words sprung to mind: "A movie is a lot easier than a mirror". For a moment he considered throwing a hissy fit but years of therapy had made him too aware of himself to indulge in such petulance.

"I feel like I'm not good enough for anyone. I have this reverse Midas thing where every relationship I have turns to shit." He paused, contemplating not so much what he'd say next, but what he'd actually said. "Fuck, what a self-piteous joke. The truth is I'm sinking into a pit of fear and loneliness, and the fear is I'll be alone forever. That I'm unlovable. So I try to make myself feel better with ... with bullshit. Cars, women, holidays, music, books, sex. But it only ever lasts for a brief period, and pfft, it's back to me. What's that stupid bit of psychobabble? Wherever you go, there you are."

Dylan nodded.

"I was thinking more about the hole in the soul. And what else have you unsuccessfully tried to fill that one with?"

Olaf exhaled, his heart and shoulders already beginning to feel lighter. It pained him to admit what he was about to but this was what friendship, honesty and trust summoned up occasionally.

"Heroin," he whispered.

The name floated between the two men. Olaf knew her power all too well. An invisible Siren, still serenading his base wants after all these years. He also knew it was always a short-lived romance, not just from his own experiences but from the tales of remorse and degradation his charges would tell. Plus ça change, plus c'est la même chose.

His eyes met Dylan's, and he felt a wave of gratitude. He knew that, quite apart from all the professional therapy, this man had an incredible ability to connect with people in crisis.

"I'm concerned for you Olaf, because now that all the other stuff is not working so well anymore, we both know that if you're not careful you'll end up on smack again."

"I don't think so," Olaf retorted with a hint of arrogance that surprised even himself. "I mean, it's been years since I had a shot."

"Exactly."

Dylan fumbled in his drawer and produced a red plastic tube. In it were a couple of disposable syringes, some sterile water, cotton buds, alcohol swipes, a plastic spoon, four condoms, some lube and two nasal pumps of naloxone. The official name was 'harm minimisation kit' but the clients called them 'smack packs'.

They were part of ITL's harm minimisation policy - made available for anyone on the site. There were always a dozen or so left around the joint in visible places to encourage safe injecting and safe sex practices. Despite the primary rule that clients would be discharged for drug use, ITL's duty of care overrode everything.

Dylan emptied the contents of the packet onto Olaf's desk and dropped a sachet of sugar next to it.

"So, just in case you've forgotten, show me how to mix up a taste. Substitute the heroin with the sugar."

Olaf wondered if Dylan had taken leave of his senses.

"Of course I remember," he said, indignant. "I must have done it a thousand times."

"Good. Then you can make it a thousand and one times."

Olaf was gobsmacked. Was this a joke?

"And if you think I'm kidding," Dylan continued, "I'm as serious as a goddamn coronary. Now do it."

He jabbed the desktop for effect, and Olaf began nervously rummaging through the paraphernalia, confused by the absurdity of the situation and his friend's aggression. He went through the ritual of preparing a shot of heroin. It may have been more than 10 years since he'd last done so, but the ritual was still second nature.

He was just about to rest the needle tip in the cotton filter and draw the 'drug' up into the syringe when Dylan snapped "stop!"

The theatrics of the role play had unsettled Olaf, bringing with it unresolved guilt around a girlfriend's overdose.

"See, you've forgotten already," Dylan said, his calming Kiwi lilt returning.

"Should I add some lemon?"

"No," Dylan replied. "But you've certainly left a lot of other stuff out."

They studied the spoon while the small wad slowly absorbed the defacto dope. Olaf pinched the syringe between his thumb and index finger, and noticed he was trembling.

"I dunno. What?"

Dylan's look of contempt had morphed into pity. Olaf hated seeing his friend look so sad, but was also at a loss as to what he'd forgotten.

"You left out your house and everything in it. You left out Xanthe and her kid. You left out this job. You left out the neighbour's cat that visits you every evening."

He paused for a second.

"You left out me, buddy."

"TELL ME about her, Olaf."

He furrowed his brow.

"What? Are you now my fucking therapist?"

"Oh, you know you should never fuck your therapist!"

They slyly checked each other out, having the same lurid thought - I'd therapy you.

"Why do you assume there is 'one' out there?" he asked.

"Because you have a beautiful sadness, Olaf. It's okay, we all have it. And by this stage of life there always is that one."

He tried not to squirm but failed. Besides, he was all too aware of the impropriety of the situation. Policy dictated that staff were never to be alone with clients, and certainly not in a closed room at 11pm. Sarah had called in ill that afternoon, and Aisha was unable to find a casual worker to cover her shift. The following day was forecast to be abnormally hot, so Olaf put his hand up, figuring a weekday at the beach was in order.

Sylvia had been in ITL for a month, but this was the first time they found themselves alone with each other. For the past half hour they had discussed mundane stuff like favourite films, art and music - a slow dance during which they tried to hide their mutual attraction.

Two blind peacocks, Sylvia thought.

Olaf's thoughts were more neurotic; he was justifying the unjustifiable. She's different. I'm honorable. I'll be transparent with Dylan around this. Nothing will ever happen.

"What was her name?"

Olaf tried not to allow his anxiety to become apparent. All his life he had struggled in the presence of women he was attracted to. He could feel his heart racing, just as it did the first time when he was seven and playing spin the bottle after school with some friends. Even though they were only kids, and he and Wendy's lips barely brushed, that was the moment Olaf crossed into a world of rushing emotions and sexual anxiety that would shadow him from then on.

"Xanthe."

"Xanthe. What a beautiful name. Was she an Amazon?"

"No, a seamstress."

They continued gazing at each other. Olaf knowing it was a dangerous situation and deluding himself he was the more responsible person in the room.

"Why did it end?"

Get a grip, dude, he thought. Here you are, allowing your emotions to be swayed by someone you hardly know. Just end the conversation now and allow her to get back to what she came here for.

"Because I'm a coward."

The corners of Sylvia's mouth rose slightly, and her eyes softened.

"In what way?"

He absent-mindedly tapped the space bar of his computer, watching the revolving logo on the screen be replaced by an aerial shot of a seaside village. His resolve left as though he'd just dived from a cliff into a crystal clear lake.

"She wanted love. Stability. Trust and emotional honesty. Her running joke with me was whenever she wanted a break she'd say 'Let's talk about thoughts and feelings' knowing I'd jump in my car and disappear for days."

Olaf's heart warmed at the memory of Xanthe's 5000-watt smile - then loathed himself just that little bit more.

"So why didn't you give her those things?"

Jesus. She was more brutal than his actual therapist.

"I've already told you that."

"You're not a coward, Olaf. And if you are, then we all are."

They remained motionless, listening to a particularly raw Alice In Chains song playing in the background.

As it faded out, Sylvia reached across and picked up Olaf's phone.

"What's your code?" she asked.

Normally, Olaf would have reprimanded a client for not only touching his property, but for also having the temerity to ask such a question.

"Six five two three."

Sylvia paused.

"Of course. Your name. I should have guessed."

The gall of her, he thought. But she's sharp.

"What exactly are you doing?" He'd never given away such information to anyone, yet here was someone he didn't know meandering into his privacy. She held the phone up between them.

"I'm getting ready for bed, Luffah."

Luffah? Olaf had enough trouble with his name but now it was being turned into a pet name? He did like the soft 'a' she put in it, though. Sylvia tapped away at the screen with a dexterity beyond his. Again he noticed the blood spot on her sclera.

"What happened to your eye?"

"It's called a nevus. It's cute, huh?"

He had no idea what she was talking about but made a mental note to find out later. Sylvia rose, leant across his outstretched legs and gently pushed her thigh into his as she put the phone back in its charger cradle. Her leg didn't move, and she pushed her hair behind her ear, looking down at him intently.

A snare drum began a slow skiffle as a resonant male voice and organ flowed out of the speaker.

Her lips opened ever so slightly, and Olaf battled the desire to lean up and kiss her.

"Night night, Olaf," Sylvia cooed and swanned out of the room, leaving the counsellor feeling like he'd been chloroformed.

Olaf killed the office lights and listened to *All Night Thing* repeatedly, each time hearing something new. Well, he thought he did. He knew that what he was actually hearing was the sound of his own desperate and confused mind. Olaf had already convinced himself that Sylvia was as besotted with him as he was with her; this was all some sort of deeply coded message that could traverse enemy lines, blitzkriegs and flak - from her heart directly to his. Every time he went to focus on writing up the day's reports and assessments, he'd be distracted by a word, or a phrase, or a tone, or a note.

Eventually he became bored. It was a great song but maybe it was just Sylvia fucking with his head. Olaf decided to apply the same principles that he drummed into his charges – identify, acknowledge and process. He identified his own neediness, accepted that it was something that would not go overnight but could certainly be dissected in therapy, and decided to take action by moving away from the delusional feelings he was experiencing. He turned the phone off, threw it into the drawer and sat in the dark lost in one of the umpteen guided meditations Dylan had installed on all the computers. Tonight's journey out onto the astral plane was an autumn leaf, falling to a brook and floating away to a serene pond.

By the time the narrator's soporific voice gave way to the chime at the end, Olaf was refocused.

He went into the next room to make a cup of tea. Slouched against the sink, waiting for the electric jug to finish its interminable cacophony, he could hear a piano being played. Olaf figured it was Marilyn, an eccentric local music teacher who lived directly across the alley. But as the neighbourhood's resident health nut who was forever reminding everyone that an early night was the key to a long and perfect life, it seemed odd for her to be tickling the ivories at 2am.

Olaf drowned an Earl Grey tea bag in boiling water, lobbed in two sugar cubes and added a thin slice of lemon. He strolled out into the garden to let the chilly night air brace his body temperature and subdue the tea's. The piano was now even fainter so it obviously wasn't she-of-the-good-sleep-hygiene. He watched a tiny strobe arc slowly across the sky, imagining it to be some bizarre vessel filled with mutants from a weird planet. In reality, it was a passenger jet cruising at 38,000 feet. Right the first time.

Back in the house, the piano sounded clearer. The occasional flat notes told him it was the old upright whose main purpose these days was more as a plant stand.

He moved along the hall, listening to an accomplished rendition of a popular piece, and relished the fact that for once there was a client whose musical tastes went beyond the jarring repetition of rock and rap. Not that Olaf disliked either, but some days just cry out for a gentle tune. He listened as the circular melody wound down to its final two repeated notes, then quietly opened the door.

He fully wanted - and expected - to see Sylvia sitting there but it was The Kid in the dim lamp light.

"I would never have picked you for a Luddy Van B fan," said Olaf.

The Kid practically jumped out of his skin and hurriedly closed the piano lid.

"No, no," Olaf continued. "Keep going. And I do love the irony of you playing that sonata on a moonless night."

The Kid looked like he'd been busted pulling off a major heist. Olaf was half expecting to see the poor guy's heart burst through his Iggy T-shirt.

"I'm s-s-sorry."

"No need to apologise for the music, although you won't win points for being up at this hour." He paused. "You play well."

The Kid scratched at his hair.

"How the fuck did you know what I was playing, man?"

"Same fucking reason you do, palooka. It's called an edumucation."

The Kid relaxed.

"You play?"

Not this again, Olaf thought. First it was Sylvia psychoanalysing his emotions, and now The Kid had found his Achilles heel. Whack. One arrow.

"No. But I always wished I did."

Olaf didn't regret telling The Kid this - one of the main principles they ingrained in the clients was honesty. As the old cliche goes - you can't bullshit a bullshitter. One of the most prescient things he ever heard was when Aisha sat him in her office five years before and laid out her personal mission statement.

"These people are the forgotten ones," she had said. "They come from all walks of life. We've had trust fund millionaires, people who live in subway tunnels and pretty well everyone in between. They ain't coming here because they're bored. They come here because they are the doomed. And nobody but nobody wants their funky asses no more. Except us. You're going to learn to give them two things. Hope. And love. All the rest we throw at 'em is just nonsense. And believe me, the only way we can provide that love and hope is with honesty."

Olaf met The Kid's stare.

"So why not, Olaf?"

"Long story short; my mother was a degenerate whose wants always came before her kids' needs. My sister was a musical freak. After a year of piano lessons she could listen to any pop song once then hammer it out note perfect. My attempt at piano was embarrassing in comparison. Maybe I could have done it, but next to her I was crap. But hey, we found a happy medium. Turned out I could sing, so we would just entertain each other for hours going through all sorts of stuff."

Olaf felt a familiar tinge of guilt.

"So man, what happened? You guys still jam?"

"What happened is I gave her her first shot of heroin when she was 17."

"Dude, that's fucking brutal. Is she dead?"

Ahh, yes, thought Olaf. Where honesty is trumped by pragmatism.

"No Jason, she's very much alive. And you have to crash."

"Man, I wanna hear about you and your sister. Sounds kinda like what my sister and I had, but different."

"And I'd love to hear about that, but not tonight. I've got work to do, and you need sleep."

The Kid headed toward the stairs, and Olaf took his tea to the office.

"Yo, Olaf. Maybe we should jam someday."

"Hit the sack kid. Now."

If anything, his mind was now well and truly away from Sylvia. He fired up the computer, pulled out the documents from his colleagues' pigeon holes and wrote six extensive client case management reports.

As Olaf strolled home through a cool morning fog, he turned his phone back on, waiting for it to go through its protracted start-up sequence. He watched a black cat sporting a red bandana scuttle across his path and tear up a tall wooden fence like some feline ninja. And he remembered that song. Sure, he had played it to death only six hours beforehand, and there was no denying it was a cool song, but he resolved to delete it from his list. It had no real bearing on his life this morning, and if he ever felt the need to hear it again, well, he could easily access it.

This was the part he enjoyed the most – the processing. Olaf always felt a sense of accomplishment when he could consciously change his behaviours. The device vibrated in his hand, and a 'boink' sound informed him of an SMS. It was from his friend, Matt, telling him that his dog Alice had died, and by chance did he happen to have any photos of her?

Olaf did, indeed, have some photos of her. He had been purging hundreds of useless happy snaps only days before and came across a series of Mr and Mrs Matt with their beloved hound. Olaf decided to keep them purely for posterity, mainly because the loving couple travelled extensively and he knew that getting them together was a rarity. He remembered how pissed off he felt at their insistence of the dog being in the pictures, but was now glad he'd kept them. These little dabs of glue that bond relationships. Maybe their presence in his photos could be some form of talisman. He opened the photo folder and squinted at the screen in the dissipated foggy glare. A spur-of-the-moment shot he'd taken of Aisha and Dylan the day before had been superseded by a frozen video frame of what looked to be a chin. He touched the large white arrow, and the image panned back to show

Sylvia's beatific face. Those gorgeous eyes, slightly crossed, and staring straight at him. Her lips flared coquettishly and her dimples grew.

"I'm getting ready for bed, Luffah."

"ALL BECAUSE of a purse. A stupid, fucking purse."

Tracey wiped her eyes and blew her nose into a tissue. She absent-mindedly started pulling little pieces off it and dropping them to the floor.

"I'm sorry guys; that's just sent me into the deepest shame spiral."

"Oh no, babe," Sylvia said, but Dylan raised his hand to quieten her.

"Why?" he asked.

"Oh, you know. I, like, get my life totally together for so long, some stupid thing happens and then I'm back to square one. It's like I'm a total failure."

"Are you a total failure?"

The question stung, but Tracey knew it wasn't true.

"Well I'm here. So I guess I must be doing something right."

Tracey had arrived the day before, a complete mess. Two years prior she'd had a career, financial stability, a loving partner and a seaside apartment with views to die for. Now it was all gone.

She hadn't intended to disclose as much as she did in the morning group, but it just came out. Tracey spoke of the alienation she began to develop despite her successes; borderline workaholism; investing all her time in being with her girlfriend; losing connection with her old support network. It had been 15 years since Tracey had used heroin or methadone. But then the purse had disappeared on a crowded train.

It had been her late mother's, the only memento of the one person who never gave up on her. Tracey was a single child, raised in an atmosphere of abject poverty but enduring love. Despite the former, she never wanted for much. A rebellious teen flirtation with drugs progressed to addiction, which in turn led her into a methadone program. At 23, Tracey had defied statistics, gotten clean and started a nursing degree. Even after her mother died from a sudden coronary,

Tracey stood at her grave and promised to honour her memory by never using drugs again.

Unfortunately, the missing purse became the catalyst for her unravelling. Tracey's relapse was simply a declaration of war – on herself. There's a theory on the streets that when people return to addiction after a decade or more of respite they go straight to the same level of using had there never been any gap. Tracey certainly lent credence to that theory. Within six months of picking up heroin again her near-perfect life had been supplanted by sex work and prison. The irony was that her mother's keepsake was returned four months after it disappeared, but by that stage Tracey knew, deep in her heart, none of this had anything to do with the purse.

During the group Zac fought a niggling distraction. He felt like he knew Tracey, but he couldn't place her. He racked his brain trying to make a connection between her face and his déjà vu but eventually gave up.

As they walked to the clinic that day, he sidled up to her and awkwardly reintroduced himself. He told her how she had a hell of a story and that, although they really didn't know each other, he was still glad she made it to rehab.

"Funny how you say we really don't know each other," Tracey said. "Because we don't know each other at all."

Her air of hostility only compounded his confusion. Anyone who knew Zac would describe him as a lovely guy or something similar. Apart from the occasional corrupt shyster he'd taken down in the popular press, he had no enemies.

"Yes, that came out all wrong, and I do apologise. It's just I have this overwhelming sense that I know you, and I can't quite place where from."

Tracey stopped dead in her tracks, folding her arms tightly. The others kept moving and, when they were out of range, she started on him.

"Listen," she said. "I don't know what your game is Zac, but I'm here to get my life back in order. So if you're harbouring some bullshit Pretty

Woman fantasy because you fucked me in a parlour once, forget about it."

Zac was mortified and grabbed her elbow as she walked away.

"And get your fucking hand off me NOW!" she barked.

"Tracey. Oh God. Sorry."

His brain and mouth had ceased to connect, and he felt ashamed and humiliated.

"It's nothing to do with anything like that. Please hear me out. I've only had five sex partners in my life. I just think I know you and..."

"I don't know you," she said. "And frankly, I'd be happy to keep it that way. So please, leave it. Okay?"

A fair enough request, he thought, and for the first time in years Zac could not wait to get his dose.

THAT EVENING'S dinner was particularly convivial due to two things - it was Aisha's birthday and Sleeve was going home the next day. Departures were often challenging for all; the individual because they were leaving the relative cosseting of rehab; their peers because they were losing one of their own; and the staff because there was always the niggling fear that this one might be the next to relapse and die. Fortunately, this wasn't a particular concern around Sleeve. When the gossip got out he was in rehab, a bunch of past and present rock musicians in Narcotics Anonymous banded together to refurbish his apartment. Sleeve himself spent a few weekends on top of a ladder painting the joint - a new skill he found both satisfying and meditative. His friends also chipped in, recarpeting and refurnishing the place and, when they weren't doing that, they were dragging him off to meetings and checking in on him daily. As he announced over his farewell dinner, he was truly feeling the love.

As was Aisha. Dylan had originally suggested he, Olaf and the birthday girl celebrate at a nearby osteria but she was insistent it be with the clients. When word of this got around the rehab, Claudia and The Kid offered to make the cake. Dylan's knowledge of cooking was non-existent so he had no idea why they had requested passionfruits, a dozen eggs, fresh cherries and balsamic vinegar.

The meal itself was spectacular - osso bucco, kingfish cutlets, crumbed tofu and three salads - but the massive pavlova was something else. As it was carried to the table Aisha asked Olaf where he had bought it. He pointed to the two cake makers as the others burst into applause. She squeezed them both in the warmest mama bear hug possible then turned to Olaf and Dylan.

"And to think you two bums wanted to drag me away from my family here to some greasy spoon dive."

As the cake was demolished, the topic came around to family backgrounds.

"What do your parents do, Zac?" Sylvia asked.

"Ooh, that's a rather personal question. But hey, we're all friends here. Basically they reside deep in their own fetid fundaments and exhibit parental love by throwing indiscriminate amounts of cash at me."

Sylvia widened her eyes and pouted.

"You say this as though it's a bad thing."

"Maybe it is. My grandfather was the epitome of grace and charm, so I can't figure out how my father became the blue-ribbon asshole he is."

"What did your grandpa do?"

"He was a dental surgeon. The loveliest man in the world. What about yours?"

"Funnily enough," Sylvia said. "My grandpa was the loveliest man in the world, too."

"And mine," said Claudia.

"Well," announced Aisha. "You're obviously all forgetting about mine."

Amid the frivolity Zac caught Tracey staring at him. He still hadn't reconciled himself to the muddled discussion that morning but their few interactions throughout the day had seemed cordial enough. It unsettled him that she appeared to still be pissed off.

Eventually she got up and headed to the fridge, taking out a Coke and a Sprite before walking up behind his chair.

"Hey, can we talk?"

Zac wondered why she felt the need to reopen the wound at this point in the evening's festivities but her subdued manner suggested her animosity might have dissipated. They went out into the garden. But this time it was she who did the grabbing, by gently taking Zac's upper arms.

"I owe you an apology."

The only thing that unnerved Zac as much as aggression was intimacy. He knew the others could see them but the chit-chat from the dining table indicated there was little interest in their private talk.

"Think nothing of it," he said.

Tracey sniffed a little and wrapped her arms around him. He returned the hug, confused.

"You said your grandfather was a dentist, and then I remembered. You were right. I am so sorry Zac. We have met. I narcanned you in a subway toilet once."

THEY TALKED about the paths their lives had taken after their initial encounter. What Tracey failed to mention in group was that she was a paramedic; a detail, Zac suggested, which could have saved them the embarrassment of that morning's misunderstanding. Although she couldn't remember the exact details of his overdose, she said she never forgot the watch and the briefcase.

"I still have one of them," he said, raising his wrist to show her the titanium-cased Swiss chronograph. "It was my 18th birthday present from Pop."

Tracey looked at the watch, a macho cluster of buttons and dials that, to her, looked out of place on Zac.

"Very action man," she joked.

He asked her why she had given him the clinic's business card.

"That was my standard modus operandi at drug overdoses. Why? Did you call them?"

Zac raised his opened hands, sweeping them at the garden and the dinner party.

"Fairly soon after. Dr Vanessa gave me my first dose, and all these years later I've decided to jump off. So here I am."

"With all respect," Tracey continued, "you're very well preserved considering all your years of abuse."

"Yes, I have the most outrageously perfect genes. Real master race shit. In fact, medical researchers have made it clear that if I ever actually die, they would love my body and brain for cloning." He paused. "Alright, so I'm a weirdo. That overdose you saved me from was a wake-up call. I was on the cusp of career and failure, but the drug milieu was never really my scene. And, to be honest, that overdose was also way out of character for me. Sure, I liked getting stoned, but I was never that big on being knocked out cold. It was a no brainer."

"So what did you do? Just use 'done, weed and pills?"

"Nada," he replied. "Just my dose and the occasional beer or wine. See? I told you I'm strange."

Tracey looked forlornly toward the magnolia.

"Is everything okay?" he asked.

"There was something else about that day and it's been bothering me. You probably don't remember, but you had a really sore jaw when you came around."

"Yeah, vaguely. Why?"

Tracey wanted to downplay it, but her guilt was overwhelming. She knew she would have to atone for it some day.

"The guy I was working with that day was a prick. Sometimes at ODs the junkies would freak out when we saved them. It's insane. They're dead. We bring them back to life and they start throwing punches. Anyway, he had this thing where just before I'd inject the naloxone, he'd smash their jaw onto a hard surface so when they'd wake they'd have a blinding pain to distract them from their bullshit about us fucking up their high. You didn't look like the sort of guy who'd get violent and I told him he didn't need to hurt you but, you know…"

Zac unconsciously rubbed his jaw before taking a swig of his Sprite.

"Hey, Trace. I dropped, you saved me. End of story. As Pop once told me, 'If life has given you a shit sandwich, you need to look at your part in the ordering process'. I honestly can't thank you enough."

They returned to the table to scoff more pavlova and interrogate the other's lost decade. Beyond their shared history of drug use, Tracey and Zac realised that, by and large, they were fellow travellers of sorts. Industrious, empathetic, non-judgemental. And damaged. All the ingredients for a wonderful friendship.

THE RAIN started late one Friday afternoon. It was sudden and torrential, and set to stay for the five days. As the activities coordinator, Sylvia had organised a community get-out-of-town on Sunday. Her proposal to drive to a national park beach for a picnic and then a lengthy nature walk was endorsed by Aisha and Sarah. Weekend activities were usually mundane excursions like going to the movies or amusement park. Occasionally the clients would begrudgingly agree to commune with nature, but the general will was to be indoors, distracted, and with copious amounts of caffeine and sugar at hand.

But when Mother Nature put paid to Sylvia's proposal, Aisha called Sylvia and Tracey into the office to offer an alternative.

"You've all been doing really well, ladies," she said, "but you can't go on a nature walk in this weather so what would you say to Sunday just being a total chill-out day back here? Take-out pizzas, ice-cream, watch movies. You can do what the rest of the city will be doing in this squall."

It appealed to them and they riffed on the whole kids' party-theme by squealing and stomping their feet.

"But I do like your nature walk suggestion, Sylvia," Aisha continued. "So let's do that on the following Monday, which I believe is a public holiday."

"That should work," Sylvia replied. "So that means Sarah will still be coming with us?"

Aisha tapped at her computer.

"No, Olaf is rostered on that day."

A frisson ran through Sylvia at the prospect of spending some time away with Olaf. Tracey had an inkling about the two of them but wasn't sure if she was reading too much into their interactions.

"Oh, okay," said Sylvia as she nudged her friend's ankle, confirming her suspicions.

LEON OPTED out to visit his ailing mother. Most outings tended to be non-negotiable events but as Mrs Murphy had been moved from a nursing home into palliative care, it was agreed that Leon should spend as much time with her as possible. His sorrow around his mother's failing condition was compounded by the fact that his addictions had not only robbed her of her only child for two decades, but his gambling debts meant she had had to forfeit her modest apartment to keep him from prison. Within three months of Mrs Murphy transferring her title deeds to a Macau-based casino consortium, Leon commenced a four-year incarceration for conspiracy to supply methamphetamine to an undercover police officer. Still, as Washington Irving noted, "A mother's love endures through all".

Karen was also excused because of the fortnightly call with her nine-year-old daughter, who had been living in foster care since she was three. Little Amber knew nothing of the detritus and waste of her mother's life and it was unlikely she would remember her own tumultuous first few years.

Her current lifestyle was one her mother would not be able to replicate. Amber lived with two other foster children in a homestead on 900 acres of lush dairy farmland. One of her carers, Don, had himself been the product of a horrendous childhood and 17 foster homes. He and George met while working at a major advertising agency, fell in love, eloped, developed an app for streamlining online shopping, sold that for a king's ransom and, after a year of doing yoga and sweet fuck-all else in the highlands of Bali, decided to 'retire', tend dairy cattle and give the unloved some love.

Their primary goal was to provide the kids with nurturing until the parents were ready to take back the reins. Despite their desire to see Karen and Amber reunited and happy, they were more than aware of the underhand behaviours some people would go to to turn their children against their carers in the deluded belief their child would be returned. The reality was the children would more than likely be shunted off to another home, and not necessarily one brimming with the love and warmth provided by these two. So the calls were monitored closely, always with the child's safety and interest at heart. Beyond that, though, they had a certain soft spot for Karen.

As did Olaf. And Aisha. And Dylan. And more often than not anyone else who ventured into her unhinged orbit. Her first admission to ITL nearly didn't happen. She turned up smashed on booze and pills, so much so that she was dispatched to the local ER in an ambulance. This would normally preclude a client from reapplying for six weeks but within two hours of the emergency vehicle tearing off in a blaze of flashing red lights and sirens Karen was back at the rehab door, compos mentis. She was admitted but the proviso that should she step an inch out of line, she'd be discharged. Behind the orange door, the staff gave her two days.

How wrong they were. Having come from a hideous existence of meth, heroin and benzos addiction, truck-stop sex work and regular arrests, the mundane and rigid structure of rehab was a godsend for her. Karen slotted into the routine immediately and threw herself into the program. In groups she would go to a level of vulnerability that was rarely seen - and not out of braggadocio, but pain. The staff had become inured to hearing tales of depravity and horror but occasionally even Dylan was caught off guard. In the relapse prevention group one morning, he was getting them to understand why they held such underdeveloped societal attitudes and mores and explained how for many drug users their emotional development slows down at the age they started using. He then went around the room getting each of them to give a precis of what age they started using, the drugs they liked then and how old they were now. By and large it followed a fairly similar pattern. Pot/alcohol/hallucinogens around 13, intravenous drug use by 16, and poly-drug use for the next 20 years or so. All of this peppered with detoxes, prisons and rehabs. Certainly there were exceptions, but not often. Karen was an exception.

"Is this by choice, or when you started shooting yourself up?" she asked.

"Well, usually the act of using drugs the first time is a choice. Let's not worry about it being a wise or poor choice, but it is a choice nonetheless. So, how old were you when you first chose to use?"

Karen stared at him blankly.

"Okay, let's forget about the 'choice' stuff, Karen. Just tell us how old you were and what you had."

"Six. Heroin. Mum gave me a taste."

Neither Dylan nor the rest of the group were prepared for that. He tried to process how to circumvent the inevitable discussion, not out of censorship but to avoid triggering others in the room - particularly those with small children. There was also the dilemma of being obliged to report crimes. And while Karen was now in her late 30s there was no statute of limitations on child abuse.

"I am so sorry to hear that Karen, and I thank you for your honesty and bravery in sharing that with us. It must be a very painful memory."

The room was dumbfounded. Karen looked around sheepishly and nobody remonstrated with Tracey when she wrapped an arm around her shoulders.

Dylan didn't need her to qualify his comment about the pain of memory. Her sad eyes and the fingernails digging into her wrist spoke volumes.

"Why the fuck would someone do that?" one of the others asked.

Before Dylan could curtail the inquiry, Karen spoke.

"So her boyfriend could fuck me."

The room broke into mutterings of disgust and even Dylan recoiled at what he'd just heard. Any hesitation he might have had about involving the authorities was instantly trounced. Suddenly, all his pacifist and libertarian tendencies were gone. He looked at Karen's forlorn face; at the pitted acne scars, the deep lines around her mouth and eyes, the sunken cheeks of dental loss, the glazed and dulled eyes. He didn't want to reassure her that everything would be alright. He didn't want to pity her. He didn't want to hug her. All he wanted was vengeance.

"WHAT WAS that incident you had with Karen last time she was here?"

Olaf shifted uncomfortably in his chair.

"I really don't want to pillory the poor kid. I mean, man. What a fucking life."

"No," Dylan replied. "Neither do I. I just vaguely remember some drama the two of you had while I was in Scotland. I'm not prying. I just heard talk of you two having a run-in and wouldn't mind knowing what happened. But if you don't want to, I'll respect that."

"She was smoking inside the kitchen door one night," Olaf began. "I walked in, told her it wasn't kosher, that she needed to be outside. Then BOOM. She went off. Started yelling at me. Calling me a fucking cunt. Screaming that she wanted to die. Challenged me to boot her out so she could go OD herself. Honestly, she was so off the Richter I didn't catch half of it. So I go into the whole open hands, puppy dog eyes, softly spoken shit - which of course only compounded it. Yelled at me to stop fucking patronising her. It's not fucking Sesame Street. More abuse. Cocksucker this, fuckwit that. I told her I wouldn't be spoken to like that and then…"

Olaf took a deep breath.

"And then she cleared her lungs and spat this fucking oyster of shit into my face. Man, it was putrid. I could feel it rolling slowly down my cheek."

Despite the vileness of the event, Olaf grinned in disbelief at the memory.

"That's revolting," Dylan said.

"Yeah, nah. That psychotic whore mother of mine used to do it regularly, and don't forget I sang in punk bands back in the day. And you don't wanna know what floats my boat in bed. Funny thing is, I clearly remember that, when she did it, my first thought was 'thank fuck she still has some humanity left in her'."

"I don't quite follow."

"When I called Aisha that evening, she asked if I was going to kick her out. I mean, it was late on a cold winter's night and she was homeless. And you know how much I hate dealing with those power-crazed assholes at the shelters. No, I just factored in that the day before some family court judge told her she wouldn't see her kid 'til she turned 18. Now that is fucking brutal. You imagine being a mother and hearing that? From some decrepit old Masonic Hall motherfucker? Man, a bit of spit is nothing in comparison."

Just then Aisha walked into the office and dumped the phone in its cradle. Dylan was slouched back in his chair, drumming his tattooed digits on the armrests. Olaf had his feet on the desk, indolently toying with an origami crane made by a former client. She figured she was interrupting something, but knew it could wait.

"Well, there's good news and there's bad news," she said.

"Please tell me those evil bastards had fucking violent deaths," Dylan sniped.

"I've just got off the phone to family welfare, who became aware of the sexual assaults when Karen was 14. Two males were jailed for raping her, they were never able to establish the identities of the other three, and her mother died from AIDS when Karen was 11."

"So what's the bad news?" asked Dylan.

"The good news is," Aisha continued, "Gene has a friend who specialises in childhood sexual abuse. She's a shrink. He's just spoken to her and she's agreed to waive Karen's fees for the first five sessions.

Her thing is dialectical behaviour therapy and, from all accounts, she's brilliant."

As though guided by some invisible cue, Olaf grabbed a sheath of papers and headed toward the orange door.

"Residents evaluation group," he said.

The door clunked shut, and Aisha knocked on her desktop.

"Hey Dylan, what's wrong?"

"Sometimes it's hard to retain one's faith, Aisha. You know that. Look at what we do. Look at our residents. These poor buggers end up here not because we are the last resort. They know we'll welcome them anytime, without judgement or prejudice. There's a reason the three of us do this stuff. God knows it's not for the money. Look at bug-a-lugs there. It's like he owns a diamond mine or something. He could be anywhere in the world, go anywhere he wants, whenever he wants. Yet he's dedicated to this place. As are we. Sure, he and I have both been there, so that gives us some kind of street cred. But look at you. Why are you here?"

Aisha looked at him askew.

"Are you after a pay rise?"

"No. No, not at all. Damn, that came out all wrong. We know you could get a gig on some board that would pay you … aaand I've done it again. It's not the money."

He paused.

"Look, we do this because we love it, you agree?"

Aisha nodded.

"And we're a niche service. What I'm trying to say is I sometimes feel we - the three of us - lose our sense of purpose and direction. We go on autopilot, and that's okay because we're bloody good at this. But sometimes …"

His head lowered and his voice trailed off. He stayed slumped for a bit then looked up.

"Oscar is six years old. He's the light of my life. I was a crap father to his mum, so I'm sure as hell going to be the best grandfather I can possibly be. And the thought of anyone violating or defiling that little boy … Christ, any child. It makes me physically ill. Just the thought."

"Hey," whispered Aisha. "I know you and Olaf see your own therapists but when did we last have clinical supervision?"

Dylan closed his eyes, took a deep breath and nodded.

"Probably about six months back, just before Olaf went to Hiroshima."

"Well it's about time Dr Ginsberg graced us with her presence again."

DESPITE THE love he had for his job, Olaf hated working public holidays. Not that he had anything better to do. It was just that it either meant sitting in a darkened cinema with a bunch of people with the attention spans of gnats, watching some mind-numbingly B-grade piece of violent doggerel, or making niceties with the clients' relatives at family visits. He could never figure out how the same people who had been hostage to their loved one's reckless, brutal lifestyle for years could suddenly turn up on the day as though they had returned from a four-decade-long deep-space probe.

"And how do you think my Murgatroyd is going, Oliver? He's such a sweet boy."

Oh, just swimmingly, ma'am. Once you look beyond the swastika tattooed across his throat, and the behavioural contract I've put him on because he insists on masturbating to rape fantasy porn on the lounge in the middle of the night, hell, he's a regular Little Lord Fauntleroy.

"That's probably a question you best ask Murgatroyd, Mrs Gronkman."

So the debrief on his desk about a road trip out of town came as a pleasant surprise. He checked it over and approved it. Picnic lunch prepared and packed by the residents. Three not attending. Six clients and one staff member. Make sure the phone is charged and the fuel tank is full. Take a first aid kit. Yada, yada.

On their constitutional to the methadone clinic, Olaf asked how they were all feeling. Most were fairly excited, with the exception of Karen and Lenny. Karen was torn because she was forfeiting the excursion for a 10-minute phone call. But when Olaf suggested calling George and Don to see if they'd be amenable to changing the time of the call, she rejected it on the grounds that she owed it to Amber to be reliable and consistent, and if she couldn't start doing that now, would she ever?

Olaf knew Karen always felt apprehensive around him after the spitting incident. She understood that one day she would have to apologise to him, but every time she thought of doing it she would be racked with guilt and shame. Today wasn't going to be that day, though. Olaf kept pace with her along the pavement.

"Hey Karen, for what it's worth, I believe you can get this."

She nodded, wishing she was half as confident.

Olaf dropped back, resting on a low garden fence to wait for Lenny. He'd arrived the day before in an ambulance, not that he needed it. Sure, he was in the early stages of emphysema, but his initial phone assessment had been three days ago, so it was apparent Lenny had friends in high places.

He was 68, wire thin and looked like a 17th century storybook pirate who had wormholed into an acid trip at Woodstock. He was a melange of ludicrously large earrings, painted nails, feathers, leather thonging, bells, necklaces, rings and patchouli oil. And a portable oxygen tank. Fifty-five years of dedicated smoking had begun taking its toll.

Lenny had done it all. Champion equestrian in his mid-teens, Vietnam war soon after, a taste for grade four elephant foot heroin while on R&R in Bangkok, smuggling runs to Afghanistan, three years in a Malay prison, down and out in the Golden Triangle for a decade. At 42, his oldest and dearest friend bankrolled Lenny's three-month stay at a private rehab in California, if only to give him a break from the chaos. The friend was Gene Prato, and that break from the chaos continued for the next 18 years. In that time Lenny settled and reinvented himself in Bali, overseeing a small team of mechanics and airbrush artists revamping Italian motor scooters into famous art pieces. Botticelli's

Birth of Venus, Warhol's Campbell's Tomato Soup can, Van Gogh's Starry Night, Mondrian's Composition. Virtually every great modern masterpiece ended up on one of Lenny's Vespas. Over five years he shipped about 200 of these crazy artefacts around the globe. When one turned up under a bikini clad model in a rap video, it was game on for Lenny. Suddenly, slews of the Beautiful People - as he referred to his gullible customers - wanted one of his bikes. The only problem was, like most things with Lenny, it was a game of three-card monte in a smoke-and-mirror tent. He would have his chosen associates arrange delivery of the consignments to the purchasers, switching the seat between the arrival port and the buyer's delivery point. This was for the simple reason the Beautiful People were buying an arty piece of crap while the not-so-beautiful people were taking delivery of three kilos of pure cocaine. The combination of crooks, side-kicks, dodgy offsiders and obligingly corrupt officials at the Tanjung Perak seaport meant that, should anyone get caught, it would be near-impossible connecting the coke back to Lenny. In that time he never lost a gram.

Ironically, it all came to a halt when some coked-up moron lost control of his sports car in downtown Denpasar, mounted the kerb and sent Lenny flying through the air and straight into hospital for a month with multiple bone breaks and contusions. A steady diet of oxycodone woke his dormant demon and, well, here he was. Again.

"Let me guess, man," Lenny said in his weird patois of Nimbin via Bali. "You want to carry my scuba tank while I smoke a joint."

Olaf couldn't help but laugh. He was familiar with Lenny although they had only met the day before. Dr Gene had been regaling the staff for years with wild and wonderful tales about his treasured friend. Most of the stories were dismissed as hyperbole but, after completing his admission assessment, Olaf concluded it was all true.

"Only if it's full of nitrous."

Lenny wheezed an emphysemic laugh which turned into a violent coughing fit. The blood-tinged spit that hit the pavement did not bode well so Olaf took hold of the tank. Lenny wiped his mouth with a tissue and peered over the top of his purple hexagonal glasses.

"Man, if that had nitrous, I'd be dosed up already and leading the peloton through the Pyrenees."

Olaf offered to see if he could arrange Lenny a take-away dose of methadone. He knew a call to Dr Gene would see it done, but the hippie was too proud.

They made their way so slowly that, well before they arrived at the clinic, the others were already returning, dosed, animated and fired up on double shot caffe lattes.

When Lenny sidled inside to get dosed, Olaf zipped across the road, bought him a coffee, and flagged down a passing cab.

"We're only going a few blocks, but I'll give you $20."

On the trip back Olaf told his ailing client to just rest easy for the day. He was about to lecture him regarding emergency procedures but stopped. After the life this guy has had, he'll be able to figure shit out on the fly.

"So, Lenny. What do you think you'll do today?" Olaf asked.

"Sometimes, man, I just want to slip into the third nap. But then, man, I think of the grandkids, yeah? I really wanna see the little guy start school. So, Olaf, just one more slice of that unforgiving birthday cake, you know."

The cabbie waived the fare.

OLAF HAULED himself up into the 12-seat bus and began his checklist. First was always the wing mirrors; no matter how much he told the others how to adjust them properly they always insisted on being able to see the sides of the vehicle. Then the seat. Am I really the only person in the world who doesn't drive around as though I'm kicking back at the dentist? He brought it back up to the 85-degree angle he favoured and slid it forward so his legs had enough play between the pedals. Then there was the pre-drive recording of the mileage and fuel on the hack sheet. It always took him back to a brief career in the Bronx, when he was illegally driving a gypsy cab for two dubious gentlemen with a penchant for gold jewellery and waving .38s around. Olaf had got into a game of pool with them in an Avenue B bar one night. If he won they'd sling him a Franklin. If he lost he had to drive them home to Islip. It was far from the fucking best of times so, naturally, he lost. However, he did get a night's respite from his Avenue D squat, spending it in a comfortable house and, over breakfast, being offered the driving gig. Ivan and Pyotr didn't give a damn that he had no licence, social security number, green card, passport, Kiss fan club card, nada. They just wanted him lurking at one of their seven lots all night, ready to take on any fare. Despite his own statelessness, he was expected to do everything by the book re the battered old Crown Vics: hack sheets, gas receipts, oil and tire checks. The Immigration and Naturalization Service would always be Olaf's problem but the brothers were damned if they were going to get shafted by the Department of Transport. One of the first things he found out was all the cars had a Saturday night special taped under the driver's seat. Olaf figured it wouldn't be just the drivers and radio operators who knew this so he would start each shift by stashing the gun under the spare in the trunk. In his six months of driving the worst he had to deal with was some kid doing a runner down into some projects in Canarsie, so it wasn't the mean streets that he finally turned his back on. No, it was the fiscal muggings the brothers doled out that hurt the most. At best Olaf would clear $40 a night. And then there were those mornings when he'd roll back into the lot with the tank unfilled. They jacked the gas price up three times. But it was kind of handy he was an illegal alien. Early one Saturday he pleaded with them to give him extra shifts so he could work off the $630 he owed them. His schtick was how much he enjoyed driving and how he regarded them as his best friends. They agreed, hands were shaken and futures toasted with bourbon. There's a lot to be said for bonhomie and bullshit; they even let him take a car for his personal use that day. Olaf drove it off the lot and never saw them again.

SYLVIA PERCHED herself in the passenger seat, shooting Olaf the warmest smile. Flattering as it was he decided he would play the day with a very straight bat. Boundaries, baby. Boundaries. Remember, she ain't like you.

"Okay guys, listen up," she called out to the chattering posse. "Tracey."

"Yep."

"Jess."

"Yes."

"Zac."

"Yep."

"Kid."

"YO!"

"Clauds."

"Syls."

"And, of course, Olaf."

He cast his eyes sideways at her.

"Present and accounted for."

It wasn't long before they hit the highway. The conversation was garbled noise centred around some crapulous TV series they were all following. Olaf had little time for television; rarely watched it and when he did it was dry documentaries and even drier political analyses. Zac, who had been a television critic at one point, started to give his take on the show but when it became obvious he didn't like it much, he was dismissed for being boring.

Sylvia fiddled with the windshield-mounted holder and removed Olaf's phone.

"What are you up to?" he asked.

"Oh, you just concentrate on the road."

"You won't get far without the PIN."

"No I won't," she said, then whispered. "So let's see where 6523 gets me. Oooh, and it appears I'm in. So, Olaf, if I were to look in your photos would I be shocked?"

Of course she wouldn't. The raciest shot in there was one he took at the Tate Gallery of a Lucian Freud nude of art curator David Dawson with his dog Eli.

"But there might be a rather lovely video of an alluring woman somewhere in there."

"Yes, and might she be bidding you a good night?"

Sylvia continued to play around with the radio and the phone. When Aaron Neville's mellifluous tenor vibrato filled the van Olaf noticed she'd faded out the forward speakers. She'd chosen a playlist called *chapel hill to pontchartrain*. He had a few dozen, but this was a particular favourite.

"Why'd you choose this one?"

"Because it's a very contrasting collection of songs. It's not obvious. All yours? Or did you get some assistance?"

"No, Ms Sylvia, it's the product of a very catholic upbringing."

About the only joy Olaf ever got from his mother was when she would sit down at her piano and play anything from Franz Liszt to McCoy Tyner. Her music was his sanctuary from the violence. The longer she played, the more her savage breast was soothed. He had two fond memories of his mother and music. The first was when she insisted he listen closely to the piano in Bowie's *Aladdin Sane*. The other was not long before her colorectal cancer completed its savage mission and metastasised into hepatocellular carcinoma. She had turned up unannounced at his house with a white label pressing of *Ecstasy*. He was shocked at how emaciated she was and, more tellingly, how terrified she looked. His childhood wishes were coming true, but now they just seemed excessive and unkind. It didn't feel right. They listened to the LP, sitting well apart and not saying a word. Lizzie had been responsible for his love of literature, but he was also forever grateful to her for fostering his appreciation of Lou Reed.

The two of them had sat there, engrossed in the album. Emotionless but engrossed. Neither said a word; they barely looked at each other. Two articulate people incapable of communicating. When the last track faded and the tone arm lifted, Lizzie returned the album to her tote and painfully inched her way up the hallway. As she prepared to step out into the blinding daylight, she turned to her son, her mistake, and said the three words he'd waited his whole life to hear.

"I'm sorry, Frog."

"JESUITS OR Marists, Luffah?" Sylvia playfully poked his upper arm.

"Neither. Lower case 'c' catholic, as in all-embracing. I have no time for all that sky daddy crap."

She continued flitting her thumbs around the phone screen, which was fucking with Olaf's head.

"Apparently you're not supposed to call it the Roman Catholic church, either," she announced.

Zac chimed in. "No, and just to add to the confusion, there's now some breakaway chapter of the Catholics who want to claim that adjective."

He was leaning between the front seats, his head obstructing the rear view and adding a further distraction to Olaf who was trying to watch the road and second guess what Sylvia might be looking at.

"Why am I not surprised in the least that you speak authoritatively on the holy church of Rome? Shall we play some U2?" Olaf enquired.

"Don't you start that nonsense again. For two years I shared a workstation with both the ballet critic and the religious affairs correspondent. So if you want to know how to arabesque with your tefillah strapped on, I'm your man."

"Mazel, Nureyev. But no thanks."

Sylvia giggled without quite knowing why. She'd misheard him, and hurriedly searched in his phone for 'defiller strap on', which only led her to a raft of porn sites.

AS A student Sylvia had dazzled but, unlike many of her classmates, she could function both as a cool kid and a nerd. Subsequently her parents never doubted that she'd be doing anything other than going to her friends' places to hang out and study on weekends. By 16 she was getting blitzed on cocaine on Saturday nights, then blitzing physics exams two days later. If there ever needed to be a poster girl for brainiac party animals, Sylvia was it. She was awarded a university scholarship, with her future set in science – forensic medicine, to be precise. To Sylvia, senior high school chemistry and biology were about as difficult as a 20-piece jigsaw puzzle and she craved the challenge of academia.

What life hadn't prepared her for was Jerry.

Jerry was a bottom-feeder who hung around the campus selling illicit substances like MDMA, ecstasy and LSD. He was the antithesis of Sylvia - a useless dolt with no prospects. He scurried around the university trying to avoid a gang of neighbourhood kids who regularly beat him up for his drugs and money.

Never sure if it was out of boredom, pity or convenience, Sylvia began dating him. Even more absurd, she began to fall in love with him, in part due to the comfort of his incessant devotion. She saw in him what no-one else ever would, mainly because it wasn't there. She was deluded; he lucked out. After the inevitable meet-the-folks dinner, her mother suggested it was her insecurities that wanted her to be in control, and Jerry's abject lack of nous made him a prime candidate for that. The observation stung for the simple reason it was true. And no-one knew it more than Sylvia.

The nature of his business meant late-night calls - lots of them. These were nothing unusual but sometimes they just didn't seem right. Sylvia began to vent her insecurities to friends, but they'd just echo what her mother had said. If she brought it up with Jerry, he'd brush it off, professing his eternal love and convincing her she was the only one. A dose of chlamydia told her she wasn't.

Much as she wanted out, her self-esteem had plummeted in the 18 months with Jerry. Things started to get weird. What was originally supposed to have been a one-off night of sex, drugs and fun with two other couples became a weekly occurrence. While the others would be in a hot tub getting primed on ecstasy, sildenafil and champagne, Sylvia would be in the kitchen throwing valium down with gin. Lots of both. Uninhibited chemsex might have been the order of the night, but for Sylvia blackouts became her preference. The more Jerry came out of his shell, the more Sylvia retreated into hers. Somewhere along the line they had crossed emotionally, and he didn't like it. He never minded her being the brains in their partnership, but it stung that she no longer cared. Jerry made plans for their future. One Sunday morning, while she groaned under a pillow, Jerry carefully administered her a sure-fire hangover cure.

When he walked out on her six weeks later, Sylvia was left with two mementoes. Genital herpes and a heroin habit.

BY THE time they'd entered the national park, Zac was enthralling his peers with the exploits of a low-life politician and Sylvia preoccupied herself collating a playlist. Olaf cut the aircon and opened the forward windows, filling the van with the scent of nature and warm air. Again he tried to see what Sylvia was doing.

"This is a very sexy sounding song," she said. "I like it. A lot. Were you hoping I'd hear it?"

He listened to the raga emanating from Derek Trucks' electric guitar and nodded.

"It won't be so seductive when the lyrics start."

"I'm not talking about the future. I'm talking about now."

He could feel her presence next to him and, despite the animated discussion going on behind them, felt curiously exposed.

"Do you feel awkward with me next to you?" she asked.

His mind somersaulted and came up with five different answers at the same time. Should I be honest? Second guess what I think she wants to hear? Make a witty aside?

"Extremely. And please don't ask why."

"I don't mean to. But you do have this vibe of honesty. I trust you."

"What? As in you feel safe with me?"

"Well, yes. I suppose so. But I meant this."

She touched her fingers to his chest and then drew them to her own sternum.

"Heart trust, Olaf."

"WHY DID you start using heroin?" Zac asked.

He and Olaf had left the others back at the beach. They were sated from the picnic feast Tracey and Jesse had thrown together and, despite Olaf suggesting the nature walk, chose to remain back, happy to sunbake and swim and listen to Sylvia's new playlist. Not Zac. He'd been itching to get some private time with Olaf, and Olaf knew Zac would be asking this question sometime. It was a popular query among the clients, not so much to find out about the staff, but to make an opening for their own dark secrets.

"I'd love to tell you it was the inevitable progression of an existential crisis brought on by liberating my inner artist and general paradigm subverting and all that other neo-hippie bullshit, but honestly? I found it stopped the persistence of memory."

"What did you survive?"

Olaf flinched. All the years of therapy still couldn't prevent the insidious recall of being restrained and flayed with electrical extension cords. He'd come to terms with having been repeatedly raped in his teens by a family friend, but his mother's sadism would simply not leave.

"The whole fucking shit show. You?"

Zac quickened the pace, stepping in front of Olaf to negotiate a narrow section of the track.

"My father was a very angry and resentful man, but he probably only gave me four thrashings in my life. He'd occasionally get pissed enough then rant and yell about his colleagues and how hard done by he was, but otherwise he was unable to provide any emotional contact. Physical affection didn't exist at our house. I can't recall ever seeing him and Mum even hug each other. To be honest, I'm not sure what was worse - his rage or his indifference"

"So, figure out which one and go to work on it."

They came to a short wooden bridge over a stream and stopped, resting their backs against the rails and facing each other. The gentle sound of the water below, the rustle of branches in the breeze and the occasional bird trill belied their childhood turmoils. Zac turned, looking toward a small cascade of water upstream.

"Maybe it'll just go away when I get off methadone," he said.

"I don't want to rain on your parade or anything," said Olaf. "But I've got bad news for you, Zaccy boy. As your dose lowers, your emotions are going to go into overdrive. All those feelings you've been suppressing for years."

"Yeah, that's not exactly what I want to hear. What do you suggest?"

Olaf moved, leaning on the wood alongside Zac.

"Well, when you've completed rehab, you're going to be needing some kind of aftercare. Now, whether that's NA meetings, one-on-one therapy, SMART Recovery groups, whatever, it's up to you. But speaking for myself, I found getting a good shrink was really helpful. I still wrestle with some internal alligators, but I realised long ago that getting smashed wouldn't heal me."

"I need to be honest with you. I keep wanting to leave. You know, just up and go."

Olaf laughed and slapped Zac's arm.

"Excellent. That's the best thing I've heard from you yet, you crazy fucker. So you should."

"Leave?"

"No, want to. That tells me you're getting it. You're being challenged by your peers; you're living in this lab rat environment with a bunch of nimrods like me watching your every move; you're doing unfamiliar things like being accountable for your actions and calling your peers out on their shit. Of course you want to leave. It's those Daisy Duck motherfuckers wandering around going 'oh rehab is great. I can't wait to finish and help all my friends get off drugs' who wig me out. They're the ones who usually go straight into the good Lord's pizza oven."

Zac squeezed Olaf's shoulder and remembered his childhood friend Charlie.

"What are you thinking?" Olaf asked.

"I only ever had one friend as a kid but my parents didn't approve, so that was the end of that. My next friend was schoolwork, then heroin. Kind of pathetic, really."

"Not at all. Kind of too familiar. For me, for our cohorts on the beach, for the countless other poor fuckers who used skag to disconnect from themselves."

"Can I tell you something weird? Just before I fell asleep last night I had this ... not so much a dream, but a sensation. I used to get it when I was a kid and it was really scary but it was also very comforting. So, as I'm drifting off last night it feels like my teeth are these huge boulders floating in my mouth, and ..."

"Get the fuck out of here. Like your head is outer space?"

"Yes! Yes! It's huge in there."

"Your teeth all feel like they are the size of fucking Jupiter or shit, and they're all light years apart but creating weird gravity in your head ..."

"Yes! You too? This is unbelievable! I told a couple of people over the years but they just thought I was crackers."

"Well we are," Olaf joked, and then became serious.

"My grandmother raised me. My mother was too busy galavanting around the globe interviewing idiot pop stars and running her nightclubs. Apparently I was more a hindrance than a child. She wouldn't even let me visit her house. So I lived in this really loving and safe world, except when I knew my mother was coming to Grandma's. She'd ring in the afternoon, concoct some drama and say she'd deal with me later that night. And she would. She'd come storming into the house at some stupid hour of the night, drag me out of bed and flog me mercilessly. A fucking monster, Zac - terrorising a small kid and a little old lady."

Olaf ran his fingertips along the grain of the handrail, looking down at the water coursing across the pebbles and rocks.

"And they were the nights when I had that same weird experience as you while I drifted off to sleep."

He turned his head, pretending to follow the hill line behind them and hoping the tears wouldn't make it past the bottom of his sunglasses. Liz may have been dead for 20 years but every welt still stung deep inside him.

"I haven't made the correlation with what the sensation was linked to, but I'm sure there is one," said Zac. "Hey, are you okay?"

Olaf contemplated changing the subject, diffusing the situation, distracting. But why? The ethics of showing vulnerability to a client were debatable but he also knew Zac was offering one of the most challenging values for any drug addict: trust.

"Yeah, I'll be alright. Thanks Zac."

They hugged tightly and, when they parted, Olaf removed his sunglasses. Zac looked into Olaf's teary eyes and gave his shoulders another reassuring squeeze.

"I'm glad that we met, man," said Olaf.

Summer

THE PHONE had barely finished ringing before there was a burst of Sylvia's maniacal laughter, followed by a camp "well, helloooooo, Luffah". It certainly brought a smile to Olaf's face, because for the past 10 minutes he'd looked at its screen, wondering why he was so drawn to the tongue-poked-out kook staring back, and trying to see a sequence within her phone number so he might, for the first time ever, actually remember one.

"Well, I did it," he murmured.

"Did what, Luffah?"

"I, ah... quit the 'hab."

This time there was no exuberance, no response. He looked at the phone to see if the line had gone dead.

"Are you there?"

The silence continued for a few more seconds, then was broken by the clicking of a lighter and the deep draw of a cigarette being lit.

"Yeah, sorry. I was, uh, just moving rooms."

Olaf began to worry. It was like everything Dylan had warned him of was coming true. He realised his breathing was shallow and that he might even throw up.

"Maybe you didn't hear me. I said I quit work."

"No, Olaf, I heard you." Sylvia's voice contained an unfamiliar air of earnestness. "I think it's wonderful, and it's an incredibly brave thing you've done. How do you feel?"

His brain screamed. How do I feel? Jesus. I've just upended my life, you gibbering fucking cunt. I've taken one of the biggest chances I ever could. It's like I put the fucking farm on black and red came up. I've decided to throw my heart into your bonfire of fucking love and already you're assailing me with some bullshit rehab-speak? Jesus fucking Christ, Sylvia. Are you really such a selfish, detached bitch?

"Ah, kind of uncomfortable, I guess."

She slowly whistled out a lungful of smoke. "Well, as I remember you saying once in group, today is the first day of the rest of your life."

Olaf wasn't sure if he wanted to strangle her, or himself.

"Get the fuck out of here. I never said that shit."

Then came her whooping laugh, and Olaf felt calm and happy and alive again.

"Oh, Luffah. You're so funny, my darling. And you know… I'm really, really glad you got out of that madhouse."

"I'm so happy we found each other, Ms S."

"Ohh, me too, honey. Me too. You know something? We're just going to have the most incredibly rich and beautiful life together. Listen, hun, I just have to do a few things here. What say I come over in an hour?"

Olaf swaggered into the bathroom and called out to the computer to play Mark Gillespie's *Only Human* album. He turned the shower jets on and, singing along in full voice and feeling almost intoxicated, entered the shower fully clothed.

SYLVIA STOOD at the front door in a light floral cotton dress that, given the darkness of the hallway and the screaming summer light behind her, left nothing to Olaf's imagination.

"You've got no underwear on."

"Yes, Luffah. And the sky is blue."

They threw themselves at each other and began a slow dance of lust along the wall. This was what they'd been waiting for - the right to express themselves without guilt or repercussions. So while they licked and bit at each other's faces and pawed at each other's bodies, Sylvia dramatically - and quite deliberately - bumped into a pile of CDs stacked on the hall table. With her head arched and Olaf nibbling at the sinews behind her right ear she listened to the tumbling clatter ring through the house. Not that she was here to destroy any of the rare

Japanese audiophile editions of 20-bit remasters or out-of-print reggae compilations. No, it was Olaf's resolve she wanted to put to the test.

He didn't even notice.

Much later, she leant on her elbows and angled her face above his, studying his curved nose, the hooded brown eyes she adored so much, and those lips. A warm glow enveloped her and she hoped she would never tire of kissing him. The music weaved around them - a slow, forlorn ballad driven by a simple chord progression and an airy male voice. She threaded her fingers into his hair and touched his cheek with her other hand. The scent of sex was everywhere, floating with the perfume of a flickering coconut-and-lime candle. Sylvia drew it in through her nose, cupped her mouth over his and gently breathed into him. Without taking her eyes off him, she ran the tip of her tongue across his mouth and let a trickle of saliva roll down. It slid into his mouth. God, he thought, she's alive with so many flavours.

Throughout the afternoon they licked, sucked and tongued every inch, crevice and orifice of each other's bodies before the carnal gave way to the spiritual. Olaf began to understand what tantric sex actually meant. He looked at the nevus on her eye and smiled at her.

"It matches your freckles," he whispered.

He lay under her, feeling more in love than he had ever believed possible. Sylvia's long hair formed a cosy auburn tent around them and he believed nothing would ever get inside it to change what they had. His eyes welled but he didn't turn away. Love is trust, he thought.

A single tear rolled down as Sylvia lowered her mouth to his and, just shy of kissing him again, mouthed "I love you".

Night had fallen. Olaf didn't know how long it was that they'd lay there gazing into each other's... what? Eyes? Hearts? Souls? He looked at the candle Sylvia had brought with her. It was a very different shape now and he was unable to work out how long it had taken to evolve into its present form.

She was lying on her side with her back to him. He propped himself against it, and draped an arm around her. In the wavering candle light, he examined the freckles on her shoulders and imagined them to be stars. Yes, that's what it meant. Her back was a galaxy and Sylvia was a portal to eternal love. He sensed his whole life had had one simple destination: this day. This woman. This ... love. Fuck the job. Fuck therapy. Without ever realising what his quest had been, he'd found it this afternoon. Sylvia was his grail. And he knew that with her, his life now had a purpose. One beautiful, total purpose.

SYLVIA, TOO, was content. She lay there stroking the back of his forearm, spent and tired from all the emotions and sex. How many times had they cum? She figured about five times over seven hours. She remembered some of the lovers in her life, some of whom had also become besotted with her. But Olaf was special. There was a kindness they shared, and she placed so much trust in these simple connections. She thought of his stupid puns and smiled. Sure, he's goofy. But he's as intelligent as me. God, he's into Chopin *and* Billie Eilish.

Her thoughts drifted to travel, and she fantasised about them strolling arm in arm and exploring the cobbled streets of foreign cities. The idea filled her with joy. She contemplated wines, and galleries, and alien cultures. Lisbon had always appealed to Sylvia, and she thought about doing a crash course in Portugese, partly so she could blow his mind when they arrived there by telling the cab driver where they needed to go. She squeezed his forearm and heard the guttural hint of a snore.

Sylvia turned and kissed him, knowing she was happy, he was happy and that, yes, today had been glorious in its own way. Sure, she awoke that morning next to another man, but at least Olaf cared for her. She looked at her sleeping Luffah, cuddled in tight, and took in his dozing face. Everything pointed to this being the beginning of a great, exquisite adventure. It pained Sylvia as she quietly told him she loved him, for the very simple reason that - deep down in her own tortured heart - she knew she never really would.

SHE SAUNTERED out to the garden carrying a tray loaded with fresh figs, a triple cream brie, chopped apple, a pot of coffee and a portable speaker. They were certainly settling in to some level of domestic harmony

"Number 41," Olaf told her.

"41 what?"

"Of all the ways I love you, this is number 41. The graceful way you bring breakfast."

She gave him a soft smile and kissed his forehead.

"And how many ways do you love me exactly, Luffah?"

He pulled her down into his lap and held her face close to his, exchanging a few soft kisses.

"113, baby."

She gazed at him, kissed him languorously.

"Hey," he whispered.

"Uh huh?"

"I'm so in love with you."

She climbed off him and sat back in an Adirondack chair.

"I appreciate that. Thank you."

Sylvia pressed the speaker's bluetooth button. Glen Hansard's version of *Drive All Night* flowed into the garden.

"Don't you just love Eddie Vedder?" she said.

Olaf's emotions were all over the shop. I love her. She loves Eddie. Out of the thousands of songs on my computer, she plays mine and Anita's song.

"And are you keeping track of all those 113 ways?"

"Sure am, baby. Got me a little black book which I'm putting them all into."

There was no little black book. He was keeping the list in his phone.

Olaf had tendered his resignation with Aisha two weeks previously. Had he not been so effusive with his pronouncements of eternal love, his employer would probably have tried to convince him to take extended leave, but she found his gushing drivel and disregard for the client/staff policy pathetic and sad. As much as Aisha wished happiness on anyone lost in the joy of a new romance, Dylan's prediction that the relationship wouldn't last more than two months seemed quite probable.

Sylvia was on the same ticket as Dylan.

It wasn't so much that she moved in with Olaf that first day; it was more that she hadn't left. Yet. Until then she had been couch-surfing between various friends' places, her life jammed into the bags she had brought to rehab. Occasionally she would bedazzle some schmuck on an online dating site and get herself a meal and, what she called, a "dirty and dangerous night" but Olaf, caught between his own fragile ego and cock, had never bothered to ask where she lived.

He was lathering a bar of lemon myrtle and mango soap into her back when she turned, pulled his face down and slid her tongue into his mouth.

"Honey, would you be okay if I brought some more clothes here?"

He smiled like a loon. He'd spent his life running from commitment, and now it was barrelling into his world like a locomotive.

"That has to be the silliest question you'll ever ask me."

Although he was keen for them to climb back into bed, Sylvia wanted to retrieve her belongings. Her wardrobe at his house comprised three dresses, two pairs of jeans, some tops and a pair of boots. He suggested they get a cab to wherever she needed to go but she insisted on going alone.

"Is it at some guy's place?"

Sylvia felt guilty. It was obvious Olaf was falling more in love with her each day, but his neediness invoked in her a feeling of revulsion. She certainly cared about him; he was bright, witty, charming, financially secure, and gave great head but he was smothering her emotionally. *Give me some fucking breathing space, hun, and we might get there.*

The cab pulled up outside the downtown bus station and Sylvia broke into a purposeful stride toward the terminus; a stride fuelled by anger. She hadn't spoken to Olaf the entire journey and any attempt he made to talk was met with a dismissive wave of her hand. Both were pissed off, but Sylvia didn't try to hide it.

He caught up with her at a bank of lockers where she was emptying one of the large ones on the bottom row.

"I don't understand," Olaf said, picking up a backpack and some carry bags.

Of course you don't, you fucking loser. Go fuck yourself.

"I'm sorry, honey. Can we talk about this at home?"

And talk they did. Well, at least Sylvia did. She laid it all out for him - her two failed marriages, her descent into drunkenness and addiction whenever life became challenging, her homelessness, no income, her lack of self-worth. Sure, she had touched on some of these aspects in rehab, but Sylvia was a deeply private person. In a way she was being more honest than Olaf; although he'd read through her psychologist's supporting letter and mental health history he certainly wasn't going to let her know he'd done that. When he was reading those reports his guilt played at him, for good reason. His obsession with her was overriding his professional boundaries, and he felt grubby at the time, as though he was looking through her diary or underwear drawer.

It scared Sylvia to be so open with someone else, but she felt if she didn't take this risk with Olaf, would she ever? She trusted him and, despite her own fear of commitment, there was a tiny part of her starting to love him. In turn, Olaf did all the right things; listened intently, nodded sagely and held her hand at the appropriate moments.

"Luffah, there's something I want to tell you," she said after about an hour, "but I'm worried it will hurt you. I want to preface it by saying I truly want to make this thing work with us. I want our love to grow."

His mind started racing like the Daytona 500, all his fears jockeying for pole position, each one slamming its way through to torture his base insecurity: abandonment.

"Of course baby. I'm here for you."

She finished rolling a cigarette and demolished a quarter of it on the first drag.

"I'm polyamorous, hun."

Olaf felt like vomiting. All he heard was there were going to be three other men fucking her in his bed that night while he watched.

"I, ah, need you to elaborate. I don't quite follow," he said, his mouth dry and the blood draining from his face.

"No, no, no," she said. "It's not what you think. I want you, Luffah. I want you more than anything. What I'm saying is I have been discovering myself sexually for the past few years - without any commitment or expectations. I didn't want to be tied down to one person. But that's changing, honey. You're changing me. I feel like I'm ready for monogamy again."

She reached over and hugged him, feeling his pounding heartbeat through her breast.

"At the moment I only want you, my Luffah."

BY THE TIME they'd left the restaurant later that evening both were well aware of each other's sexual histories. They'd laughed about the wildest and lamest fucks of their lives and, for all the intimate details, neither felt jealous. A light rain began as they strolled home. Olaf took off his jacket and gave it to her before serenading her with the Rolling Stones' *Winter*.

"What was that, Luffah?"

"A love song for the incredibly gorgeous Sylvia."

She tightened her hold around his waist and pushed her head into his shoulder.

Maybe, just maybe...

Unseasonably cool weather and heavy rain gave them every reason to stay inside and the next few days were spent treading a circuit from bed to shower to kitchen. Music constantly filled the air - a seven hour playlist Sylvia made of their favourite songs; a mixture of predictably sexy cheese and alt-country, with two songs in particular - by Patti Smith and Chris Stapleton - serving as a kind of Pavlovian fuck trigger.

When she asked whether she should be loading their bedding into the washing machine or an incinerator, Olaf was lost at his computer.

"Have you got a passport?" he called out.

"Sure do. Why? You taking me to Lisbon?"

"Nah," he replied. "I'm not big on Portugal."

Sylvia fossicked around in the laundry cupboard, on the hunt for stain remover. As she reached for a tell-tale pink plastic container she felt Olaf's arms wrap around her from behind.

"Hey, my beautiful, let's spend New Year in Paris."

ALTHOUGH SHE'D never been to France, Sylvia's French was extraordinary. Olaf had an inkling she could speak some but he was floored by her fluidity and accuracy as they passed through customs at Paris-Charles de Gaulle. What started with "passport please" became a conversation in which she found out where to change trains and, more importantly, where to get a decent coffee in the airport.

An hour later they were dragging their bags up the steps at Maubert-Mutualite metro, headed for the boutique hotel Olaf always stayed in on Rue du Sommerard.

The owner, Paul, greeted him and they chatted in a combination of broken English and French before he introduced Sylvia.

"Pardon, Paul, mais c'est ma femme, Sylvia. Chérie, c'est Paul."

Paul and Sylvia launched into a conversation punctuated with so much humour that it even had one of the salon waitresses in stitches. Olaf caught every fifth word or so but, rather than feeling left out, all he felt was pride in her.

It was early evening and the flight had worn them out. Sylvia was thrilled to finally be in Paris but Olaf suspected the jet lag would soon override her excitement. To celebrate their arrival she opened a bottle of champagne and put on a Camille album. As Olaf showered, he could hear her singing along to Ta douleur, complete with the grunts and blown raspberries. By the time he emerged Camille was still going but Sylvia was splayed out across the bed, still in her boots, snoring loudly. Paris peut attendre, babe.

Because of the late booking, and it being Christmas, Olaf was only able to get business class flights within an eight-day period. He always went away for a minimum of five weeks but this vacation wasn't about him; it was all for Sylvia. They spent the next few days in a tourist whirlwind, visiting the Louvre, Notre Dame, Sacre Coeur, galleries, museums, brasseries, restaurants, river cruises, and lots of walking and shopping. And seeing in the New Year at the Arc de Triomphe.

They strolled from Musée d'Orsay along the Left Bank, crossing the Seine on the Pont des Arts. Olaf explained about the thousands of inscribed padlocks attached to the bridge and, without missing a beat, both shook their heads at the mere thought.

"We might be romantic," Sylvia said. "But not *that* romantic."

They recrossed the river at the Pont Neuf, stopping to listen to an elderly saxophonist play a rendition of *West 42nd Street*. People passed by without appearing to pay attention, some occasionally flicking a coin into his instrument case. When the last note floated away, Sylvia started chatting away to him in French. The musician looked perplexed and, in an unmistakable New York accent, said "sorry, je ne parle pas français. I ain't from 'round here". He watched Olaf drop a 20 Euro note into his takings.

"And you, my man, definitely ain't from 'round here."

Olaf pumped his fist at the musician who in turn bumped his fist back. The two then went into a routine in which they slapped palms, knocked knuckles and gripped fingers. Everything but actually shake hands.

"Lamik Tobias, my man. Wassup?"

"Olaf Shapiro. How ya doing?" he replied in an unfamiliar tone that surprised Sylvia. The two of them got into a rave about Coltrane's music, discussing at length the great man's role in Miles Davis's legendary quintet and the albums they made together. They also touched on the gentrification of Brooklyn and baseball. There may have been a 30 year or so age difference between them, but in the course of their five-minute conversation it was apparent they had a lot in common.

"Yo, Olaf," said Lamik as Olaf went into a rant about Jackie Robinson and Sandy Koufax. "I could spend all evening talking about The

Dodgers and the primary colours of be-bop, but that ain't gonna feed my ass. What say we swap phone numbers and meet up another day?"

After they did, Sylvia and Olaf continued their walk toward the Jardin du Luxembourg.

"So why do you make such a production out of not shaking people's hands, but you did that whole hand thing with Lamik?" she asked.

"You got me, baby. I try not to do it with the rehab clients and people I don't want to get to know. I know, it's inconsistent, but ... you know," his voice drifted off.

She tightened her grip on his arm.

"Then there's baseball and jazz? You really are full of surprises, Luffah."

He wiggled his eyebrows a la Groucho.

"You ain't seen nothing yet."

A few minutes later they were watching two men playing chess in the gardens. This was a game Sylvia didn't get and, just as she was about to take a picture, Olaf placed his hand on her forearm.

"Don't, babe."

He guided her back a few steps, concentrating on the board.

"Do you know what's going on?" she whispered.

"Yeah. The guy on the right is fucked. The black bishop has forked his knight and queen. Classic Marshall trap move."

Sylvia was as amazed with his understanding of the game as he had been with her linguistics. Within two moves the white king was prone on the board.

"Will you show me how to play chess?"

The idea of tutoring Sylvia appealed to Olaf.

"I'll teach you anything you want," he said. "And the idea of chasing my queen around 64 squares has a certain ooh la laa to it."

She took his hands and pulled him in closer.

"Olaf, I have never felt more sure of us than I do now. J'espère que notre amour vit pour toujours."

SYLVIA WAS engrossed in a French soap opera and declined Olaf's invitation to go for a stroll around the neighbourhood. Although daylight was fading he headed for a nearby sculpture park. For years he had walked past it, but was always in too much of a hurry to go in and check it out. He sat opposite a bronze replica of Lupa Capitolina - the she-wolf of Rome suckling Romulus and Remus - and wished she'd been his mother.

He began a brief reply to an email from Zac, then checked the phone's world clock. It was noon in DC.

"Surprise! This is a voice from your past."

"Given you're in Paris, you're actually in my future."

"You're too clever by half. You free to yak?"

"Of course. I actually have a lieu day so I've been out shopping and bought all this stuff which I probably don't need."

"Like what?"

"Oh, you know. Some Deutsche Grammophon LPs; a gorgeous hickory wood salad bowl; an outrageously expensive sport coat; a stupid baseball cap."

"I hope it's a Yankees cap."

"Nah, some thing with a cartoon duck on the front I think. Baltimore? I dunno. I'll never wear it anyway."

"Then why the fuck did you buy it?"

"To fit in? Who knows? Everyone here wears them. All the men here want to look like some brat from a 50s TV show. It was only four bucks. I'll mail it to you."

"Don't you fucking dare. I struggle enough with my low self-esteem. Anyways, apart from becoming a consumerist seppo, how is ya?"

"Oh, you know. Ummm. Missing you."

"How ya mean?"

"Well, just that. I miss you O. Heaps."

"That's, ah, real nice of you to say that. I... I miss you too."

"Sorry, that was hard for me to say. Maybe I shouldn't have."

"No, no Zac. That means a lot to me. Truly. It just took me by surprise. Hey. In all seriousness, are you okay? Generally?"

"Yeah nah. I dunno. Maybe we should talk about something else. I just, ah…"

"Come on Zac. What's going on for you?"

"Well, I… Are you sure you wanna have this conversation?"

"Of course I do. Say what you're feeling."

"Okay. This is probably going to come out all wrong, but there's a big part of me that wishes I'd never come here. That I'd stayed at home and, well… just got to know you better. But - and believe me, this is not a value judgement - but I could see how in love you were with Sylvia and I, umm, I guess I just got a little jealous. Not that I felt she was a threat or anything. But you know, I just wanted a little bit of that part of you too. But, um, that's not going to happen."

"Hey Zac."

"Uh huh."

"We have an incredibly deep bond. In fact it's almost scary how alike we are. I have never had an intellectual relationship with anyone else that even comes close to what we have. And I mean that. And I'm of the opinion it's just going to get stronger."

"You mean that, don't you?"

"Of course I do. Why? Does it worry you I don't?"

"No. It's just… Jesus O, I want to say something and I worry it'll stuff things up."

"Just say it, amigo."

"Okay. I don't like labels but I guess I'm bi. I've had flings with women and men. But as you know I've never had a proper relationship. The idea of waking up to the same person every day horrifies me. And if there is anyone I care about I push them away, so I can… um, I can…"

"Protect yourself from getting hurt."

"Exactly. I know, it's pathetic, isn't it?"

"No, not at all. I've spent my whole fucking life doing it. I fully get it."

"I'm going to say something O, and not to scare you off, but just to, um, honour us I guess."

"Mmmh."

"Oh God. I uh… Look, I fantasise about making love with you. It's not that I want to. Well, yeah, I do. But I know that's not likely to happen. Shit. I. Um. Look I just wanted to be straightforward with you. Shit. I'm so sorry, O."

"Don't apologise. I get how hard that must have been for you. I've been there myself."

"What? You're bi?"

"No, no. You know my friend Bette I've talked about. I went through this exact same thing with her a few years ago. I pretty well told her what you just told me. And she said to me what I'm about to say to you."

"Which is?"

"It ain't ever going to happen, for the simple reason that once we start fucking, our friendship is compromised. It stung like a wasp to hear that, but having watched her go in and out of relationships since then I am truly grateful we didn't fuck it up, so to speak. Of course, my ego would still love to end up in bed with her, but today I care more about our friendship. As I do about ours. And just for the record, I am boringly heterosexual."

"Wish you weren't."

"I know you do. But I want you to understand one thing Zac. What we have amounts to a lot more than - and I'm going to quote Johnny Rotten here - five minutes of squelching noises."

"Could we shoot for even two minutes?"

"Ha! It's funny, you know. I'm in a park at the moment, and in this dim Parisian light I can just make out twins sucking on a wolf's tit. You and I are like twins."

"Considering what became of those two, could we be more like Luke and Leia?"

"Only if we get matching Mum and Darth tatts."

"You're a funny bugger. Hey O?"

"Yeah?"

"Thank you. My fear around broaching that stuff was you would freak out and push me away. I mean, you still might, but…"

"I promise that will not happen. You're my friend. I love you like a brother. And I respect you for being so brave and telling me that."

"That means a lot to me Olaf. Ta. So, ah, you need to go now?"

"Are you out of your mind? We're not only in the same hemisphere, but the same day. We've got to make the most of this. What books beside your bed are you currently not reading?"

THEY HAD 36 hours left in Paris. Sylvia had been moody and bad tempered all morning and, rather than ask her why, Olaf concluded it was her menstrual cycle. She was glued to her phone, rabbiting on in French to God-knows-who, and Olaf wasn't interested. He had finally got a call back from Morty, a Brooklyn artist he'd met in Morocco. Like all good bohemians, Morty couldn't stay put for 10 minutes. Fortunately, he was the sole recipient of a $10 million family estate so being an artist wasn't exactly an existential struggle. As a personal joke, he had bought a house in Berlin simply because it had a garret - albeit one with an incredible view. Morty moved from city to city on a whim, yet Paris had won his heart. Olaf was one of maybe six friends who knew his background. Others just figured his art was more successful than it ought have been.

It turned out that Morty knew Lamik so he arranged for them to lunch at a bistro on Rue Montorgueil. Although Olaf really wanted Sylvia and Morty to meet, he figured her capriciousness was best be left in the room with her and her French friend.

Lunch was hilarious.

"Une baguette avec paté et cornichons. Et aussi les escargots, merci chef," Olaf ordered, only to have Morty shoot him down in flames.

"Oh you pretentious asshole. Escargots. Those vile fucking things are only an excuse for the French to pig out on garlic and butter. And do you know how paté is made?"

Olaf replaced the paté with salami and camembert but stuck to his guns on the snails.

Lamik and Morty demolished four beers and a bottle of red while Olaf paced himself with a large bottle of mineral water. The conversation covered everything from US politics to the parlous state of modern art, music, the Yankees (again) and Paris. After Lamik asked what Olaf did for a living, talk went around to drugs, and the effect they were wreaking on societies. Olaf asked if there were any methadone programs in Paris, and Morty explained how a lot of Paris's addicts congregated around Porte de la Chapelle, so if there was any treatment happening it would be up in the 18th arrondissement. Lamik added that there was also a lot of dealing going on around Madeleine and St Lazare metro stations, so it could be possible there were drug services near there, too. Although Olaf was keen to meet with his fellow Parisian drug workers, he felt he may have left his run a little too late.

"So, my man. Where is that adorable young lady of yours?" Lamik asked.

Olaf had tuned out from the conversation. Five Greek women at the next table were having a very amusing and boozy lunch, and it reminded him of how much Xanthe enjoyed socialising, and would have loved meeting Morty and Lamik. He recalled a conversation he'd had with Dylan - pre Sylvia - in which the wise mentor challenged him around his fear of commitment. Xanthe presented everything Olaf was terrified of - companionship, emotional stability, honesty, family.

Love.

He clearly remembered Dylan's words.

"You know what your problem is? You're a tragic combination of arrogance and delusional thinking, wrapped up in a soggy tissue. You think the next one will be better than the last, instead of accepting that what you already have is great. And that's what is so sad. It's about time you grew up and stopped running from yourself."

Dylan was right. Olaf had always run from the safety of a loving bond, never quite sure of how he should behave in it. Xanthe saw beyond all his Peter Pan bullshit and loved him regardless. Not that she didn't call him on his failings; there were times when he felt like she'd scorched him with napalm. But the closer they got, the more terrified he became. The prospect of telling her he was scared was too daunting for him. Dylan had encouraged him no end to open up to her and be honest, but his own fear was way stronger than his courage.

Besides, Sylvia certainly wasn't Xanthe.

OLAF BLANKLY stared through the dusty wall of glass at an old display cabinet full of antique tattoo guns. The walls of the tiny shop were covered in hundreds of illustrations of skulls, dice, hula girls, daggers, tigers, devils, cartoon characters and every other cliched image people have indelibly inked onto their bodies. He looked at the gurney toward the rear of the premises and contemplated the cycle of life for a heavily inked inmate on death row.

"Ca va," said a large man leaning in the doorway and sucking on a clove cigarette. "Are you wanting for tattoo, man?"

This snapped Olaf out of his stupor.

"Oui. Pourquoi pas?"

Olaf went inside and drew an uneven valentine heart with the numbers 113 inside it. Twenty minutes later he looked proudly at his latest art purchase.

"C'est bon. Combien, monsieur?"

The tattooist laughed.

"113 Euros, of course."

Sylvia wasn't at the hotel when he got back, which suited Olaf just fine. After leaving the tattoo studio he had booked a table that night at the restaurant in the Eiffel Tower. Sure, it was expensive and clichéd, but what the hell. Something to tell the grandkids.

He had the place to himself and was writing an email to Zac when her SMS came in: 'all good luffah. us x'.

Olaf called her but, again, it went straight to her messages.

Lamik's friendship with John Coltrane, and the crazy stories he told about their exploits, sparked a desire in Olaf to hear some 'Trane, so he typed John Coltrane Radio into the music streaming app. The list was perfect. Dizzy. Wes. Alice.

He hit play, expecting it to come out of the portable speaker. It didn't. Figuring it had been turned off Olaf searched the room for it. He checked cupboards and drawers in case the cleaners had put it away and looked inside the suitcases. A pile of cash and an expensive watch on the bedside table told him there hadn't been any pilfering.

There was music coming from his phone but it certainly wasn't jazz. A pedestrian techno beat thumped away while some guy banged on about velvet tongues, designer voodoo and phone sex. It was *le vin de l'amour est chard* - a song list Sylvia had made for them to fuck to while in Paris, playing from her phone.

He smiled at the thought of her shopping and listening to her favourite erotic songs, then wondered why she would be carrying a speaker.

Panic struck.

He redialled her number repeatedly, to no avail. Pop Smoke's *Mood Swings* started; the same song that was playing the night before when she viciously bit his chest and snarled "me souiller".

Olaf flung her suitcase open and rifled through it looking for the drawstring bag in which she kept her sex toys. It was gone.

He fell onto the bed, head spinning, heart pounding. All he could think of was that his Sylvia was naked and writhing with another man, at that moment, in the very city he had brought her to to celebrate their love. He was too terrified to even cry.

It was getting dark and Olaf wasn't feeling any better. He'd spent hours torturing himself, watching the songs cycle into the next, and sending endless text messages. Declarations of love, forgiveness, understanding, respect, pain. Promises of a happy future. Of course, the underlying emotion was cowardice. Not hers, his. He knew he should have just upped and left.

Somewhere in the fog of his distress he remembered a technique to avoid relapse which he would drum into clients at ITL - remove yourself from dangerous situations. He headed out into the city, walking aimlessly for at least an hour. Eventually he came across a station entrance and headed for it, hoping a train ride might help break the agony.

Olaf recognised stops like Bastille and République, but he was so confused he couldn't even guarantee he knew which city he was in. Another stop. Madeleine. He stepped out and waited for the train to leave. When it did he was left alone on the platform. For no reason he clapped his hands once and listened to the echo. Nup, I'm still here. He remained motionless, observing the madness of his thoughts. Failure. Notre Dame. Heartache. Chess. Xanthe. The rehab. Swimming. Tattoos. Airports. Some French bastard with a huge cock performing analingus on Sylvia.

He looked up to the illuminated blue and white Sortie sign.

"Fuck it," he said to the silence. "It's now or never."

Olaf's grief and insecurity around Sylvia's infidelity was now replaced with excitement and raw fear. It had taken him less than five minutes to find a dealer outside the station and he was now heading back to the hotel in a cab with a quarter of a gram of heroin and a used syringe. His knowledge of safe injecting practises went out the window as he flushed the needle once with some of Sylvia's vodka. He pierced his vein for the first time in a decade and, as he did so, remembered Dylan's sage advice about what actually goes into the spoon - then sneered.

"Fuck you, you cunt," he muttered.

To Dylan.

To Sylvia.

To himself.

THE ELECTRIC lock clicked the door open just after sunrise. Sylvia looked wasted; she reeked of booze and tobacco and was carrying her boots.

"Are you okay, baby?" Olaf asked.

She stripped off her clothes and crawled into bed.

"Where have you been? I was worried sick."

She said nothing. Just wrapped a leg over him, held him and softly kissed his mouth.

"I am so, so sorry Luffah."

She continued her kissing.

"Will you ever forgive me?"

He could see tears building up and finally returned a kiss.

"I just want to know you're okay."

She started sobbing.

"No I'm not. I've just treated the most gorgeous man I've ever known like shit."

Olaf raised his index finger to her lips.

"Shhhhhh."

They continued their canoodling, which culminated in the most vanilla sex they'd ever had. No accessories; just a quiet, gentle missionary fuck. The heroin was stalling Olaf's orgasm and Sylvia continued gazing into his eyes with her mouth slightly open. All his anger toward her abated. He didn't care she'd been fucking someone else an hour ago. He just felt secure she was back in their bed. Alone. Together. As it always will be.

She licked his mouth then tenderly bit his lip.

"Us."

Sylvia decided that if they were to talk about what happened, it would be without guilt or judgement, and best done on a farewell walk beside the Seine. Olaf, for all his emotional gutlessness, agreed. She admitted she'd been flirting on Tinder with someone called Armand for a few weeks, mainly to improve her language skills. Olaf couldn't believe he was buying this crap. She insisted that they'd spent most of the afternoon and night bar hopping and talking, and that the sex was a bland afterthought toward the end of the evening. That certainly didn't jerry with the playlist going all that time but Olaf was open to any of her bullshit.

While Sylvia showered he had checked out her bag of tricks. The rubber dildos always seemed sticky, but the chrome butt plug was still in its vacuum plastic packaging, and a tube of French lube was still sealed. He kidded himself she might be telling the truth.

Olaf insisted on seeing the guy's profile pics, and that was the biggest shock. He'd had in mind a swarthy hunk but Armand, with his receding chin, crooked overbite, sunken chest and gormless stare, looked like the last man Sylvia would have ever slept with. Olaf scrolled through their chat history, to confirm he was her one-night stand.

"Why are you grinning, cherie?" she asked.

Olaf handed the phone back.

"I was expecting a porn star. The only thing that fuckwit could star in is a documentary on hillbilly inbreeding."

THEY BOUGHT coffees and sat on some steps opposite Notre Dame cathedral. It was cold and they cuddled into each other, holding hands and looking up at the enormous church.

"I've got something to tell you," Olaf said.

"Mmmmmmhhhh?"

He took a sip of his café au lait and looked away.

"I used heroin last night."

Sylvia released his hand.

"You're kidding?"

"I wish I was."

"I hope it wasn't because of me, hun."

Olaf couldn't believe what he'd heard.

"Oh you've got to be fucking joking."

She got up and stood before him.

"Listen, I won't be held responsible for your actions. I take full responsibility for what I did yesterday but I will not let you throw your guilt on me or shame me because of who I am."

Olaf looked at her boots, then up to her steely face, and wondered how hard he'd have to kick her to send her tumbling into the icy Seine.

"It's not about shaming, Sylvia. It's about how things went pear-shaped yesterday and how badly we both dealt with those things."

"Well, I've apologised to you for my actions, and I guess you owe yourself one, too. It's your shit, Olaf. Not mine."

She stormed off, launching her paper cup into the river.

ENSCONCED IN their comfortable business class seats-cum-beds, Sylvia and Olaf were still finding it hard to get settled. They'd barely spoken since that morning and were now a few hours into their flight home. Sylvia had already thrown back a few champagnes and a couple of vodkas but Olaf, despite his lapse, was sticking to mineral water.

"So I guess you'll want me to get out soon?" she said.

Olaf was on his side, looking across the console between them.

"Well, unless you brought a parachute, I'd say best you stay a while."

She smiled, and made an awkward attempt to reach across to him.

"I mean it," she said. "I'm willing to change for you. Us."

Olaf just nodded. There was so much he wanted to say but she'd heard it all before. Besides, he was too preoccupied with the ease with which he ran back to heroin.

"I'd kill for a sleeping pill," she said.

The cabin was dark, except for the faint violet strips of light along the sides of the ceiling. Olaf fumbled around in his pocket and pulled out a small plastic bag. He placed it on the console.

"Pssst," he hissed, tapping his finger next to the bag.

Sylvia looked at the bag in awe.

"Are you fucking crazy?"

"Well, you know, international airspace is a recovery-free zone. And besides, it's primo dope."

He produced a credit card, racked up two lines and handed her a rolled banknote.

"Ladies first."

They slumped back down into their pods and closed their eyes. Olaf was feeling content, slipping into an old and much-missed euphoria. He imagined the plane hurtling through the inky black sky at light speed, bending starlight and warping time.

"Luffah," Sylvia whispered.

"Clouds," he drawled.

AS SOON as they walked through the front door, familiar routine was reinstated. Windows were opened, a pot of strong Yorkshire tea steeped, a Don McGlashan LP played, kisses were stolen and there was even some impromptu waltzing.

They took their tea to the garden to have 'the talk'. Sylvia made a commitment to monogamy and, as an act of contrition, asked Olaf to change the passwords and emails on her four dating apps then delete them. For his part he promised to give her more breathing space and go back to therapy to deal with his abandonment issues. They agreed their little bout with heroin was just that, and he was now back to his abstemious lifestyle. Sylvia promised to moderate her drinking and, apart from an occasional spliff, no other drugs.

Within 10 days they were sharing a gram of heroin a day. By week three this had doubled. The drug was delivered every morning at 8am, the only time Olaf was sure Sylvia would be at home. Not that he cared. Their pathetically intimate ritual of shooting up together lasted a week. They barely spoke. Communication went the way of music, companionship, food, sex, love and joy - straight into their syringes. As soon as the drop had been made, Sylvia would fly out the door to her job, whatever that was. Their motto might as well have been "don't ask, don't tell".

It eventually became too much. Any discussions degenerated into screaming matches. Olaf verbalised his paranoia and mistrust while she toyed and manipulated his insecurities with mindless pronouncements like "I'm honouring my commitment to my truth" and other veiled lies. It came to the inevitable; they agreed they couldn't take any more of the hostility and set out to dissolve the relationship. Somehow that particular get-together was conducted with respect and sensibility and they decided they get back on methadone.

"GUTEN TAG, In The Light rehab."

Olaf felt sick with remorse when he heard Aisha's voice. He and Sylvia had been dosing for six weeks and trying to moderate their narcotic use but they knew they couldn't do it alone. His throat tightened and he struggled to talk. He was just about to hand the phone to Sylvia when Aisha spoke.

"I've been praying you'd call, Olaf."

"Aisha, I … we need help. We're fucked."

She gave him space to break down and, when he'd regained his composure, told him to put the kettle on and unlock his back gate. She'd be over in 10 minutes.

"The biggest hindrance will be your relationship. No sex or any other form of intimacy. You are both entering the program as individuals. Neither of you will receive any preferential treatment. You will treat each other the same way as you'll treat the other residents. You will be expected to do reflections on each other, and hold yourselves accountable. It will be harder for you two than the other clients, for obvious reasons. Particularly you, Olaf. You probably know the rules of this program inside out. God knows you honed it into what it is today, so you won't have any excuses. Any questions?"

Aisha had spent an hour with the two of them, drinking tea, finding out about what they'd been up to for the past three months and typing notes into her tablet.

"What if things get difficult for us?" Sylvia asked.

Aisha peered over the top of her spectacles at Olaf.

"Tell her."

"We'll have to have a conflict resolution, probably with Dylan or Aisha."

"That could be weird." She flicked the ash off her cigarette and took a long drag. " When can we start?"

Aisha tapped away at the screen.

"What is it? Thursday. I want you to see Dr Gene tomorrow, I'll tell him to increase your doses, and you can come in next Monday. You at 9am Sylvia, and you at 11."

Aisha got up, gave Sylvia a hug and then held Olaf tightly, kissing him on the cheek.

"That's the last time you'll be getting one of those from me for a while. Please don't disappoint me, kids. Monday."

Autumn

IN THE FOUR MONTHS between Olaf resigning then returning as a client, there was a new community of residents - which in itself wasn't surprising. One of the main problems they faced was making it through the Christmas/New Year period without spending it with their families or partners. Due to the increased risk of alcohol use and relapse, the clients were not permitted to go home for celebrations, but many opted to discharge regardless. The recurring problem was some relatives did not understand the nature of addiction ("Come on, a couple of beers wont hurt you."); and the clients had little resolve ("I guess one's okay.").

Sylvia and Olaf had been back in ITL for just over a fortnight. Both were committed to getting off methadone and, prior to readmission, they had made a pact that the life they wanted to share would be one without the complications of drug use or infidelity.

Olaf was finding it hard to adjust to being on the other side of the orange door, but he was determined to make it right. For both him and Sylvia. He watched his peers as they wandered into the group room and took their seats. Across from him was Mozz. Mozz was a repeat offender; Olaf had last been his counsellor 18 months ago. When he finished the program that time, his future looked great, and was for the next year until he decided to boost his dole with a bit of drug dealing. Unfortunately Mozz's loathing of the police made him one of their preferred targets. Sergey was a former soldier in Chechnya who discovered the only thing that would suppress the PTSD he suffered from was copious amounts of heroin. Until Sergey accepted he'd be needing lots of therapy, rehabs would remain his second home. Carly was an attractive young woman who got tangled up in moderate drug use and had only moved over to methadone recently. Her dream was to start a family - a big family, like the one she came from. Frankly, given what little exposure she'd had to addiction, there was nothing to stop her. On the other hand, Marianne was a total mess. Although she was middle-aged, she looked in her 70s and her veins were so damaged from decades of drug use that whenever she needed blood tests a pediatric nurse would have to be summoned. Olaf adored Marianne for the simple reason she was totally beaten, but had an indomitable desire to get well and start living. Her favourite cliché, rasped in her 30 cigarettes-a-day voice was, "It's good to be here. It's good to be anywhere!"

Then there was Dave. Dave was Olaf's roommate. He arrived at the rehab the day before Olaf and was in awe that he'd only recently been a counsellor there. Both men immediately warmed to each other, so much so that on their first night Dave admitted to Olaf that he had brought in four grams of high purity heroin. After Olaf explained to him that if he intended to hold on to the drug, then he might as well pack his bags and leave now, Dave handed the packet to Olaf who headed out to the bathroom next door. The immediate sound of the toilet flushing gave Dave an enormous sense of virtue; Olaf came straight back into the room and at that point they both knew they had each other's back.

DYLAN WALKED around the perimeter of the group and parked himself next to Carly. There was a nervous vibe in the room, generated by gossip.

"Okay, people. Let's all settle and get started."

Carly read through the roll. Three were missing. Dan, Joe and Sylvia.

"What'll I put down for the three not here?" she asked.

"Joe's over at Dr Prato's, so mark him off as 'medical'. Unfortunately, it appears Sylvia and Dan left during the night, so mark them down as 'discharged'."

Olaf wanted to be sick. He looked at the empty chair Sylvia usually occupied, willing her to magically appear. His heart began to race. There was nothing to indicate she and Dan had left together, but he knew. His frontal lobe suggested he should be concerned for her health and welfare but his amygdala envisaged her indulging her darkest sexual passions with Dan, seducing him with her 'dirty-and-dangerous' routine.

Now Olaf did want to vomit. He wanted to purge his heart and soul of all memory of Sylvia. He never wanted to see or hear from her again. Those treacherous cunts deserve each other, he thought. I hope they fucking die an ignominious death in some shithole. I want to slit that prick's throat from ear-to-ear while I rape him with a broken bottle. I want to...

I just want to make it right again.

Olaf's chair toppled over as he raced to the door. Somewhere through the fog of his distress he could hear someone call his name but he didn't care. He slammed the door behind him in a rage. As the others looked around, perplexed, Dylan raised a hand.

"Come on guys. We need to focus. Let's just continue with morn..."

"What's going on with Olaf, Dylan?" Marianne queried. "He seemed okay before."

"Olaf has a lot going on at the moment. Just let him process what he's feeling and avail yourselves to him when he needs you. Just be there."

Marianne raised her hand but Dylan cut her off.

"I know you all have a million questions, but why don't we afford Olaf the respect he deserves and have a conversation with him rather than gossip?"

Olaf did throw up. He barely made it to the lavatory before spending a few minutes hunched over the bowl, retching. Part of him wanted someone, anyone, to be there with him, but he knew they all understood the dynamics of Stephen Karpman's drama triangle. Every few weeks he would conduct a group around how people in chaos fall squarely into the category of persecutor, victim or rescuer. He'd smugly think how it wasn't part of his life anymore, yet now...

I'm the victim, the victim and the victim. He wished Sylvia was there to see him.

After he washed his face and rinsed his mouth with some warm tap water and a squirt of toothpaste, he wandered aimlessly from the bathroom to find Aisha in the hall. Olaf figured he was wearing a mask of pathos by the equally crushed look on his former boss's face. All he wanted to do was break down, to be held, to be loved.

"Come with me," she said, taking his hand and leading him to her office like some child lost at a fairground.

Olaf watched in silence as she made coffee for them both. He remembered the times he had sat on this plump, red sofa while he and Aisha regaled each other with tales of Berlin, concerts, the awfulness of snow, the homeless and the broken hearted.

Ahh, yes. The broken hearted. His mind drifted back into that long, dark alley called Sylvia. He could smell his bile- and caffeine-scented breath and imagined it to be the sulphurous stench of the unlovable. Well, of course it stinks; I've been eating shit for the last six months.

Aisha could neither smell his breath nor read his poisoned imaginings. All she could see was the shell of a formerly vibrant colleague, someone who once commanded respect from both the staff and the clients. She cursed the callous way heroin preyed on the most beautiful of people, especially the vulnerable and open-hearted. Sure, some borderline psychopaths had darkened the rehab's doors over the years, but by and large her charges tended to be the innocent by-product of cruelty and evil. She remembered the time she ordered Olaf home to change a T-shirt that said MOTHERS MILK LEADS TO HEROIN. He had challenged her and by the time he'd finished she wanted that shirt for herself. By then, though, he had announced that he hadn't factored in the nuances of his stance and how it could have triggered some of the clients. He went home and changed it.

If only life was as simple as changing a T-shirt.

Her phone rang.

"Come in," she said and, moments later, Dylan slid in and seated himself at the other end of the sofa. Olaf grabbed a cushion and pulled it into his stooped frame. He couldn't bring himself to look at the two of them so he continued to stare a hole in the carpet.

Olaf was terrified of what was coming. Will they kick me out? Tell me they hate me? Ask me what the fuck am I doing here? Or worse, demand to know what that morning's little performance was all about?

"Someone. Anyone. Fuck. Just say something," he implored.

"You just did," said Dylan. "Keep going, buddy."

Olaf squeezed the cushion, and clenched his jaw.

"Fuck off with your pious buddy bullshit, will you? Jesus. You weren't around for me the few months I needed you and now suddenly you're Mister I Give a Fuck?"

Olaf was on the verge of a breakdown; every part of him was trembling, yet all he could do was fixate on the thought of Sylvia being with someone else. Despite the humiliation of having thrown everything away to be with a client, he had no excuses. He didn't know what Aisha and Dylan expected of him at this point, but the only thing he felt he could offer would be a blood-curdling scream. He desperately wanted to conjure up some confected lie, and searched his memory for a lame-assed excuse someone had used on him under similar circumstances. But he could no longer think straight.

Worst of all, he had reverted to type. When did I become him again, he wondered. When did Dylan become my enemy? He looked at his friend, releasing his grip on the cushion.

"I ... I'm sorry Dylan. I don't know what's happening to me."

"Well, we do," Aisha said, "but we'd like to hear it from you."

Olaf felt like he'd taken his first parachute jump. An inner voice told him there was no way he could ever get honest around his feelings. That Olaf was long gone.

"You knew it was never going to work with Sylvia," Dylan said.

Olaf was now free falling into a hell of his own making. He'd jumped - but forgot the parachute. His gut knotted a fraction more and the ringing in his ears grew. Then a wave of calm flowed through him, washing most of his anxiety and fear aside. He realised that at the time he'd only been deceiving himself, and now he felt better that he didn't have to keep lying.

"How... how long did you know about Sylvia and I?"

Dylan angled himself toward Olaf, draping his arm along the top of the sofa. Olaf recognised the classic counselling move, adopting a relaxed position with non-threatening body language.

"It doesn't matter," Dylan said.

"Everyone did. Except you," said Aisha.

Olaf started to panic.

"Now I get it. You two have now stooped to doing the good cop/bad cop schtick."

He snorted and was about to take wing for a second time that day, when Dylan's hand gripped his shoulder.

"Hey … hey Olaf. We're not cops. We're just two people who love you and are concerned about you."

"Olaf," said Aisha, wiping tears away. "We knew about you and Sylvia from the moment she turned up here. And I'm glad you finally got honest around it, because as I told Dylan at the time, I was looking at having to fire you."

The hand on his shoulder tightened briefly, causing Olaf to hug his cushion tighter.

"We agonised how we could help you. But as you well know, there is nothing we can do for others in crisis if they don't want it. Do you know how many times I drove past your place at night to see if the lights were on? Because that was the only confirmation I could get that you were still alive. You never returned one call or text message. And that's okay; I get addict behaviour. So when Gene told me you had gone on the clinic's books I was ecstatic. Because I knew that as long as you were dosing, the risk of a fatal OD lessened."

She paused for a sip of water.

"I'm going to tell you something I told Dylan years ago. And I mean this. You are like a son to me. You are like the son I always dreamed of having."

Aisha blew her nose and continued.

"When I told the board you had applied for admission, all five of them recommended you go elsewhere. But I wasn't going to take that risk. I wasn't going to lose you again. Never in my years of working in the health sector have I felt so passionate and so compromised at the same time. And Olaf, this is not a guilt trip. I just need you to know how loved you are. How loved you are by the two people in this room."

Aisha sniffled again and turned to Dylan.

"Tell him."

"She was going to sack the board," said Dylan.

Olaf was shocked. If there was one thing in this world he knew Aisha prided herself above most things, it was the three women and two men who presided over the agency. Two doctors, one judge, a restaurateur and the CEO of a bank. She spent years persuading them and structuring that board; they were the brains and machine behind the whole operation.

"You didn't, did you?"

"No, but only because Gene was able to cajole the bejesus out of them. The point of all this is that now you are right where you need to be. Olaf, I can't begin to tell you how sorry I feel for you about Sylvia. I know you loved her. She's a wonderful woman, but she has her problems. And in another time and place maybe you would have made a lovely couple. But you knew from the start how damaged and broken she was. And what's the result? Now you're just as damaged and broken. Look, we'll always give you another chance. You can walk through that front door a hundred times and I will never turn you away. But please, please, please, don't become one of those clients. For your sake."

Olaf felt like a heel. Part of him still wanted to run. Sure, he could go back to his house but, like him, it was virtually an empty shell now. Far emptier without Sylvia.

"I need you to answer me just one thing," said Dylan. "And I am not interested in any lies or bullshit. I just want you to be honest. Where are you at now with her? Emotionally?"

Olaf felt nauseous. Again. His breathing was shallow, his heart was racing, the anxiety he'd been held hostage by for the last few weeks was tightening around his throat like a garrote. What in fuck's name was honesty anymore?

"It … it's hard to explain. I… I…"

The office fell silent.

His chest tightened and sadness enveloped him. He wanted to be free of his suffocating emotions. He wanted it to all end now. He wanted to be honest. He looked up at the corner of the silver frame around the organisation's mission statement - *To foster recovery and respect in a loving environment devoid of judgement, regardless of who we are or what we have done.*

"She's like fucking heroin. When we're physically together, I feel okay. I feel safe. When I was living in Napoli, I saw this grafitti. Eroina è calda - heroin is warm. And it was the most sensible description of it I'd ever seen. And she is warm, too. But only when I've got her. When she walks out the door - to go to her parents', the shop, work, the toilet, wherever, I panic. My head says there'll never be any more dope. That that was the last shot. So, you know, I start jonesing. I crave her. It's just the fucking same. I call her incessantly, send texts. It's fucking madness. And because she deals with her own demons by being emotionally cruel, it hurts me even more. The more I want her, the less I can have her. Until … she wants me. Her insistence on an open relationship, disappearing for days on end. And she's forever reminding me she loves me but she's not in love with me. It's absolute conditional love."

"Except there's no love."

"No, there is."

"Olaf!" snapped Dylan. "Stop kidding yourself. You have perfectly described the dysfunction of your 'relationship' - and I use that word very loosely. To quote you, she is like heroin. So, what do we do when the drug has become too much?"

Olaf's anxiety was giving way to anger. He wanted to scream and throw a tantrum, mainly because this was all his own doing.

"Are you enjoying this? I'm here drowning in a pit of quicksand called shame, and all you can do is harangue me." He looked perplexed. "I'm sorry. I shouldn't have said that."

"I don't know if you've forgotten where you are," said Dylan, "but you're not drowning in some Hollywood studio fabrication. You are sitting in a room called 'my consequences'. And no-one put you here but you. Not us, not Sylvia, not the authorities. You. So, again, what are you going to do about your obsession with her?"

Olaf felt like he was going mad. His emotions were catapulting around like a pinball. He remembered his relaxation therapy training, drew a long breath, held it, then slowly released it.

It did nothing.

"Put my heart into detox?"

The other two nodded.

"How will you do that?" Aisha asked.

"I don't know. Help me guys. I just want this to stop. Please."

He flinched when Dylan squeezed his hand. It wasn't exactly professional, but comforting all the same.

"Well, buddy. First thing you'll need to do is get rid of her. Any photographs, social media accounts, love letters, texts, emails, all of it - gone. I'll help you."

"One of the most important things I heard," said Aisha, "was how she told you she loved you but wasn't in love with you. Can I just say, that is the most manipulative and cruel thing anyone could say to someone who obviously loves them. If she actually did care about you she would have wanted to build a relationship with you. That's what couples do, they make plans together. Her plans didn't factor you in one iota. I'm sorry, Olaf, but the fact is Sylvia didn't love you. If anything, she probably despised you, and her actions support that."

Olaf knew Aisha was right. He wasn't too keen on Dylan's Stalinist revision of history but in another time he would have been advocating the same tactics. He sensed a change come over him, a ripple of relief. Nothing major but, still, it felt reassuring.

"So, what happens now?"

"You tell us," Dylan said. "What do you want to do?"

Olaf grinned at the memory of Dylan explaining to him once that you always allow the client to answer their own questions. He turned to his friend and took his hand.

"I want to stay. I want to get well again"

Aisha beamed. "Nur für Heute, liebling."

Olaf knew it was about a darling, but hadn't a clue what the rest meant.

"Ich verstehe dich nicht," he said in an appalling German accent.

"I'll tell you tomorrow."

Dylan wandered over to the coffee machine.

"How do you want to play this out, buddy?"

Olaf squirmed. He knew there were two ways - the right way, and the lie.

"Let's go into a house group and get it over with. I'll tell them Sylvia and I had been in a relationship, we were planning to get married, we didn't have sex while we've been here."

"Why don't you just say the two of you had been in a relationship, then explain why you are still here. Don't muddy it with all that soap opera crap."

The last quip stung but Olaf was aware what Dylan was up to. He knew he couldn't just turn off his emotions around Sylvia, so his friend was going to do his darndest to help him. Was it soap opera crap? At this moment, no. But if I examine it more closely.

"How are you feeling?" asked Aisha.

The question caught him off guard.

"I feel heart-broken, scared, happy you guys won't give up on me, nervous of the group, a small sense of freedom. I don't know. I'm not sure how I feel."

Suddenly, the mood was broken by Dylan clattering a spoon inside in a coffee mug. He took a brash slurp, expelled an unnecessary "aaahhh" and reminded them that they'd better get everyone to the clinic for dosing.

THE HOUSE group wasn't nearly as dramatic as Olaf had feared. He followed Dylan's blueprint and, if anything, there was an air of ennui in the room. This may have had to do with the fact most of them had just downed a horse-stopping dose of methadone. Joe fidgeted for a few seconds, worrying whether he should speak up. He was in his early sixties, had never been to prison and, in his heyday, had been a cook in some of the world's leading restaurants. His propensity for narcotics, however, kept him from ever advancing beyond sous chef. Because of his age the other clients rarely held Joe accountable for anything, and he was quite aware of this. He came to ITL knowing if he didn't give up drugs now, he never would.

Joe admitted to the group that Dan had told him he knew Sylvia and Olaf had been an item a long time ago, but Sylvia had asked Dan to respect Olaf's privacy because of his history there.

Olaf couldn't work out if Sylvia did actually love and care for him or if she was merely manipulating Dan for her own needs.

Dylan stressed to the group that neither Dan nor Sylvia were there, so any discussion around them was nothing but gossip, and that they needed to support rather than ostracise Olaf. He asked the group to vote, and the eight of them were unanimous in their decision for Olaf to stay.

As they left the room, Dave beelined to Olaf.

"I need to talk to you about something."

They headed up the side of the house to the magnolia tree. Dave checked to see they were out of earshot.

"Listen, when I came in and you flushed that dope of mine, it really ate at me. I'm not blaming you, but I was dirty on myself for letting you get rid of it. And now I respect you for that. Anyway, I just want you to know that any differences we may have had, well, my part is I had a resentment around that. But dude, I can't imagine what you must be going through with Sylvia and everything. So I'm just letting you know I've got your back, brother. Let's work at helping each other. I figure I owe you one. We good?"

Olaf hadn't ever given much thought to their niggling differences, but between Aisha and Dave's confessionals, he was - as they say - feeling the love. He mock-punched Dave on the sternum and nodded.

"Yeah brother, we're good."

FROM THE outside, it appeared Olaf was letting go of Sylvia. As each week passed, he would consciously try not to discuss her. He thought about her incessantly but he also figured it was boring for his peers. When one day he yet again mentioned her in group and saw that everyone looked stultified it was the last time he brought her name up. Occasionally he'd refer to her while out in the garden or on an afternoon walk, but the reception was usually the same - feigned interest. He was getting the message.

His friendship with Dave began to bloom. At night they'd lay on their respective beds sharing stories for hours; Dave was fascinated with the fact that Olaf had been a counsellor there, then ended up back as a client. Olaf rarely spoke of his life before he started working in drug and alcohol counselling, partly because he found it hard to reconcile the junkie he had become with the person he now was. Drugs had certainly led him on a wild and crazy life, but deep down he always felt a sense of regret. Dave was the opposite. He was still zapping from every demented event on his journey of weird and, like all good criminals, needed to function like a detective in order to get out of his own way. He had an extraordinary ability to garner and retain information, and after much probing Olaf finally let slip that he'd been the famous radio announcer Harvey Buxton's producer.

"You're kidding! You really worked with Harvey Big Bux?! I loved that show. Every morning my clock radio alarm would wake me with 'Live! From Studio Nine One One - The Rock and Roll Emergency Room. You're tuned into Harrrrvey Buxxxxton!' Man, I fucking loved that shit. And then they'd blast straight into something really cool like *Rearview Mirror*."

What took Olaf back was not so much Dave's unbridled enthusiasm for the late, great Harvey, but his ability to mimic the voiceover guy's intro. The station paid something like five grand to get that recorded but Dave's rendition was way better.

He would incessantly quiz Olaf about the celebrities who had been on the show, and every time Olaf dropped some rock star's name, Dave's response would always be "Get the fuck outta here! You met so-and-so?! What's he like?"

Of course, the allure of fame had worn off within a month of starting work for Buxton. Having to be up at 3am to start work at 4am before legions of people were blasted awake with the same 8-track cartridge tape that left such an indelible mark on Dave was not that glamorous. Most of Olaf's time at those hours seemed to be spent on phones, hassling publicists to get their charges into the studio. Then there was the ignominy of dealing with some coke-addled shitheel stinking of booze, urine and sex, insisting that the near-comatose 15-year-old girl in tow was an integral part of who he is, but if one word of this gets out motherfucker they'll never find your ass. Olaf thought it best he spared Dave that sort of detail. Not so much because he was worried about the reputation of some moron who had mastered five major guitar chords, but because by the end Olaf himself had a ticket on that very same ride.

Not all the guests were like that but the majority had their issues. As would anyone in their early 20s suddenly having millions of dollars to burn and their face on every magazine cover. For Olaf it became the old 'if you can't beat 'em' …

Olaf was far more interested in how Dave got his MBA and a university degree in prison, was released, crawled his way up the hierarchy of a junk food corporation, started drug dealing on the side, only to end up back in prison. Then restart the whole charade again. The two of them began to fall into step with each other's similarities, in that one man's cup of tea with The Thin White Duke was not much different to the other man's cell door slamming.

Their discussions became deeper and personal. Before his fall from grace, Olaf had always felt he'd been adept at getting the clients to open up to him. And he had. But as he grew closer to Dave and saw how the other clients interacted, he noticed that most of them rarely gave everything away. He, too, started doing this. In one session with Dylan, the subject of how he was coping emotionally around Sylvia came up. Olaf said how bereft he felt deep inside, but realised this was also an opportunity for him to grow and get some acceptance around it.

"I remembered something I read in a book that you lent me, actually. It said 'when you can share your story and it doesn't make you cry, then you know you have healed'. I honestly feel like I'm breaking through my grief."

Olaf was, he knew, still emotionally stunted. And he was still sobbing himself to sleep every night.

BEING A client in the institution he'd been working in four months earlier came with its challenges. Despite his wealth of experience, Olaf was now just 'one of them', wading each day through the intoxicating haze of methadone. In Olaf's case, however, instead of feeling a step closer to recovery every five days when his dose would drop 5mgs, he felt a step closer to relapse. Aisha hinted that, once he completed the program, he might want to move away for a couple of years, lose himself in a simple job and psych himself up for returning to his true calling. As enticing as this sounded, Olaf knew not to get too ahead of himself. It gave him pause for thought, though.

The house was 'running rough', as Aisha was fond of saying. When Olaf started working at ITL, she explained that the clientele are on a see-saw, rolling to-and-fro between cohesion and chaos.

Despite that, they were also meant to be self-regulating, harmonious and transparent. Major infractions like drug use were to go straight to staff and, given the fragile environment of detoxification they inhabited, always did. Less trivial matters like leaving clothes or dirty dishes around, disrespecting others, et cetera, were dealt with in the morning group. Partly out of frustration, Olaf decided to lift his game. It came while he and Dave were having one of their late night tête-à-têtes. Both of them were getting tired of the general lack of enthusiasm in the house. Some of the men weren't flushing the toilets, someone was pilfering the coffee, and everyone knew Carly and Sergey were fucking. That one was going to be particularly hard for him to address, especially after his charade with Sylvia. The other tricky part was going to be Sergey. He was a wild card who'd fought in the Chechen army, spent years in military prison and was prone to violence. Two consenting adults having the occasional late-night fuck might not seem a big deal but it was splitting the house.

Olaf felt it was his duty to lead the community back toward cohesion but, as he told Dave, the prospect of getting suffocated in his sleep by the formidable Russian did not appeal to him.

"I've got it," said Dave. "Sergey's girlfriend is close to my friend Tony's wife. I'll deal with him."

What also became apparent to Olaf was that many of the interactions in group were not as impromptu as they seemed and were, in fact, highly orchestrated. As a worker he and the others had had their suspicions but as a client he began to see new examples of how the system worked.

The first order of the next day was Sergey. They gathered at the end of the garden, away from the staff and, more importantly, where they could smoke. In classic jailyard style, Dave sidled up to him and mumbled something before they wandered up to the magnolia. Olaf glanced up at them while listening to Mozz holding court about some drug caper he pulled off in his late teens. This in itself was frowned upon; any celebrated discussion of past drug use or related capers was called negative raving. If Olaf was going to be as principled as he intended, he'd later be calling Mozz out with a reflection around his 'neg raving', but at that moment he was too distracted by Sergey and Dave's interaction.

Sergey's flailing arms and puffed-out chest indicated he was ready to explode but Dave's ice-cool attitude seemed to be keeping a lid on things. Eventually they both relaxed, shadow boxed a few punches at each other and came back through the garden talking about some guy from 'inside'. As close as Olaf was getting to Dave, they'd never have that fraternal bond that prisoners develop. And it worried him that this worried him.

"I'll make it brief," Olaf announced to no-one in particular. People stopped chatting and looked around.

"As you know, I used to work here and I believe we're going through a rough patch. We have people not talking to each other, all sorts of shifty behaviour going on, and basically we're gonna end up losing people. Anyone feel like splitting? Or using dope?"

He was met by blank faces.

"I'm not going to drop anyone to staff, I'm not like that. I'm one of you guys. I'm on the juice too, and I want to get off it. So does anyone feel like leaving or scoring gear?"

Carly, Dean and Mozz raised their hands and Marianne said "yep".

"Okay, here's what I propose. I'll get the ball rolling today. No-one has been doing reflections, so Dean, I'm going to chop you with one today about not doing the laundry yesterday."

Dean bristled.

"You're fucking kidding, aren't you?"

Before Olaf could respond, Dave chimed in.

"Guys, Olaf and I came up with this plan together. He's cool. We're doing this for us. You heard Dylan give it to us yesterday morning, and he's right. One of us will be out the door soon, and dead before we know it. We're a good crew, and Olaf knows this shit inside out. We'll do one today, another tomorrow, a couple more the next day, and so on. Let's just give it a go, eh?"

Mozz still didn't look happy.

"Why don't I give you one instead?" he asked, staring at Olaf. "We all waited half an hour for dinner last night because of your fucking around with the vegetables."

The hunter had become the hunted. Whatever it takes, Olaf thought.

"Excellent idea," he said. "Thanks Mozz."

CARLY CALLED for reflections and Mozz raised his hand. As did Joe. But when Carly raised hers, too, a chill ran through the room. Everyone loved Carly. She was fun, witty, engaging, loyal and about as sharp as a bowling ball. Even Sergey, who normally exhibited two emotions - aggression and aggression - looked concerned.

"Mozz, please share your reflection."

"I noticed, Olaf, you were very late with our dinner last night. This concerns me because we are expected to eat at a set time, and some of us like to go for an evening walk, and we don't get that long to do that. I am willing to support you in reflecting on this by helping you prep and cook the next dinner you are rostered to do."

Everyone thanked Mozz, and then Carly called Joe.

"I noticed, Marianne, you keep stamping your cigarettes out on the ground. This concerns me because there are ashtrays nearby, and it's kind of disrespectful to our place. I am willing to support you in reflecting on this by kindly reminding you to use the ashtrays when we're having a smoke."

Carly handed the folder to Dylan, who shook his head at her.

"Not my responsibility," he said, to nervous laughter.

Carly placed the folder against her chair leg, then turned toward Sergey and Mozz.

"I noticed, Mozz, you didn't wash any of our bed linen yesterday. This concerns me because it only gets done every three days, and because some of us are detoxing we sweat and stuff at night and it starts to stink. I am willing to support you in reflecting on this for the next two washing days by reminding you it needs to be done, and I will also gather the women's sheets and pillowcases for you."

Dylan knew there was something underlying the collective tension - and he had his suspicions - but whatever it was did not get brought up in the reflections.

"I noticed one of the smack packs has gone missing from the downstairs bathroom," Dylan said. Although the staff had a liberal approach to harm minimisation and endorsed clean and safe drug using practises, for the residents it was invariably a near-catastrophic event. To them, it meant one of their own had fallen and was in crisis and they loved to red line to drama.

"Just a reminder guys, if you see one missing or opened, let staff know straight away so we can replace it. I don't need to remind you there is no shame attached to taking one. If all you leave here with is a better understanding of safe injecting and OD practices, well then good. Sorry to interrupt, Carly."

As Carly stooped to retrieve her folder, Olaf chimed in.

"Hang on, a smack pack has gone missing and no one cares? What's going on here?"

Everyone looked surprised, and nobody as much as Dylan. If anyone should understand the rationale behind the provision and accessibility of the smack packs it was Olaf. After all, it was he who drafted and rewrote the rehab's policy around it soon after he started working there.

"Olaf, no cross talking please," Dylan said. "This actually isn't cause for major concern. As I said …"

"Great, so one of us is on the brink of relapse, and all you care about is some ass-covering policy bullshit."

Dylan was puzzled. Olaf wrote the policy and now he's relegating it to an exercise in ass-covering?

"Hey, Olaf. We understand your concern, and it's a very healthy concern, but as I said, we try not to attach shame to this."

"Yeah, yeah. I get it, but I just feel we're pulling together as a team and it upsets me that someone among us is struggling and we're not doing anything about it."

Dylan looked at his friend sadly and wondered when Olaf's reasoning went south. As a counsellor Olaf had been exemplary. As a client, however, he was just an archetype.

"And I understand that. But as you … we, I mean … we all know, we're not about witch hunts here."

As soon as he said it, Dylan wanted the words to fly back inside his mouth. Too late.

"Witch hunts?! Jesus, I never said any such thing."

"That was a stupid thing for me to say," admitted Dylan. "It was thoughtless and disrespectful, and I apologise unreservedly to everyone."

Just as Olaf was about to fire up Carly made the 'time out' gesture and announced "respect time" to the room. It was a tactic used for whenever conversations got heated or aggressive and was generally effective. Everyone looked at Olaf, whose body language - clenched jaw, leaning forward, leg jiggling - spoke volumes. Dylan addressed the silence.

"Hey, Olaf, would you be open to holding this conversation over until tomorrow morning?"

Olaf sighed and sat up, relaxing slightly. However, his face was a portrait of emotional pain. He looked around the room and gripped the sides of the seat.

"Dylan knows this story, but what the fuck. I've only ever told him and one other person. When I was 19, I had this amazing girlfriend. Sonja. She was an incredible musician and the sweetest person. We were using heroin together. One night, we got some really good dope. Afghani brown rocks. It was late, and we walked around the neighbourhood for ages trying to find a place that would sell us a lemon so we could dissolve the smack. As we did, and I'll never forget this, we talked about how much we loved each other and how we should go to detox and plan a future together. We had the dope, and there was no urgency to use it. Sonja's cocktail napkin plan that night was 'we stay clean for a year, then start a family'. Out of the fucking blue - let's have a baby. It was beautiful and weird. Two kids in love on a cold, wet night. But you know, as soon as the woman at Ray's all-night pizzeria gave us that lemon, we tore home like maniacs to get high. And we did. I woke up the next morning fumbling beside the mattress for the dope. It was on Sonja's side of the bed. We hadn't used all of it, but as I leant over her I could see the packet was empty.

"And then I realised that this gorgeous girl, my best friend, my lover, was cold. Her skin was all waxy and blue. And the last thing she said to me was 'let's have a baby'.

"Why I'm telling you guys this is that I've seen lots of people die from drugs. An average of three clients a year leave here and drop within a week. Most don't affect me, but when they do ... man, it cuts."

Olaf looked into every person's eyes. It was a technique he used to regularly employ when he worked there and, for a second, he had forgotten where he was. Or rather, who he was.

"I dig all you cats. You're all fucking great. I know - I fucking believe - you will love me back to recovery. And I'll do the same for you. Believe it or not, at this point in time, we're all we've got. We get each other. We know what we are going through. So whoever feels like having a shot, please don't. Please, just don't. You know, we used to have this guy who worked here years ago, and he always would say 'Hey so-and-so, remember you are loved'. And it took me ages to get what he meant. But man, what a beautiful message for any junkie. So whoever is thinking about a shot, remember, you are loved."

Dylan felt a tinge of resentment. This was what had made Olaf such a great counsellor. He could get right to the clients' hearts without any bullshit. They always understood he was one of them, hence the trust. But now he really was one of them, and that hurt Dylan. Not because he had relapsed, or was now on methadone. He was in a protected, healthy environment, being cared for. He was safe. No, what stung Dylan was that, statistically, the odds were stacked against his friend making it 'back'.

A FEW days later they were all hanging around outside in the garden, having the usual erratic discussions. On one hand their common experiences were the decadence of addiction and crime, yet they were now trying to get a handle on the prospect of a drug-free life. Some felt like it was all a revolving door of doom, where rehabs became sanctuaries of respite. Mozz fell into that camp. By his own estimation, this was the 12th time he had been in rehab. Mozz was 34.

His father, Kevin, had been a notorious underworld figure who was forever being linked to crooked politicians, dubious corporate high-flyers and the beautiful people. His closest allies, though, were the three lawyers he kept on massive retainers, and it paid off. Kevin Morris was forever being called before judges, but he always left the courts via the same door he entered.

Mozz's mother, Kiitta, had been a fashion model who made the transition into acting. Subsequently, young Mozz was an extraordinarily handsome man, but being the product of psychosis and beauty had left him a confused individual.

One evening, in a booze- and coke-fuelled rage, Kevin Morris decided his wife had been sleeping with someone else. These paranoid fantasies usually culminated in a beating but on this night he took to his wife's face and temple with the butt of his Glock .40 handgun. It was the fifth blow to her head - across her left temple - that ended her life. Morris immediately knew no amount of bribes or lawyers were going to be getting him off this charge so he fired a bullet up through his chin, tongue and brain, leaving 16-year-old Mozz an estate worth $11 million.

By the time the department of taxation and Morris's circle of lawyers, friends, associates, low-life mates and general hangers-on had got their cut, Mozz was left with a nondescript, urban townhouse.

YEARS OF drug use and violence had taken their toll on Mozz. Olaf remembered how handsome he was when they first met five years before, but his head was now pitted with small scars, his face hardened and pock-marked, and that million-dollar smile was now in need of some urgent dental attention. Olaf was fond of Mozz and it concerned him that he was losing his sense of self. All the bravado and tough guy crap could never hide the wounded little mummy's boy. They sat in the garden that morning, under the sporadic descent of autumnal maple leaves.

"I fucking hate this time of year," Mozz announced.

Olaf knew why, too. He remembered Mozz breaking down in group a few years beforehand, saying exactly the same thing. His father murdered his mother around this time of year and Mozz had recalled how he was supposed to have been heading into a winter of fun and excitement in the snowfields with his parents and three of his friends. Instead he waited out the vacation break at the boarding school, playing chess with a geriatric Jesuit.

"Your mother, eh?"

"How the fuck you know anything about my mother?"

"Yo, Mozz. I used to work here. You shared this with me years ago."

Mozz took a drag on his smoke.

"Oh yeah. Thanks for remembering, bro. That, you know, means a lot."

Olaf wanted to continue the conversation; wanted to gain a level of trust with Mozz, and lose the us-and-them vibe he still carried. But he knew it could wait.

The community dined on shepherd's pie that evening.

"Favourite meal of that old geezer in the Stones," said chef Joe as he doled out the portions. "Except we don't have any of that HP sauce. No brown sugar here tonight, you rock-and-roll stars," he drawled in an exaggerated British accent.

Dave shot Olaf a look that made him want to laugh. He used all his self-control but the more he tried to suppress it, the more he trembled keeping it in. Dave, too, started to snigger, and soon Marianne and Carly were catching the bug. Even Sergey cracked out some weird excuse for a smile.

Unable to contain himself anymore, Olaf snorted.

"What the fuck are you on about, dude?"

Joe pouted like a trout, waving his pie tin and spatula round, wiggled his hips and, in the most gratingly tuneless way possible, sang the beginning of *Jumping Jack Flash*.

At which point they all lost it.

"I'm sending you to Dr Gene for a meds review first thing tomorrow," Aisha announced. She smiled as she looked around the table and Olaf felt its wattage increase when she looked at him. It was the first real laugh he'd had in ages.

As a result, the dinner conversation was lively, centred mainly on their differing music tastes. The surprise was Joe, who loved big band jazz orchestras like Duke Ellington's and Count Basie's but, because hardly anyone there was au fait with either gentlemen, he went back to riffing on Keith Richards' dietary habits. According to Joe, the guitarist hated cheese - a spot of trivia which cracked them up even more and, when Aisha mentioned she'd once read cheese described as 'heroin for the ruling class' it was too much. The gags cartwheeled into the obvious and the absurd and it seemed Dave and Olaf's plan to get them back into cohesion was working. It felt right.

Until dessert, when Olaf broke a patch of silence to ask Mozz how he was coping. Mozz had just taken a bite out of his apple and simply stopped chewing.

"Why would you bring that up now?" he asked through the half-chewed fruit.

"Well, because I care about you, Mozz. And it being the anniversary of your mother's death and all, I just ..."

Everything on the table rattled as Mozz brought his fist down on it like a gavel.

"Fuck, Olaf. What is your fucking problem?"

"As I said, I care about you, Mozz. And I'm not convinced it's not you who has the smack pack."

Amid a chorus of "let it go" and "for fuck's sake", Mozz rose from the table and headed toward the bedrooms. Aisha also rose from the table.

"Excuse me, people. I need to do something before I go home. Olaf, come to my office please."

Once there, Aisha wasted no time.

"This obsession with the harm minimisation kit ends right now."

"But, Aisha, did you see ..."

"I am not interested. It ends now."

But Olaf wasn't ready for it to end.

"He is emotionally on edge. Trust me. I think he should sleep on the couch tonight so Sarah can keep a watch on him. Please. You have to trust me on this. I know. I don't know why, but I just do."

Aisha wanted to buy into his drama but also knew this wasn't how things were done.

"No Olaf," she said. "You're not an employee here, you're a resident. And, frankly, it's about time you realised that. Now, please leave, and I'll see you tomorrow."

"SORRY BROTHER, but I'm with Mozz," Dave said to Olaf as they readied for bed. "What's going on with you at the moment?"

"Honestly? I don't even know why I fucking bother," Olaf snapped. "Sometimes there is a major shit storm descending, and all the indications are there. Fucking twisters throwing cattle and tractors all over the state, armafuckinggeddon writ large. Man, you could have goddamned billboards everywhere saying 'duck, motherfuckers' and cunts just roll on oblivious to it all because they have their heads jammed so far up their own asses they don't know where they are. And then it hits. POW. Like a fucking nuke. And everyone will be like, 'oh, maybe Olaf was right'. Well, fuck you all. I'm going to write to my friend in Washington. At least he understands me."

Dave decided it might be best for Olaf to have some space to think it over.

"Alright, brother, you do what you feel you need to. And if you feel like talking later, wake me. Okay?"

Olaf, looking a bit sheepish, turned in the doorway.

"I will. Thanks Dave. Love you bro."

He headed to the chill-out room and fired up the computer. Olaf opened his email account and scanned the list, hoping desperately to find a message from Sylvia. His heart nearly stopped when he saw an email from two days before. **Sylvian, David.** *Blemish* **reissue**.

He started a new email and began typing in Zac Watts' name. Then, in the subject line, typed 'the missive of weird', cracked his knuckles, and began typing furiously.

DAVE WOKE at 5am the next morning. It was still dark, but he could make out Olaf's sleeping mass by the diffused light from a street lamp. "I hope you got a good rest, ya crazy fucker," he mumbled, and headed off for his morning shower. Fifteen minutes later he was down in the kitchen with Mozz, Marianne and Sergey.

"Where's your wife?" Dave teased Sergey.

"She want divorce. And I happy to give to her."

It was no secret that Carly and Sergey had put an end to their nocturnal activities, and neither of them seemed the slightest bit fazed about the cessation.

"How's Olaf?" said Mozz.

"Oh, you know. Who knows what goes on inside that nut's head. Throws his life away for some chick, ends up in here, she runs off with some steroid clown, he won't let go of his old self, thinks he still runs the joint. A million bucks couldn't get me to spend five minutes inside his scone. He was up til all hours writing to his boyfriend in Washington."

"Funny how he's so worried about me," said Mozz. "I'm just as worried about him."

"Yeah, well, he'll be okay," Dave said. "Let's just hope that nasty bitch sticks it out with GI Jerk. Here, make me a cup of tea for him. We'll help him kick start his day afresh."

Dave placed the mug of tea next to Olaf's bed.

"Here you go, brother. Two bags and milk. Just the way you like it."

He turned his bedside light on, trying not to wake his roommate too suddenly. As he was hanging his towel on the side of the wardrobe the clock radio clicked over to 6am, and the syrupy cheese of Toni Tennille reminded him that love will keep us together. Dave and Olaf had agreed that the worst way to be awoken was with sudden, violent noise, so their radio dial lived on the local hits and memories station.

Dave started to make his bed, deliberately snapping the bedspread as he shook it.

"Come on, brother, you can't stay in bed all day."

He continued bopping and singing along to the song as he tucked in the covers. In the dim light he could see Olaf was still in the hoodie he'd been wearing the night before. Dave flicked the overhead light on and then saw it: next to Olaf's pillow was a colourful, unfolded square of glossy paper. It was a part of a woman's face and the criss-cross folds indicated it was a makeshift envelope fashioned from a magazine - it was the packet in which Dave had smuggled in his heroin. The heroin Olaf said he had flushed.

Dave gave him a formidable nudge.

"Come on, get up, you unit."

A blood-tinged syringe puncturing his roommate's forearm was the giveaway.

Olaf was dead.

ABRAHAM LINCOLN looked down at Zac Watts, who in turn was looking up at the 16th president's celebrated address. "The world will little note nor long remember what we say here but it can never forget what they did here." The furthest thing from Honest Abe's mind on November 19, 1863, would have been the insecurities of a reporter from the future, but that didn't prevent Zac convincing himself that no-one would ever remember what he did there. Or more realistically, didn't do there.

How had he gone from being a zealous newshound to a lonely hack riven with self-doubt? The hangover he was battling gave him a partial answer, and the desire to zone out with a spliff under a tree rather than be back in his shoebox of an office reading about suicide prevention programs for Uncle Sam's misguided children - as the marine corp was known - completed the answer.

He wandered out of the memorial and looked along the Reflecting Pool at the Washington Monument. If this glorious nation truly had courage, he thought, they'd replace that stupid looking phallus with an LGM-30 Minuteman-III ICBM. Primed. And ready to launch.

He squeezed the baggy of weed in his pocket and descended the stairs toward Constitution Avenue. Despite the day's balminess, there were few people around. Zac fixed his eye on a particular grove of trees and decided that was as good a place as any to get high.

Jesus, where did I even get this weed? Zac thought back and remembered he'd spent the previous afternoon at the African American Civil War Museum. While he may have been struggling with the convoluted vagaries of Capitol politics, his thirst for history was certainly being sated. He knew he had stopped in at a bar on U Street for

a quick beer at around 4pm, and left there with a woman called Hinata
about six hours later. He vaguely recalled them fucking on a bed, but
couldn't remember if it was his or hers. Then there was another bar and
lots of Long Island Teas. He had woken in his bed, with Hinata, and
started the day with coffee, Tylenol and a soixante-neuf.

None of it explained where the weed came from though.

He lay on his front with the sun behind him. Through the trees he
could see the pool; above, the air traffic descending into the airport. A
southerly breeze carried the slight hint of avgas, which only made Zac
keener to get away from the city. As he broke the sticky bud of skunk
weed into the two papers, his phone dinged. It was an email from Olaf
Shapiro. His first thought was that Olaf's communiques were best read
high but the subject line - 'the missive of weird' - had a strange element
of urgency about it. He put the weed and papers back into the plastic
bag, and tapped the screen with his thumb.

*yo, clark kent. how's life in that open sewer? listen, i trawl that rag you
work for and i gotta say, bowie had your number. you need a new career in a
new town, dude. really - a gig review of some hillbillies in an amphitheatre?
what the fuck? you smokin' that river root too? though i gotta say, an open air
concert in a national park sounds pretty fucking cool. and wolf trap. groovy
name. just a pity about that band. i checked 'em out on youtube. nuh-uh. move
on. besides, that keyboard player in all that black leather. if he went within a
block of a school the cops would be within their rights to shoot him. repeatedly.
like twenty times.*

*speaking of which, we went and saw sleeve a while back. oh how the mighty
fall. all that love and shit he got from the save the oceans concert went to his
head. he managed to pull together a band of bigger burnout fuckweasels than
him and... well to put it mildly, it's pathetic. he played at francois' rock lounge.
i can't believe that dump hasn't been condemned yet. so we go backstage... fuck
i kill me. backstage. we went into this putrid stinking box called a dressing room
and he's carrying on like he's james brown or someone. mr superstar, but with
no star, and fuck all super either. so he's all "how was it?" and of course sylvia
was all "you're so brilliant, we're so proud of you" bullshit. he looks at me and*

asks, "what did you think, o?" i'd had a few bourbons and stupidly said, "you should call this "the bring out your dead tour." suffice to say, he probably wont speak to me again. in fact, i can guarantee he wont, but more of that later.

hey, i heard a joke you can use over there. what's the difference between a cowboy hat and a tampon? cowboy hats are for assholes. yeah, a million laughs, i know. i'm lenny bruce phase II. maybe i should make stand-up my next brilliant career move.

so, so much has been happening. too fucking much. i don't want to bore you with the intricacies of what's been going on with sylvia and i, but i will. i'll keep it brief. so paris was a fucking car crash. still, when we got back we set up the spare room so she could have her own studio space blah blah. all that shit you would have seen on the book of faces. so the plan was for us to spend another year here, she finish her university degree, then sell the house and move down the coast to fucking hippie world. except... skag. it's okay. i'm okay now.

no i'm not. i'm fucked. i'm in the fucking rehab - as a client. but it's good. christ, i feel so sorry dumping this on you, but... well, you know.

so we started using together. it wasn't anything major. we were both putting about a hundred dollars each up our arms daily, but then she got all bolshie about it and said she needed to get work to pay for her own dope. told me she resented feeling dependent on me. so she ends up working in some cathouse assuring me "i'm only the receptionist", but you know, her libido disappeared and she ended up with blisters all around her mouth. "stress related", of course. and for some reason her habit was waaaay bigger than mine. it was hideous. man, stevie wonder could see what the fuck was happening.

so, we both went to the clinic and got on the 'done. after four weeks we made a pact to go into rehab - but not as a couple. we would temporarily split. (i hope to christ this isn't reading as deranged as it sounds. but i know it is.) yeah, so the cunning plan was get into rehab, get clean, and get back on track. then go back to plan a - move down the coast, paint, write, grow our own vegetables. the full utopian wank.

that's all good. we hadn't fucked for ages so some enforced celibacy in the 'hab wasn't gonna be a problem. it worked well. occasionally we'd have little private chats outside at night, whisper sweet nothings and talk about the future. then one day *poof* she's gone. she just took off into the night - with some neurone deficient ape. that was just over a month ago, and now i'm left broken like some bloke in a jackie leven song.

it's been in a living hell since then, zac. every waking minute i obsess about her. is she alright? is she being treated kindly? i fantasize that she's back at university. or moved to paris. that city is so her. grace and style. she was born to sashay down the champs elysees.

i sneaked out late a few nights after she left and went over to the house. all her stuff has gone, but the jewellery i gave her is still there. a gold bangle, some rings and a rolex watch - still on her bedside table. all the framed pics of us are there. it's like 'we' never existed. the safe has all sorts of valuable shit in it, including twenty grand cash. all there. her passport has gone, but nothing else touched.

and it's not about the caveman or whoever it is she might be fucking. i just hope for her sake she's okay. but i know she's gone. forever. and that's what causes me so much agony. i was never going to be able to keep her down. and that is so sad. you know all that "if you love somebody set them free" shit. she'll always have freedom. but i guess i don't fall into her definition of it. i've tried to call her sister, but she's obviously blocked my number. and really, what's the point of calling anyway? sometimes we just have to get the message. i think maybe i should remove the rose-coloured tinting off my rear view mirror when what i should actually do is yank the whole fucking thing off and throw it under the next oncoming truck.

by the way, i've sent a registered letter to your cousin tim. i got one of those do-it-yourself last will and testament kits and filled it out. i told dr gene this bullshit story about how i needed to do it because of my risky lifestyle, and he agreed it was a good idea and witnessed it. so the original is with yr cuz, and the copy of the will is in my safe at home. it's in the bathroom floor under the bathmat. the instructions for opening it are in the bottom drawer in the kitchen. the combo for it is 11 31 13. yeah, yeah. i know. shut the fuck up.

i love you man. you are the brother i never had, and i'm not just saying that. we have a bond that is extraordinary and i can honestly say i have never felt an affinity with anyone the way i do with you. i know our friendship has only been relatively brief, but it's magical. as i type this, i have my phone propped up against the front of the computer. there's a photo sylvia took of us, and i don't think you've ever seen it. she took it in that vietnamese vegan joint one night. our heads close together. i'm looking straight at the camera. i clearly remember that moment. i was looking at her, but i was thinking how much i really cared about you. you're half leaning away with your eyes shut. you must have blinked. but i remember at the time i was concerned you weren't gonna make it, and that moving to dc was too soon. too big a risk. but there you are. sure, i give you shit on social media, but you know that's just me jerking yr chain. i'm so proud of you zac. and i mean that. sure, you don't have the same high-profile you had here, but i know that will change. i have faith in you. major faith. i fucking believe in you, amigo.

you have a dogged tenacity that will get you far. and you know i know what the fuck i'm talking about. so no matter what, i want you to keep going. follow that path yr on, dude. damn the fucking torpedos. hey, i'll put that pic on instagram now, so you can see it. i'll tag you.

now, here comes the hard part.

please don't think cruelly of me, zac. ever. i'm not a weak fucker. i'm just a very lonely and scared little boy who now realises no amount of therapy is ever going to get me through the hell of abandonment. after that day when my shrink explained to me i'm the way i am because of that evil cunt who i was cut out of, well... everything changed. i truly believed sylvia was some kind of guardian angel. i have accepted that i don't deserve love, and if i do, well, i'm selfish. i only ever wanted it from her. as i once wrote to her, eternity exists because of her infinite beauty. and if i can't be with her here, i'm going to wait for her in the cosmos. when you see sylvia - and you will - please tell her i'll be waiting for her on a planet near sirius.

technology is both a beautiful and hideous thing, my friend. the luddites were definitely onto something. one of the beauties of computers is you can delay stuff. i delayed the transmission of this email by four hours.

i'm sorry zac, it's nothing personal, but i'm gonna OD myself straight after i hit the send button.

i love you my brother. go well.
olaf xxxxx

Zac stared at the screen in disbelief, but deep inside he knew it was true. His heart raced and his mind began a cacophony of mad reason. "He's still alive." "It's some sick fucking joke." "Why would he do that?" "Call his phone." "Some moron is playing a prank." "Call Sylvia." "Race back home." "Is he alone?" "Where did it happen?" "No-one else knows yet."

He looked back through the email, looking for some kind of clue. To what, he had no idea. Rehab. His house. Art. Heroin. Tim. Hippies. It was all blurring into an incomprehensible mess and the louder and more discordant it got, the clearer two things became.

Olaf was gone.

And Zac wanted him not gone.

A memory of the two of them wandering along a beach not long before Zac left for DC barrelled all other thoughts aside. He recalled Olaf's smiling face as he checked out Sylvia's derrière, raising one wiggling eyebrow then sweeping his arm toward the ocean. He remembered how Olaf sang a few lines from a song about slow boats, then yelled "Ralph." Him and his stupid rock trivia. What the fuck was that song? Who was Ralph? Why the fuck did you have to …

Zac gripped at the lawn as his face fell into it. His sobbing fluctuated between body convulsions and gentle sniffles, while occasionally moaning "Olaf". After half an hour he was exhausted. As he got up Zac noticed the bag of weed in the imprint of his frame in the grass. What better time could there be to roll a big, fat spliff? The idea of heading back to the apartment and getting utterly fucking blitzed was just the ticket. I'll even grab a fifth of bourbon to expedite the anaesthetising process. Zac bent down to retrieve the dope but Olaf's voice echoed from some past relapse prevention group: "If you don't pick up, you won't get a habit."

"So, what the fuck happened to you man?" he asked.

The hum of Washington continued. The murmur of cars, the sound of a distant police siren, faint voices from over by the pool, a far-off jet.

Zac left the bag where it was and began the longest and loneliest and saddest walk home.

"I guess we both just fucked up."

HE OPENED the door, baulking at the state of his apartment. A chair had toppled with the weight of his clothing across its back. There was a distinct smell of booze and stale sex. The bed sheets and comforter were strewn on the floor, the remnants of a bottle of burgundy staining them. A red thong on the pillow just said 'tacky as'. Zac thought of his mother's mantra throughout his teens - "your room looks like a brothel" - and considered taking a picture to send to her.

He turned on the coffee percolator, cranked some music and threw himself under the shower. After 20 minutes of trying to scald the day's pain away he gave up, poured the coffee and lay naked and wet along the couch. He opened his Instagram account to see if the photo Olaf mentioned was there. It was. Zac's eyes were indeed shut, but it was still a great pic. He made a decision to not cry. Sure, there'll be more tears - lots and lots of them - but for the time being let's make it about us. He took in Olaf's sly glance. This, he decided, needs to be printed and framed. He contemplated where it would eventually hang just as J Mascis began his cover of the mournful *Fade Into You*. Zac had so much hurt to endure.

"ULLO," the clipped accent answered through a fog of static.

Zac paused, looking at the array of emblems on his screen, contemplating whether to end it now by touching the white handset on the red disc.

"I don't know if you remember me," he said. "It's Zac Watts."

"Of course I remember you, Zac." Dylan paused. "How are you, buddy?"

It had been three hours since the email, thought Zac, so maybe Dylan wasn't aware of Olaf's death. Or maybe Olaf was okay; maybe someone got to him with some Narcan.

And just as fast as that freak wave of joy hit, it receded back into the cold, black ocean of reality.

"I, uh, listen. I've got some pretty sad news, Zac."

"Yes, I know. He sent me an email."

They listened to the crackles and blips of the ether. Zac wondered whether the telco was bouncing their satellite signal off Sirius or indeed if Olaf was listening in. His eyes welled.

"Hi," he said sombrely.

"Hi buddy."

Zac cleared his nose and wiped his eyes.

"Sorry Dylan, I was talking to Olaf. I mean, I … Oh fuck. I don't know what to say. I just don't know what he… Why? Why did he have to die?"

"That's the tragic part. He didn't have to."

DISMAL DIDN'T even begin to describe the atmosphere outside the chapel. Aisha looked at the crowd, wondering who half of them were, and hoping the rest would ignore her. She heard a salvo of laughter and turned to see two middle-aged men shaking with mirth. Her aching soul was telling her to storm over and slap their faces when Dylan sidled up and took her hand.

"He'd have wanted more of that," he whispered.

She tightened her grip on his and moved in so his other arm could provide the comfort she craved. The sobbing began and Dylan did the only thing he could; he held her. Aisha heaved against his chest, desperately trying to stifle any sounds without smearing her lipstick on his T-shirt. She rested her hand over his heart and looked at the image of Bob Marley, the words NATTY DREAD emblazoned above his head.

"You know I met him?" she said.

"I do, which is why he's here. For all the spirit guides our boy needs, I reckon old Bob will take care of him the best."

Dylan released her and took a pen and paper from his coat.

"Eulogy. You just reminded me of something."

Of the hundred or so people gathered Aisha only recognised a handful of them – mainly former ITL clients, a few she vaguely remembered from parties at Olaf's house and a couple of his ex-girlfriends. One of them caught her eye and acknowledged her. Aisha felt anxious; she'd always liked this woman and, in her ersatz maternal love for Olaf, had hoped she'd be The One for him.

Saskia was dressed in an elegant black ensemble with a pair of patent leather heels that accentuated her 1.8 metres. All her years of modelling were evident in the way she glided over.

"Oh Aisha, I can't begin to tell you how sorry I am."

"Thank you," she replied. "Me too."

They made polite chit-chat about Olaf and were reminiscing about a night they'd had at a Catalan restaurant when Aisha noticed Saskia's wedding ring.

"I didn't realise you'd married."

Saskia looked at her ring, then back at Aisha.

"No. I ..."

Dylan used to refer to her as Sad-Eyed Sass, and never was that moniker more apparent.

"Sorry, that was inappropriate of me."

"No, it wasn't. All I wanted was a happy life with O, but you know, some guys you just can't tie down. I mean, I love my husband – he's a great guy and all, but ..."

"You don't owe me or anyone an explanation."

"I always held out hope that one day we would, you know ..."

Aisha nodded. She knew.

ZAC WATTS tapped his credit card against the electronic terminal and waited for the 'beep'.

"What, no tip?" the cabbie asked.

Zac fumbled to get out of the taxi. He slammed the door with rage.

"You should have thought about that before you took me on that tour of Shitsville, cunt."

Walking through the car park, he felt nauseous and angry. It was 11am, and he'd already had 20mg of benzodiazepine, six nips of bourbon, and there was a point of heroin waiting in his wallet. Like everybody else at the chapel Zac didn't want to be there. But unlike everybody else, he was taking his friend's death very personally. For three weeks he had tormented himself with a recurring question: why didn't he just fucking call me?

Of course, the irony wasn't lost on him. As their friendship bloomed, Olaf would impress on him that the most useful tool a recovering drug user can have is connection with another person. Things not going well? Call someone and talk about it. Feeling angry or resentful? Call someone and talk about it. Want to use drugs? Call someone and talk about it. It was a private contract they'd made with each other – and neither abided by it. So here he was, marching up a pebble concrete drive in a suit and tie on a blazingly hot day to have his guilt rip his heart asunder. What was it Olaf used to say? "Consequences, baby." Yeah, right.

At the chapel there was an overspill of least 30 people. I've thrown in my apartment and career to be here today, he told himself, so I'm fucked if I'm standing outside. He shoved his way through the other mourners, as though at a concert rather than a funeral. He was met with a few indignant mumbles but didn't care. He spied a pew and parked himself on the end of it.

He looked around the room, trying to reconcile how someone with so much verve could be despatched from the mortal coil in such drab surroundings. Why not floating down Mother Ganges on fire? Placed atop a Native American burial tree? Dynamited on a light tower at a rock festival? Shot from a cannon into space?

He pondered whether it was the heat or emotion that would not allow his mind to be still, then decided to concentrate on the woman holding court. She spoke of his friend with respect but obviously didn't know him. It was all "Olaf this" and "Olaf that", but then she said something that totally threw him – and no doubt most of the other people in the room.

"Olaf and I both got our doctorates of divinity after a sojourn in Arizona 20 years ago. Although we're both atheists, we made a deep spiritual connection at that sweat lodge and decided to broaden our horizons by studying at an online college. So, as sad as today is, it is also a tremendous honour that we can farewell our friend in a manner he would have wanted." She jerked her thumb over her shoulder at a wooden cross mounted behind her. "Meh to that nonsense. And with that, I call on Olaf's dear friend and mentor, Dylan."

Dylan moved to the lectern, produced some papers and looked at them as though they were written in Sanskrit. It was apparent he was struggling to keep his emotions in check.

"I'm not going to read what I've written. Well, not yet, but I thought I'd share a story with you. A few years ago we were in what Olaf called the druggy buggy taking the clients to a lunch organised by some politician. They were all excited because they were being feted at some fancy restaurant, but our friend in the box here was less than impressed. Like so many things in his life, he did it under sufferance. Anyway, we're beetling along, got some good music playing, when there's a burst of police sirens and red and blue light. He pulls over, tells everyone to make sure their seatbelt is on, then - and this is the weird part - says, 'y'all better leave this to me'. I mean, who else was going to be dealing with the police? He was driving the damn thing. Anyway, the policeman comes to his window and looks in, while Olaf just stares ahead. Finally the feller taps on the window and says 'open the window please, sir'. So Olaf opens the window a fraction, still looking ahead. The policeman then says, 'can you open it more?' Olaf replies, totally deadpan, 'no, I'll get cold'. It was the middle of summer. So the policeman then says, 'I need to see your licence, sir'. Olaf finally looks at the policeman and says, 'is that a request to actually look at it, or some banal statement of no relevance?' The policeman then sternly says, 'I demand you show me your licence, sir'. Now, for the record, this feller looked about 18 years old. Fresh from the farm. So Olaf mucks around looking in the glovebox, checking his coat pockets, under the sun visor, in the centre console. The officer was starting to get annoyed, and says, 'I order you to produce your licence now, sir'. With that, Olaf reaches into his jeans, pulls out his wallet and holds his licence up near the window crack, making the policeman put his fingers through to get it. He studies it for a minute, then asks, 'is this your correct name and date of birth, sir?' Olaf replies, 'sure, sonny'. The officer then asks, 'and is this your current address, sir?' Olaf replies, 'sure is, sonny'. The policeman then looks at Olaf and says, 'don't call me sonny'. With that, Olaf lowers the window and says, 'do I really look like the Queen would tap a sword on my shoulders and give me a knighthood and a suit of armour?' The officer looked a bit confused and replied, 'no'. With that Olaf points at the licence and says, 'well use my name, and stop calling me sir'. And, this is the weird part, he hands the licence back and says 'have a good day, Mr Shapiro'. Olaf says, 'you too, officer, and you can call me Olaf. We're all friends here'.

"Now, I can guarantee you, had any of us tried that caper we'd have been handcuffed and taken down to the station. But that's what our Olaf was like. Later on I asked him what the point of that was, and he said it was an exercise in education. Some of you may not know this, but one of his good friends here today is a senior detective who trains up-and-coming detectives in social skills and mores. Apparently, this was Olaf's way of taking the edge off that police academy testosterone. Sure, it's a risky gamble to take, but that's what he was about. It was very kind of you to refer to me as Olaf's mentor, Katherine but, really, I learnt more from him than I believe he learnt from me. He had that ability to not only access someone's character, but move his in with theirs. I can't tell you the number of times we had clients come to us in the first week of treatment complaining about Olaf's brusque style, and two weeks later asking if he could be their counselor. And the saddest part of it is …"

Dylan wiped a tear away.

"… the mad bugger refused to believe in his own ability."

He turned toward the coffin, picked up his papers and waved them at the room.

"I won't read through this. It's a maudlin rant that he'd hate. Indulge me while I work around its basic theme. Our Olaf was an incredibly complex man. Frighteningly bright, but sometimes unbelievably stupid. And I say that with love and respect, but God, sometimes … that anecdote about the traffic stop was a classic example. And what used to infuriate me is he got away with so much. As cavalier and amusing as those stories are, he knew that stuff often held back his emotional growth. He had that ridiculous Peter Pan complex that he refused to let go of. Now, I know a lot of you are here with a rough idea of what killed him. I believe his friends from his days in radio and his bands are of the understanding it was a coronary. To the people at the rehab, it was a heroin overdose. I had someone call the other day asking if it was complications from hep C. The more romantically inclined will think it was a broken heart. Maybe all those things contributed to his death, but the overwhelming cause was fear. Olaf was terrified of what he'd become. He was great at what he did, but he could not see that side of himself. The poor bugger had one of the most brutal upbringings of anyone I've met, and believe me, in our line of work we get to see some real doozies. But I've never met anyone who survived for so long running from love. He was like one of Harry Harlow's monkeys, desperately looking for someone who could fill in the gap called "what's a mother?" To a large degree, he got some of that maternal love from our friend and colleague Aisha. When they'd go off to the opera or an orchestral performance, his excitement was wonderful. Totally electric and infectious. For all his wild days singing in punk bands, I bet many of you don't know he was an authority on string quartets, particularly Beethoven, Schubert and Mozart. And that's what we loved about him. He was a man of deep contrasts. Lived in jeans and T-shirts but didn't think twice about dropping two grand on a paisley tailcoat. Regarded Saturday night drunks as humanity at its lowest ebb, but would always stop to talk to a street addict or derelict - and slip 'em some cash. Loved rock music, but his shelves were full of books on art and history. He hated pretentious bastards, but careful if you ever got into an intellectual argument with him. He became the most pretentious of all. And my favourite, and I'm gonna be naughty here. He called himself a feminist, but only went out with glamorous women."

A chorus of laughs rolled through the chapel, and Dylan caught the eyes of at least two of Olaf's exes. He knew there were a few more there.

"But most importantly, and ironically, it was love that he brought to so many of us. There are many of you here who contacted me over the past few days to tell me that they truly believe that had they never met Olaf, they'd still be stuck in the cycle of drug addiction. And I believe them. One woman told me she rang him at 2am one night - she was on the verge of using heroin for the first time in years - and he drove across town to a cafe where he sat with her for an hour. They barely said 10 words, but that was enough. He had that ability to care so deeply. But as I said before, the ability to give himself some of that affection was almost impossible. Working as a counsellor gave Olaf an incredible sense of worth. I've watched people come into this game with all the greatest intentions ever, only to leave a year or two later totally jaded, cynical, burnt out and full of disdain. With him, he was way ahead of everyone, but in his heart he knew he had hardly scratched the surface. He transformed people's lives without batting an eyelid, yet baulked at helping himself. Sure, we all know he did lots of therapy, but I bet it was he who was running the sessions. So, when we leave here today, let's not dwell on his sad demise. Let us carry in our hearts the love he fought so hard to attain, and send a little bit up to him when we think of him. And we will. For a long time. I'm going to finish with something I just heard outside. I was talking to one of the rehab boys - hi Sergey - and I expressed my sadness at having lost such a much-valued and dear friend. Sergey said, 'but now the Olaf has feathers and is flying above'. And despite his evangelical atheism, it gives me hope that our friend is indeed flying around, in feathers. I think that's a beautiful image, so what more can we expect now? Adieu, good buddy. We love you."

Dylan stepped away from the lectern, walked across over to the magnolia covered coffin, kissed two fingertips and softly rested them on a framed picture of Olaf.

As he returned to the pew, the room filled with a gentle drum rhythm followed by a series of repetitive single piano notes. Polly Harvey's *We Float* trundled along as a large, wall-mounted TV began screening a montage of Olaf's life. There were pictures of him as a small boy dressed in a cowboy outfit; proudly holding his first skateboard above his head; cuddling a cocker spaniel; a school portrait with a missing tooth - the usual collection of snaps from one's childhood. Except Olaf wasn't one for sentiment. The closest he got was posting a few pictures of him with rock stars on his social media page, taken in his radio days. It pleased Dylan that most of the people there would have been amazed such pictures even existed. The slide show rolled on through his life - happy snaps of him at various international landmarks; candid pictures taken at parties and other ordinary social events. It was obvious Olaf was not happy being photographed. Regardless, the song brought a heavy air of melancholy to the proceedings, accompanied by loud sniffs, the occasional wail and general sobbing - as any good funeral should sound. Just as Ms Harvey began singing about losing one's way the slideshow froze on a photo of Olaf impishly grinning, and his mortal remains began their final journey into the crematorium.

THE WAKE was held at Kashmiri Paradiso, a fusion Pakistani/Neapolitan restaurant. The purpose was two-fold; it was Olaf's favourite noshery, and they didn't serve alcohol so the ITL residents could attend without compromising their recoveries. The proprietors, Ciro and Saeed, went all out not only in their catering, but the decorations. Olaf would have loved it. They had cleared the main body of the restaurant of furniture, placing the tables around the edge to groan under the weight of all manner of incredible dishes and delicacies, thereby lending the room a heady perfume of spices and aromas. The walls and ceilings were festooned with the loudest coloured drapes and silks, like some psychedelic high-camp harem tent.

For the first 30 minutes people wandered in, awkwardly nodding at those they'd never met and searching out those they knew. Although Aisha comported herself like the unflappable executive she was, Dylan was all too aware that she was on the verge of breaking point. He'd suggested she head home after the funeral, but she was insistent she honour Olaf at his wake. Dylan, in turn, promised to not leave her side.

Neither of them was prepared for the shock of seeing Zac. It was apparent he'd lost a considerable amount of weight, and self-care was obviously no longer a priority. The now ill-fitting suit needed dry cleaning, his gaunt face was sporting an unruly five-day growth and an ugly cold sore next to his left nostril. His eyes were rheumy and he carried a stale odour of booze.

It had been three weeks since Zac and Dylan had spoken. In that time Dylan had had to negotiate a police investigation into Olaf's death, the overwhelming shock and grief both he and Aisha felt and keep the rehab running as smoothly as possible.

"How you holding up, buddy?" asked Dylan.

"Yeah, well. You know. How are any of us holding up, eh?"

Zac reached for Aisha's hand but she threw her arms around him and thanked him for coming back for his friend's funeral. Then, to compound the situation, she took his face in both her hands and kissed his forehead.

"That's how we're holding up, Zac. It's just all too awful for words. Are you back here for long?"

"Well actually, I've moved back here. DC didn't quite pan out."

Aisha gasped. "No."

"Well Zac," said Dylan. "Maybe we can catch up later and look at setting some goals to help you resettle here."

Zac knew this was code for "let's try to get your shit together", and he agreed. They continued making mundane conversation until they were unexpectedly distracted. For, standing outside looking discombobulated, was Sylvia. She checked her phone, then cupped her hands around her eyes and peered in through the window. She made a phone call, but it barely lasted 10 seconds. Everything about her said anxiety. Dylan was just about to go out to greet her when she sauntered in and eyeballed the familiar trio.

"Well, hellooo!" she said. It was, given the circumstances, totally inappropriate. Dylan could tell she was pretty well much in the same boat as Zac, only with cleaner clothes.

The conversation was stilted. Usually former clients who are doing okay are enthusiastic to regale you with tales of their newfound lives and the challenges and rewards they're experiencing without drugs. But when they're back on dope, it's more often than not an exercise in deceit and lies.

"Zac," she said after a while. "I was wondering if your cousin was here."

Zac wondered why Sylvia would be asking after his cousin when the penny dropped.

"Of course. The will."

Dylan, whose prevailing temperament was calm, felt his anger rise. Sure, his late friend may have believed Sylvia was the embodiment of fairytale love, but he was of the opinion she was nothing but cruel and vicious, locked into her own sick behaviours. The endless demands she'd placed on Olaf, her relentless cuckolding of him in the guise of 'positive sexuality', the emotional torture of refusing to commit to their relationship beyond any one day - and now here she was with cap in hand, before his body had even finished burning. Christ. She couldn't even be bothered coming to his funeral. Dylan wanted to rip her a new asshole. The fucking arrogance.

"Actually, he's not," Zac said. "He had to go to court at the last minute, but I'll give you his personal number. He did mention you two had spoken."

As Zac started to send the number to Sylvia's phone, hers let out a 'ding'. She flipped the leather cover open to reveal the logo of a popular online hook-up site flashing onto her screen. Almost mockingly, she tapped away at the phone and raised it to her ear.

"Marcus, you naughty man. Be patient. Listen, I'm in a particularly delicious moon phase today so, while you're waiting, grab us a bottle of champagne, and I'll meet you in twenty." She looked distantly around the restaurant, then giggled.

"Oof! Then you know what else you better grab."

As the phone went into her shoulder bag, it signalled the arrival of the lawyer's number. Her face hardened.

"It's a pity you couldn't have let me know earlier that he wasn't going to be here; it would have saved me a lot of fucking around."

With nary a condolence or farewell, Sylvia stormed out the door and into a waiting taxi.

(another) Winter

THE SCUFFS around the toes of his hand-stitched brogues belied the basic sense of style for which Zac had originally acquired them. A year earlier, he would lovingly polish and buff them every third night, taking pride in the intricate patterns and stitching of the classic shoe. It was another way of him staying connected with his late grandfather, a true gentleman. Pop had doted on Zac and schooled him in all manner of social mores that would change - and in some cases become redundant - in time. The offering of one's seat on public transport to one more deserving; saying "how do you do" rather than "nice to meet you" when being introduced to a stranger; accompanying the elderly across intersections; not placing your elbows on the dining table. And then there were the more practical skills - changing a tyre; repairing a faucet; hanging a painting; cooking a steak; throwing a punch; learning to tie both a Windsor knot and a clove hitch. Whenever Zac saw a male wearing leather shoes without socks, he'd imagine Pop's look of horror. At 12 years old, Pop took him to an old friend's wedding. His debrief the night before was more of his sage advice.

"My boy, we're off to Barney's nuptials tomorrow. I guarantee it will be more painful for me than you. This will be his fourth marriage and, we all suspect, not the last. I also guarantee you will be bored rigid with the whole ceremony; we Wattses are a restless lot anyway. However, you won't yawn, wander out, play on your Gameboy - you will sit attentively and feign interest. This isn't about going to a wedding, it's an exercise in discipline. But I promise you the party afterwards will be a hoot."

Zac learnt a major lesson the next day as he climbed into his grandfather's immaculately restored 1966 Ford Mustang.

"Young man, we're going to a wedding, not the beach."

After that, Zac never wore sneakers again

HIS FEET were propped on the corner of his desk, crossed at the ankles. He continued examining the scuffing and contemplated how the little things had fallen away. It was a no-brainer. He had failed in Washington, his only friend was dead, he hated work, was back on heroin and methadone, drinking every night and eating pills to fall asleep. So why would he give a stuff about keeping his shoes clean? His eyes followed the line of his leg back to his waist, and noticed a prominent dark stain on his tie. Ketchup? Ink? No. It was a bloodstain from where he'd tied his arm off for a shot then unconsciously wiped the injection point. He didn't care about any of it.

He looked at the photo of him and Olaf tacked on the divider. Part of him pined for his departed friend but the overwhelming feeling of drug-coddled ennui ensured he wasn't going to be experiencing too much emotion today.

He listened to the furious clicking of dozens of his colleagues tapping out tomorrow's paper. It was a sound that usually filled him with pride; a mysterious, plastic symphony which might bring about unforeseen change. His own eight paragraphs of drivel sat untouched on his screen. Zac swung his feet off the table, shut his computer down and glanced across the partition at the paper's art director.

"Yo, Josephine, I'm heading out to lunch."

It was 10am.

"MY DEAR Mr Watts. It's been far too long. What brings you back to these cursed climes?"

Of course Gene Prato knew exactly why Zac was there. His arrival was about as unexpected as sunrise. Still, he was one of the few clients he felt he could engage in any semblance of sensible conversation.

"I need to go up on my dose, Doc. Now."

It had been six months since the doctor had last seen Zac, so he'd been expecting them to gambol into some rambling discussion about the state of the world and to hear tales of DC, but Zac's insistence told him things were not good.

"When did you go back on methadone?"

"As soon as I got back from Washington. You're not going to start giving me a hard time for this, are you?"

"Zac, we're all reeling from Olaf's death, in our own particular ways. The last time I saw you, I congratulated you on getting off methadone, and wished you well in your endeavours. I have no idea what has been going on in your life since November so let's have a polite chat. All I know is I was just informed you were dosing here again and Dr Asher is your prescriber. And for the record, I don't judge you for anything."

"Jesus, I'm sorry Gene. It's just that I'm … not coping."

Zac felt a ripple of self-pity and decided to restart the discussion.

"Okay, look, I apologise for being an asshole just then. I'm on 65mg, and using heroin on top of that. I skip my dose some days to use the smack."

"Thanks, Zac. What else?"

He did a quick inventory of his recent drug use.

"A bottle of wine each night, a few Xanax here and there, valium at bedtime, odd shot of coke. The heroin of course. Some weed. Occasionally a stiff scotch."

For the next five minutes, they figured out a game plan for Zac's return to some form of recovery. Gene wanted him to go to detox for a week but Zac was emphatic that his work situation was so dire it would cost him his job, so he committed to not using any illicit substances, try not to drink more than two glasses of wine every couple of days ("at dinner") and stay on the prescribed benzos at bedtime. Gene offered to talk to Dr Asher and have her push his dose up to stave off his heroin cravings - a suggestion Zac readily agreed to.

The rest of the consultation was spent catching up. The reporter regaled the doctor with anecdotes about his sojourn in DC and Gene told him about a report he'd read on controlled opioid use in narcotic addiction. Although they didn't discuss Olaf, Zac knew they would someday. Hopefully soon. He stepped out of the clinic door into the noise and filth of the street, looked to the clouds and sobbed. You've got your feathers now, Olaf. You're free. Only this time, my brother, be like Daedalus.

BACK AT the office, Zac stared blankly at his computer, preoccupied with Dr Prato's prognosis. Of course, I could rebuild my life. I did it last year, so I can do it again. I went for years without even thinking about heroin.

A purpose - that's what's missing.

Last year it was work, so let's make it about me now. Gene is right. I deserve this. Frittering my life away in a mire of intoxication is below me. Just settle back into a routine of having only my dose and concentrate on work. What was his formula? Recognise, rationalise, relax, refocus.

He looked at the copy on his screen, half expecting his muse to sweep him up in a flurry of inspiration. It didn't. But he did find he was concentrating on what he'd already written and there was already the kernel of a damn good article in there. It was only following up a story his colleague had already broken but why not? It's not like I'm the be-all and end-all of reporting around here. The public suspects Leroy Harrison is one of the shadiest crooks ever. He's forever lurking in the shadows of corrupt dealings and it's about time we - I - zapped him with a spotlight.

Zac felt a tinge of excitement; maybe he was getting his mojo back. He downloaded every article that had ever been written on Harrison, and furiously began taking notes in longhand. He cross referenced people who'd even had the most minor association with him and sourced their contact details from the paper's computerised teledex. All afternoon Zac Watts attempted to transform himself back into Zac Watts - and felt all the better for it. On the few occasions he went to the bathroom or made a coffee, he found himself keen to get back to his desk.

Josephine's scarlet talons gripped the top of the divider as she leaned across it toward him.

"Come on, let's head down to Langer's. Fiona's 40 today and we're going to help her drown reality."

Night was falling and most of his colleagues had left. The idea of a scotch and some laughs was most appealing.

"Give me a few minutes. I just want to tie up a few loose ends."

The few minutes rolled into an hour. Zac discovered his quarry had gone to school with one of the most sanctimonious bastards ever - a property developer who'd hid behind a guise of pious goodwill while encumbering the poor and gullible with debt and low-grade constructions. Without any warning, the scumbag went to God while guzzling mai tais in a Hawaiian pool bar.

Zac called Harrison's widow to see if she was aware of, and willing to discuss, her late husband's possible friendship with the unctuous fraud. Expecting to be dismissed, Zac was caught off-guard when she said that the two were friends, he'd been a regular guest at their dinner table, and she'd loathed them both equally. Denise Harrison also mentioned a couple of other people Zac might want to talk to and suggested they discuss this at length in her lawyer's office the following week. Zac was beside himself. What had been a mere candid snap of two men in a gossip column from a decade ago was now his lede.

He threw his notes into the drawer and shut the computer down. A libation at Langer's was enticing but he kept going back to the conversation with Gene. Fuck all that muse bullshit. The fact is, I am good at what I do. Yes, I lost my way and screwed the pooch in DC; besides, the sum of my parts is way more than being a junkie.

He wrestled with the idea of joining his cohorts at the bar and decided to give it a miss. Maybe I should … what? Go to a movie? Ring Leon or Tracey and go have a bite with them? Head home, try to get a semblance of order in the apartment? Watch TV? Have a long shower?

For a few minutes Zac toyed with his fountain pen and conscience, then called his heroin dealer.

"IT'S DENISE HARRISON, again, Mr Watts. I've left you numerous messages and sent texts. Much and all as I would like to assist you with your enquiries, I fear your tardiness will be nothing more than a hindrance in the future. Therefore, I am withdrawing my offer to discuss my late husband with you, and request you do not contact me again. Good day to you."

"FUCK."

In rage he launched the phone across his apartment, watching it curve above a lampshade and head straight toward the centre of the balcony door. It hit the door pane, which in turn shattered into a thousand-piece mosaic.

Zac was shocked by his malicious outburst. He waited for the glass to make some strange cracking noise then rain down into the carpet and balcony. It didn't. It stayed fixed in the metal door frame, taunting him. In a strange way it set the scene. His apartment looked like it had been ransacked. Perched on the far arm of the couch was a half-eaten bowl of instant noodles with some hideous fuzz growing through it. The floor was strewn with clothes, books, cutlery, soda cans, beer bottles, a towel. His computer rose from a pile of crap covering the dining table - plastic food containers, a soldering iron, screwdrivers, magazines, tubes of glue, a can of motor oil, a bottle of duty-free cologne, speaker wire, a broken vase, unread books, ear plugs, Indian ink. Even his keyboard was propped up on a book about the Japanese art of chindogu.

All this squalor accurately reflected the chaos of Zac's mind.

He clicked on his mouse and the computer's startup told him it was late on Thursday evening. The appointment with Mrs Harrison had been scheduled 10 hours beforehand. Zac conjured various excuses for missing the meeting, noticing each one was more ludicrous than the previous. I thought you meant next week. A family death. In hospital with a congenital blood disorder. He even toyed with the truth - I've been on a three-day heroin and booze bender, trying to reconcile my pathetic fucking id with the reality of my innate failure as a human.

Zac rummaged through a cupboard and pulled out a roll of red gaffer tape. Carefully he applied long lengths of it to the shattered glass, forming an elongated asterisk. He opened the door very slowly and began mirroring the tape on the outside. His concentration was broken by the jangling ring of his phone, which had somehow survived the impact. It was Tracey. As much as he didn't want to answer it, he felt some weird obligation to take her call. After all, it was her who steered him away from junkiedom all those years ago.

"Trace. Wassup?"

"Thank God you're okay. I've been worried sick about you."

Zac thought she was being a tad dramatic but figured there would have been a dozen other missed calls in his 'absence'.

"Yeah, all good. I've been fairly busy with work and everything."

As he spoke, a siren's escalating howl cut through the canyon of the street, which in itself wasn't so strange, except it was equally deafening through his phone.

"I'm actually out the front of your building. Buzz me up."

He went into an instant panic. There was no way he could let her see the carnage of his apartment.

"Hey uh. Listen. Just wait a few minutes. I've got nothing on. Hang around down there. I'm actually just heading out."

The line went dead. He looked at the phone, assuming she had sensed his lies, and given up. Or had it been in its death throes? Nup. It was glowing like Christmas.

Zac ventured to the balcony railing and looked down onto the street. There was no sign of Tracey. Good, she's left. He'd call her the next morning. At least by then he would have figured out a plausible lie. He had returned to taping the glass when the apartment shuddered with a thumping on his front door.

Shit.

As Zac opened it, his slight-framed saviour barged past. Three steps in, she stopped dead and surveyed the shambles.

"Jesus. You really have taken this addict-living shit to a new level."

Zac was about to launch into some cockamamie story involving thugs from his past settling old drug debts but even through the funk of his inebriety he remembered he didn't start to fraternise with low-lifes until recently.

From the corner of his eye, he caught his profile reflected in an unshattered pane. His shoulders were stooped, his stomach distended and he was way too thin. He wondered if the pathos was the image he saw, or the hole in his soul.

"Fucking both," he mumbled.

"Both what?" Trace asked as she relocated an armful of crap from the armchair to the table.

She looked pitifully at the emaciated shell her friend had become. When Tracey first encountered him in that toilet stall all those years ago, he had youth on his side. Good job, questionable health, panache. Her one wish that day as she handed him the Paradise Palms card was he would not spiral into a formulaic life of drug addiction. So no-one was more pleased than Tracey when she re-encountered him in rehab seven months ago to see that he hadn't. But then these past eight weeks happened. The poor guy had certainly made up for lost time.

They adjourned to a local diner, sitting in a booth by the window. It gave them the opportunity to distract themselves with passers-by when the inevitable tracts of silence would occur. Zac kept trying to steer the discussion toward his work but Tracey neither knew of nor cared for the people he was researching. She was a health professional and couldn't give a damn for a bunch of self-absorbed crooks. The human condition was what floated her boat, particularly when it involved people she cared about.

"Have you considered quitting and taking a year or two out to get clean and find yourself?"

Zac looked at her incredulously; she might have well suggested he cut his arm off right there and then with the butter spreader.

"Are you out of your mind? I'm a professional fucking journalist. I'm one of the best there is, in an industry that is goddamn imploding. I just can't fucking take off and go contemplate my navel for a year."

One of the things that Tracey had respected in Zac was his reluctance to use profanity.

"I'm not talking about navel contemplation, I'm suggesting you take yourself away from the stresses of your life to decompress. No-one is questioning your professional capabilities. All I'm saying is go to rehab, get sober and try something different for a while. Get to know yourself. And when you feel centred and refreshed, well ... *then* go out and bring all those crooked shysters down."

Zac poured the equivalent of eight teaspoons of sugar into his coffee, glaring at Tracey with contempt.

"Is that what all this is? To get me to go back to fucking rehab? Have they got you on a retainer or something? You get a spotter's fee?"

Tracey fought a sudden urge to throw her drink at him. She studied his face, wondering if it was slack from narcotics or merely the look of the smug and arrogant. She took a deep breath, held it, then slowly let it out.

"Zac, I consider you a friend. I'm here because I value you as such but I cannot stand by and watch you kill yourself. I know where you are; I've been there numerous times. I implore you, please consider rehab again. Not for me, not for your career, but for you. You're a great guy with tons of potential and, I promise you, you get yourself sorted out and you won't know yourself. I spoke to Dylan today and told him I was going to talk to you tonight. They'll offer you a bed. All you have to do is call Aisha."

Zac downed his coffee in three large gulps. He rose, pulled a $20 note out, threw it onto his half-eaten burger, and fixed Tracey with a venomous glare.

"Do me a favour, you duplicitous cunt. Lose my fucking number. I never want to see your ugly, pinched face again."

NO MATTER how hard he tried, Zac was incapable of focusing on his work. His mind kept wandering back to Denise Harrison's message. Not so much the kiss-off regarding her assistance with his investigations, but how his tardiness would become a hindrance. A hindrance? Jesus, it was beginning to look like the wall of Jericho.

He toyed with the idea of contacting her and making some excuse but whatever he said was going to sound feeble. Zac opened his notepad and stared indifferently at his notes. There was nothing in there. Josephine and the chief of staff were swanning across the office with a ream of galley proofs, obviously amused by something, yet all he felt was contempt. Who the fuck gave those two bitches the right to be happy?

Zac checked himself. What has happened to you? When did you become this judgemental asshole riven with loathing and hate? He knew the answer, but it didn't suit the deluded narrative running through his unravelling psyche. So he opted for the easy option. He stared at a postcard of the Capitol and directed all his regret and self-pity at what that represented. Maybe I went there with far too many expectations. The woman I was replacing should have given me more of her contacts. Why were the others in the press gallery so dismissive of me? I wasn't given enough time to settle into the culture. Not once, however, did he consider his arrogance had any part to play in it.

He looked at that photo of him and Olaf. What would you do, O? What advice can you give me? For a split second Zac really wished he would get a sign, but he was so irritable his mind refused to offer one cogent thought his dead friend might say. It was then he remembered one of Olaf's favourite aphorisms – the longest journey is from the head to the heart. For a brief second Zac felt a modicum of emotional relief. My body and mind may well be degenerating into a chemical stew, but I am still able to feel both loss and love for my friend. He sat with that emotion, then took a picture of the photo and made it the screen saver on his phone.

"Hey Zac, when you've got a minute, pop into my office."

"What's cooking, chief?" Zac asked as he dropped into the sofa in Carol Sanchez's office.

"You tell me. And spare me any crap."

Zac squirmed, wondering if it was his recent three-day absence or the lack of progress with the Leroy Harrison expose.

"I, uh, don't follow."

"Really? Well, pay attention."

With that, Carol launched into a diatribe that started off with the time and trouble the company had made putting him through rehab before relocating him to Washington; his inability to perform his duties once he got there; the fact that in the two months he had been back he'd had a total of 11 very ordinary stories published – and three of those only made it in because ads dropped out at the last minute. She culminated this by calling into question everything from his appearance, his attire, his physical disarray and, as a rancid cherry on top, his body odour.

"Normally, I'd go into a spiel now about what a great journalist you are, how you've been presented with challenges of late. But you and I both know that's all indulgent bullshit. Zac, I don't know what particular brand of shit you're poisoning yourself with and, frankly, it's none of my business. But what is my business is your performance here as a staff member. And it's pretty well non-existent. So let's compromise. I'm putting you on 10 days leave without pay starting today. What you choose to do with that time is your own business, but unless you turn up here on Wednesday week with an obvious improvement in both your health and attitude, well … don't bother."

He couldn't bring himself to look at her.

"Do you want me to go to detox?"

"Detox. Disneyland. Dunedin. It's up to you. But wherever you end up, do something about your drug use. You need to get it through that miasma of whatever shit you're on that this isn't a sheltered workshop for junkies."

As he levered himself up from the sofa, he felt like all 15 kilos of weight he'd lost in the past few months had suddenly returned tenfold.

"Oh, and Zac. Good luck."

THE HIRE car came to a grinding halt in the dirt and gravel. Zac looked at the wall of trees before him, wondering why exactly was he there. Well, he knew why. Olaf had told him about it being his safe place; his happy place. Zac drove there hoping he might capture some of that solace himself.

He began negotiating the nature walk, a rough incline heading up from the car park. As the waxy-leaved shrubbery began to dissipate, Zac understood why this area held so much meaning to his friend. By the time he reached the peak, he was faced with a breathtaking view of the Pacific Ocean. To his left was a v-shaped crag, falling a couple of hundred metres into a surf-pummeled rock formation. The land before him rolled down for about 20 paces before becoming a precipice. Jammed right in the middle of all this beauty was a park bench.

Looming beyond the horizon was a cloud bank made up of pinks and greys and whites, made more spectacular by its reflection on the sea. Beside those reflections were the countless undulating greens and blues of the ocean, rolling and melting into the shore. Zac removed his shirt, stretching his arms along the back of the bench and hungrily filling his lungs with restorative sea air. He looked from a faraway headland to the right, up the jagged shoreline, to the land's hazy vanishing point way off to the left.

Then caught sight of his arm. While the elements celebrated all the beauty and the majesty of nature's hues, the purple and yellowing bruises on his arm brought him crashing back to reality. It had been three hours since he'd last had a shot in the stinking bathroom of a truck stop. Zac had sat in there for 10 minutes making useless bargains with his soul and willing himself not to get high, but an impatient long-haul trucker banging on the bathroom door and bellowing "hurry the fuck up" made the decision for him.

A wave of melancholy flowed through him and he remembered Sergey's belief that Olaf was flying above us. With feathers.

"Are you, man? Are you flying above me?"

The combination of the surrounding beauty and never-ending loss was too much, and Zac broke down and cried.

"You know, I think I'm getting past the loss, but why did you … why did you do it? I mean, as the Mexicans say, amores perros, but fuck, O. Was she really that important?"

He leaned down and pulled up a long blade of grass, tickling it below his bottom lip.

"Anyway, it's academic now, isn't it? You got time to talk?"

Zac looked around to make sure no-one else was there. He took stock of himself - who are you talking to? He's dead. Get a grip. When did you start believing in this ouija board bullshit?

A fat gull glided past him and disappeared over the grassy edge below.

"Was that you jerking with me? Huh?"

He grinned at the absurdity of it all, snorted some snot back, and restarted the conversation.

"I miss you Olaf. So much. And I don't know if it was your leaving when you did, or the inevitability of my life. But now I … I feel like the prodigal son. I'm fucking lost, in pain, nothing makes any sense to me, and all I want to do is go home. But there ain't no home. The closest thing I ever got to a home was your love and friendship. I never knew shit like that existed. You taught me so much. Really. I was sitting in this patisserie at Dupont Circle one day, and I had this epiphany. I knew things were going to shit in DC and I thought I'll get Olaf over here. I'd been unravelling anyway, but it wasn't 'cause i needed you to save my ass. I just missed your company. Honestly, all these mind-blowing museums and shit. The fucking National Portrait Gallery, man. It's worth it just for Kehinde Wiley's painting of Obama. You'd have loved it. I was going to write you from that cake joint and say get your ass to DC, but I stalled for a week. And instead, you wrote to me. You fucking fuck."

Zac doubled over and sobbed uncontrollably, letting the blade of grass take to the breeze.

"I've come up here for one reason. I just wanted to honour you and tell you how much you are loved. And missed. And I don't know if we'll ever have another one of these talks again, but now seems as good a time as ever. I think of you always, Olaf. Every day. Your presence in my life is indelible, like your stupid tattoos. Remember what you told me? The truth is always better than the lie. Anyway, that's all. I just had to come here tell you the truth - that I miss you. Full stop. Send me a sign if this is real. Or don't. Bye bye, my brother. I love you so much."

He put his shirt on and continued watching the cloud bank. It had turned quite dark, as had the water beneath it. Deep inside the clouds were electrical flashes of diamond white, heralding an expected storm. It was probably a good hour away but Zac decided to head home. His intention had been to stay a night; he'd certainly brought enough heroin and methadone, but he was feeling calmer now that his purpose had been fulfilled.

From further back up the path Zac could hear a man with a Scottish accent singing and playing an acoustic guitar. He had a wonderfully rich voice and, although the song sounded like a paean to desolation, the lyrics resonated with Zac.

Maybe this was Olaf's sign.

Actually, it was a blonde woman in her 50s, in double denim and hiking boots, taking in the view and drinking a can of beer. The music was coming from a portable speaker.

"Lovely song," Zac said as he ambled toward her.

She squinted at him, and gave a half smile.

"I'm sorry," she said. "I hope I didn't disturb you."

Zac shook his head.

"No, it's a fitting end to being up here. Who is it?"

She shrugged.

"Just a feller singing a song."

"I like the lyrics. Does it have a special meaning?"

"Lyrics mean nothing to me. It's just a song."

Zac figured she wanted to be alone and turned away.

"Hey," she said. "I didn't mean to be rude. It's just that I got some bad news today."

"I'm sorry to hear that. Everything okay?"

The woman had a deeply forlorn look on her face.

"An old lover died six weeks ago. Sometimes that bad news doesn't travel as fast as they say it does."

"No," he agreed. "Again, my condolences."

They nodded to each other and Zac wandered off.

By the time he'd reached the main highway, he'd found the song, Colin Hay's *I Just Don't Think I'll Ever Get Over You*, and was playing it at an unsuitably loud volume. On repeat. He kept thinking of the woman. Her attire. Her nonchalance. The penny dropped with him and he looked out toward the storm.

"You motherfucker."

He had just encountered Olaf's ex-lover, Anita.

AFTER FIVE hours of driving, the fervour of the coastal sojourn had well and truly worn off. A two-point shot of heroin had also dulled the experience somewhat. Zac looked around the carnage of his apartment, contemplated a late night-cleaning frenzy, then opted for a drink.

The half hour stroll to Langer's bar gave him the opportunity to get his circulation flowing and get in a bit of much-needed exercise. The downside was it also took the edge off his high. It was a balmy evening, and he enjoyed taking in the city lights and observing others out perambulating. He tried to conjure the feeling of connection he'd been feeling with Olaf earlier that day; he looked up to the night sky, willing that bond to return but something told him it was back on that bench, being nurtured by the ocean storm and its occasional whiff of ozone.

He beelined through the bar to the far corner popular with his newsroom colleagues. The usual gang was there, along with a few of the photographers. Prior to going to rehab and DC, Zac had arrogantly told one of them, Puccino, how to take a picture of some striking transport workers. Zac was capable of capturing some nice pictures on his telephone but he was certainly never going to be the recipient of a slew of photographic awards for doing so. Puccino had. His image of a young Hong Kong girl looking in terror at a riot cop's gun pointed an inch from her face had become iconic.

Zac asked if anyone wanted a drink and when he returned with them it was Puccino who asked, "are we good?"

The question threw Zac off guard because it was he who had been in the wrong and had, while at the bar, been summoning up the courage to apologise.

"Yeah, we're good. I was in the wrong. I can only plead ignorance."

"Think nothing of it," said Puccino, raising his glass. "We've all done it to some degree."

They clinked glasses and downed a gulp.

"Let's move over there," said Puccino, pointing to a semi-circular booth in the corner. They settled into it; Zac sipping at his drink while Puccino absentmindedly fiddled with a cardboard beer coaster.

"Listen man, I know it's none of my business, but what did you think of In The Light?"

Zac was flabbergasted. Part of the deal with him going to rehab had been, with the exception of the editor and one of the human resources staff, that no-one at the paper would know. What weird-ass head trip was this guy pulling?

"So tell me, mate, when did my private life become fodder for office gossip?"

The photographer raised his hands in quasi-surrender.

"Oh shit, no Zac. Fuck, man. Sorry, my friend Leon was in there with you. I promise I haven't told a soul. You know I went there myself?"

"You were on the 'done?!'" he asked.

"Eight fucking years, man. Ninety a day. I never thought I'd get off that shit. Then, six years ago, I went to our favourite rehab."

Their conversation drifted into 'war' stories, how easy it was to get on methadone, and how hard it was to get off it. And, of course, tales of rehab.

Puccino headed to the bar and returned with two beers and four shots of scotch.

"Here my friend, a little boilermaker."

They each threw a shot back, drank some of the beer, then dropped the extra scotches into the remaining beer - shot glass and all.

"Hey Zac, what's the story with that Olaf guy? Leon said he just upped and left one day. Word was he'd taken off after some wacky chick who'd been there a week. Bullshit or what?"

Zac studied the diffused image of the shot glass in his beer. The mottled foam reminded him of the surf and clouds he was so lost in earlier that day. He wondered if his friend was down there in his drink. He tossed the remainder of it down and went to the bar.

"Same as before, Sal," he called to the barman.

Sal poured the beers and lined up four shot glasses.

"You two take it easy, okay."

"Oh, believe me, this is us taking it easy," he replied.

"Good to hear, because after these, it's lite beer only."

Zac put down the tray of drinks, to the bemusement of his drinking buddy.

"Fuck, mate. You're the original go-hard or go-home dude."

Forsaking ceremony, Zac tossed back two of the shots, slamming the second glass down on the table hard enough to startle a few patrons.

"Olaf killed himself six weeks ago. Just slipped out the back door quietly. He was my best friend, Puccino. My best. Fucking. Friend."

"Maybe you better have one of these," said the photographer, sliding a shot across to Zac. "Oh, and call me Pooch. All my friends do."

Zac downed the scotch.

"Then Pooch it is."

In that space of confusion and drunkenness and tension and whatever other weird energy they had going on between them, they began grinning.

"Hey, Pooch. More bad news. Sal said he's moving us on to low octane."

"Well, fuck Sal. I've got an eight ball of coke. You interested?"

Zac eyeballed his new-found associate.

"Let's go back to my place and find out."

ZAC STOOD at the stove top, impatient for the moka pot to brew its restorative black water. He was admiring the sparkling light of the morning sun through the shattered door, when he noticed the large silver ring pierced through Pooch's perineum. He vaguely remembered them having sex. He clearly remembered them shooting a mixture of heroin and cocaine, possibly the most dangerous thing they could have done given the amount of booze they'd consumed. Speedballs are a recipe for disaster at the best of times, so it was purely dumb luck neither of them had dropped.

Given the general night of fun and depravity, Zac decided to wake his guest appropriately. He took Marianne Faithfull's *Blazing Away* LP off the turntable, and replaced it with Lou Reed's *Street Hassle*. As the rhythmic cellos of the title track bubbled away, so did the coffee.

Zac spotted the baggie of cocaine next to the bed and spirited it into the kitchen. He dipped the tip of a gravity knife into it for a quick heart starter, then tore off a large piece of silver foil, emptying most of the drug onto it before folding it up and hiding it above the cupboard. Zac opened the fridge, took out a small brown bottle, cracked the seal and drank the 18mls of methadone in it. He then poured their coffees and headed over to the bed. Scooping a formidable bump of coke out with the blade, he shook Pooch awake.

"Here you go, sleepy head," he cooed as he angled the drug under the photographer's nose. "Big sniff."

With his eyes half open, Pooch automatically pushed one nostril closed with his finger and inhaled the powder. Zac leant forward to kiss him but Pooch pulled away.

"Not such a good idea. I can still taste your piss on my breath."

Zac dived on top of him, driving his tongue into his mouth.

Their morning fornication was hard and fast, so much so that their coffee was still hot after they'd both cum.

"It's not every morning I wake up next to a world famous photographer," said Zac.

"Well, it's not every morning I get deliciously fucked by a guy holding a switchblade," Pooch replied. "So I guess that makes us even."

They showered then headed out for brunch. The conversation was staid, revolving around work, colleagues and the decaying state of journalism. No mention of Olafs, Leons or rehabs. Pooch made it clear he was keen to get back to the office and work on a series of black-and-white studio portraits he'd shot of a visiting Italian ballerina. Zac made noises about going to visit his parents but really he just wanted to get back home and chop into the cocaine.

By 1pm Zac had demolished half of the stash and was feeling decidedly jangled, gripped by a hideous level of anxiety. The euphoria of the drug was now giving way to his own feelings of inadequacy. He worried about how lucky he'd been in life, continually saving his ass at the 11th hour, but an overwhelming sense of doom was looming. Maybe I'll just get a good night's sleep, spruce myself up and swan into the newsroom tomorrow as though nothing ever happened. As they say, today is the first day of the rest of your life.

His deranged commitment to get his life back in order by sunrise was thwarted when he checked his bank account to find he only had a few hundred dollars in it. He began to jot down a list of debts. Overdue electricity bill - $422. New washing machine - $700. Money owed to colleagues - $800. Credit card debt - $2,200. Of course, it was all bullshit - Zac was simply preparing a tale of woe for his over-indulgent parents.

The list was a pointless exercise. The ensuing phone conversation with his father lasted less than a minute. Watts senior was entertaining lunch guests and, probably more as a performance for his audience rather than concern for his son, he interrupted Zac's bogus list to say there'd be $5000 in his account within the hour. And there was.

As part of this newfound lease on life Zac booked a glazier to repair the window and spent the afternoon cleaning the apartment. Living skills, as they were called in rehab. Of course, what was alien to his cohorts in ITL was second nature to him; he'd always been houseproud. Rugs were vacuumed, floors were mopped, garbage vanished, crockery sparkled. Mind you, the pulsating techno soundtrack and cocaine helped greatly.

Zac made his way across the car park outside Anthony's, a local meat market fraternised by ageing desperadoes and the occasional junkie selling caps. All he was interested in was a quiet beer and burger before an early night. It was just going on sunset and he figured the joint would be quiet enough to scan the day's tabloid and take the edge off the coke. He'd finished it and was now feeling edgy and uncomfortable. A homeless man approached with his hands out.

"Excuse me, brother, have you got any spare change?"

Zac rarely hesitated to sling the neighbourhood homeless a few bucks, and if he didn't have it he'd always make a mental note to recompense them next time.

"Nah," he drawled.

"Anything, sir. I haven't eaten for ..."

Zac turned and snapped.

"Hey fuckwad. What part of 'no' don't you understand?"

The guy looked shocked; he'd had numerous interactions with Zac and this wasn't what he'd been expecting.

"Please don't speak to me like that."

Zac walked back to the man.

"Then don't start fucking conversations with strangers," he replied, jabbing the man's chest.

"And please don't touch me," the homeless guy said, taking a step back.

Zac looked at the man with contempt and again jabbed him.

"Or you'll what?"

The punch sent Zac reeling backwards. Try as he might, all he could do was frantically wave his arms to break the inevitable fall. Everything went into slow motion; he felt his left heel jar against the kerb and twist agonisingly as the asphalt rose to slam the left side of his face – right where the punch had landed. He instinctively curled into a foetal position, raising his arms to protect his head from any further beating, but none came. When Zac finally lowered his arms his sparring partner had gone.

He held his throbbing jaw and probed the back of his teeth with his tongue. There was a pronounced gap and a sharp bone in the top front. Zac panicked, pushing his finger into the bloody socket, willing his missing tooth to reappear.

He hobbled toward Anthony's but the slow head shake from the bouncer told him burgers were off tonight's menu.

ZAC TAPPED repeatedly at the illuminated disc with his security card, but it just kept flashing a red X.

"Here, let me see that card, Mr Watts," the security guard said.

Expecting her to wave some special security guard device over it to make it work, instead the guard dropped it into a drawer and lifted a phone receiver.

"I'll just get you to sit over there, Mr Watts."

"Sorry, is there some kind of problem?"

"Mr Watts is here in the foyer now, Ms Sanchez," she said into the phone.

He got the message. A few minutes later Carol emerged from the elevator, accompanied by a rent-a-cop carrying a cardboard box.

"I don't understand what's going on."

The guard ushered the two of them into a frosted glass window office, stood outside the door, and told the chief of staff she'd be "just here".

"Let me guess. You're firing me."

Carol looked crushed. It was patently obvious what was going on but she still couldn't comprehend it. Zac's lip was swollen and scabbed; he was missing one and a half of his front teeth; his eye was purple and grazed; he'd obviously made an effort with his clothing - it was clean and pressed. But why in God's name was he wearing a blood stained jacket? And had he lost even more weight in the past 10 days?

"Zac, do you really think you could have continued working here in this condition?"

"Listen," he said. "Drug addiction is a disease, and I can't believe that you … you, Carol, of all people, are going to persecute me rather than help me."

Her pity evaporated.

"Sorry, Zac, but as I reminded you the other day this organisation spent the better part of a year putting you through rehab and relocating you to Washington. At a personal level I have covered for you from the get-go. The moment you hit DC you became a liability. Most of your articles were padded out with wire services copy, you were pretty well incommunicado and then you come back here and tell me you don't want to go back. And like the fool I am, I pleaded with Sue to give you another chance. Oh, he's got some struggles. He'll deal with them. He's done it before, he can do it again. And then, then - I hear instead of you drying out or whatever the hell you were supposed to be doing, you've been shooting up drugs with Puccino who, I might add, is now recuperating in a cardiac ward. Disease? Jesus, Zac, you're the fucking plague."

They sat silently. Zac knew it was pointless. As brutal as Carol's pronouncement was, it was also very accurate.

"Look, I'd give you another chance, but you and I both know the ball is in your court. I really hope you get your life in order. I don't know, maybe you should have stayed on methadone. The thing is only you can help you. It pains me to see you so … so fucked up. Sorry to be blunt, but you are. Please, please please try and get your life in order. And you know this isn't you, Zac. I could go on but …"

He nodded morosely.

"We've given you four weeks severance pay, and you had just under five weeks vacation pay. It should all be in your account now."

He picked up the box and caught his reflection in the glass wall. Not only could he not look at Carol, he couldn't look at himself either.

AFTER A week, Zac knew he had to leave the apartment. His problem was two-fold. Not only had he not had his methadone, but he also hadn't had a bowel movement in that time. Of course, both these predicaments were due to the same thing - heroin. Yet again dumb luck had sailed into his life - this time in the form of money. His father's generous deposit and his termination pay had left him with a grand sum of just over $38,000 in his bank account. So really, he had no need to venture out. Modern times, baby. Pick up your phone and the mean streets will come to you. The apartment was now back to its previous state - trash dump chic. A dozen or more used syringes and a bent soup spoon on the coffee table were testament to his burgeoning habit. As Dylan used to reiterate in the relapse prevention groups, there'll be a lot more than skag going into that piece of silverware.

Gene Prato beckoned Zac into his office and shook his hand.

"You look like crap."

Zac was expecting something along those lines but the huge shot of heroin he'd had an hour beforehand stopped him from giving a fuck.

"Yeah, well spotted, Doc. I've been hearing that a lot lately. What are you going to give me for it?"

Gene tapped away at his computer.

"So, are you quitting the program? Here for a social visit? Want to do something about that constipation?"

The last question jarred Zac from his stoned complacency.

"How do you know I'm constipated?"

"Because of that faeces-tinged halitosis of yours. When did you last have a bowel movement?"

Zac gave Gene an honest rundown of his excretions (or lack of), diet and drug use over the previous week, and brought him up to speed with his other ailments. The doctor took a brief, distant look at the busted tooth and started scribbling away at a prescription pad.

"This is an osmotic laxative to clear your pipes, and I'm also going to give you some bisacodyl to help move it along. I'm not mucking around, Zac. If you haven't gone to the lavatory within 12 hours, or you start vomiting shit, you are to go straight to the hospital ED. And here's some amoxicillin for that infected gum."

Zac took the script, shaking his head.

"You can vomit shit?"

"Yes, and given that gum infection, you don't want to be doing that. Oh, and go see your dentist asap."

Zac folded the prescription and went to leave.

"Whoa, Nellie. Take a load off there. The main act hasn't even started yet."

He kept tapping away at the keyboard, then kicked his chair back from under the table.

"How much heroin are you using?"

Zac thought for a minute, but it was hard to figure out exactly.

"I bought half an ounce a week ago, and I have very little of it left. Maybe a couple of grams a day."

"I'm going to increase your dose to 100mg a day, and we'll see how that goes."

"What makes you think I want to stop using heroin?" Zac asked.

Gene looked back at him, bemused.

"Oh, I don't think for one second you want to stop using heroin, Zac. I mean, you come in here looking like death. Hell, you're even smelling like death. Your teeth are falling out. Who'd want to put a stop to all that?"

Zac glared at him.

"This, old bean, is called duty of care. I'm going to put you on a large dose to stop you overdosing. I don't know what your personal circumstances are, and they're none of my business. But look around out there as you leave. That lot in the waiting room aren't dropping a few grand on drugs every week. You are in what I call the danger zone, and I'll do my darndest to usher you out of it."

"But I keep naloxone on hand."

Gene felt his blood pressure rise along with his eyebrows. Zac may have been one of his smarter patients, but he could also be the poster boy for how drugs screw up one's thinking.

"And who's going to administer it if you've OD-ed? By the way, are you still working?"

He shook his head glumly.

"Good, because you're no longer getting takeaways. You can come in here every day."

ZAC CONTINUED to dose at Paradise Palms, mainly because it gave his empty days some semblance of structure. He'd arrive there at 6.30am purely to get it over and done with. It also meant he would not run into Dylan or any of the other rehab people and, most importantly, the efficacy of the methadone was reduced by the late afternoon, thus he could feel any heroin just that little bit more.

His mornings fell into routine. Dose, buy a triple shot caffe latte then head home to eat a banana with a large bowl of bran. The rest of his day was spent vegetating in front of the TV, watching mindless soap operas about Mexican drug cartels, drinking wine and whiskey and waiting for the clock to tick over to 5pm. He would then administer a hefty shot of heroin, loll on the sofa for a couple of hours, have a smaller shot then order a chicken kebab roll at 10pm. Rinse and repeat. Daily.

Zac's dealer was an interesting piece of work called Thumper. Given the scars around his eyebrows and knuckles, it was a fitting nickname. Many years ago, he'd gone through ITL, got clean and remained that way. The dozen or so tattoos adorning his neck, face and shaved head precluded him from working a straight gig, so he returned to doing what he knew best.

When they were introduced, Zac's first words to him were, "I'm sorry about Bambi" - a daring gambit received with a smile and - about the only time Zac ever saw Thumper exhibit one. When Zac upped the ante from two gram baggies to half ounces, the dealer was most grateful because it meant he could offload a large chunk of his product quickly. Most of his runners were ne'er-do-wells he recruited from bars in the city's red-light district. Unfortunately, many of these halfwits were struggling to stay drug free themselves, so tearing around town with bum bags full of cash and dope inevitably led to the obvious, resulting in a painful comprehension of their boss' moniker. For all his business acumen and prowess at avoiding detection, Thumper had the people management skills of a goat.

The drops became routine. Zac would call him and ask if he wanted to catch up for a beer. If Thumper replied "maybe one night this week" it meant he'd be at Zac's within the hour. If he said "I'd prefer a coffee" that was code for call back tomorrow morning. They never opted for coffee.

Two and a half ounces into his escalating habit, Zac's already precarious mental health began to really unravel. He'd spent years investing everything in his persona as Zac the Journalist and now he was unemployed. He would not accept Olaf was dead; on the rare occasions he ventured out onto the streets he'd scan faces and crowds vainly hoping his friend would reappear. And the more he knew he wouldn't be seeing him again, the more he contemplated suicide. Late night visits to the toilet were accompanied by irrational thoughts of what Olaf might be doing now, only to roll into bleak notions of joining him before sobbing back to sleep.

He awoke naked on the couch one Monday morning shivering uncontrollably. At first he wondered why he was going into such a heavy withdrawal, then saw he had left the balcony door open, coinciding with winter sending a sneak preview during the night. Zac hadn't been to get dosed in three days and, given the state he was in that morning, a fourth wouldn't matter. He checked his bank balance. There was still well over $20,000 in it, so he figured he was doing okay.

Zac braved the chill of the balcony and surveyed the city. He knew something had to change, but what? I could just jump, he thought, but the cars he'd inevitably land on five floors below told him he'd probably just end up a mess of compound fractures and in traction for months. He went back inside, turned his computer on and created a document: 'The Pros and Cons of Being Me.' For the next hour he sat there wearily typing the odd word or phrase. It was turning into a shopping list of self pity and not really getting him anywhere. He opened his music

streaming service, chose a list called *faithlovesfate* and cranked it so loud
that Trixie Whitley's voice filled not only the apartment but most of the
neighbourhood. Zac agreed with her sentiment about wreaking havoc
with a blunt knife and took his first shower in days.

Somehow the song was on repeat, so by the time he reached for a
towel he'd lost count of how many times it had played. His skin was
a deep crimson, his fingers all wrinkled. The scalding water was like
a salve for his soul, the staccato drum rhythm a perfect backbeat. Yet
when he turned the tap off his malaise returned.

He donned a pair of boxer shorts, two T-shirts and prepared a shot.
There wasn't even any ceremony left in his drug use now. Simple rituals
like changing the cotton or flicking the syringe to rid it of air bubbles
were disbanded. It had become as rote as taking a piss. Even the amount
he doled out was unchecked. Where he once used a gold coke spoon
for a level measure he was now cavalierly scooping some out with the
switch blade and dumping it into the charcoal-tinged soup spoon. And
if any missed, then so what?

Overdose wasn't a concern anymore because, like the etymology
of the drug's name, Zac felt indestructible. Each passing hour was a
taunting reminder that the end was approaching; everything had
become a bleak testament to futility. His futility.

He contemplated his stint in DC, and what a spectacular crash-and-
burn to his once stellar career that turned out. He thought of the last
time he saw Tracey. Zac knew he was a good person, but his bullshit
veneer of street bravado was overtaking him. Maybe I should call her
and apologise? Nah, fuck her.

His parents. Well, that was just a never-ending tale of juvenile angst
where they should probably have never bred and anyway, he should
have severed that umbilical cord years ago.

And, of course, there was Olaf. No matter how stoned he was, Zac
would always feel a tinge of heartache at the mere memory. He stared
at the two of them on his phone screen. Is it pathetic that I pine for
someone I hardly got to know, but felt like we'd known each other
forever?

For the first time since Olaf's death, Zac didn't tear up. He tried, but couldn't. He dwelled on their conversations, the dinners and strolls through the city. He admonished himself for not being there for him, but really, Zac wasn't even there for himself anymore. *If only I hadn't taken that DC posting.*

He dipped the knife into the dope and snorted a lump.

"Best restock," he muttered, before cutting an X into his bare thigh with nary a flinch.

Night fell, and through his narcotic fog Zac decided it might be an idea to give Trixie Whitley a rest. After all, the song must have played a hundred times during the day. He hit stop, and immediately a neighbour's bellowing voice echoed from outside. "About fucking time." Zac jerked his middle finger toward the window and rang Thumper.

THE DEALER plonked himself down in the armchair and parked his feet on the coffee table. He produced a ziplock bag of white powder from his leather motorcycle jacket, waved it by its top and lobbed it to Zac.

"It's a bit under. Let's make it two and a half large."

Zac peeled away five notes and placed the remaining roll of cash on the table.

"You okay, Zacco? You look a bit buggy tonight."

Buggy didn't begin to describe how he felt. Zac's will to live had slowly been seeping away for weeks, but today it was akin to rushing down a storm drain. The worst part? He didn't give a fuck. About anything. He'd rehearsed what he wanted to say to Thumper, and had even come up with a plausible excuse to justify it.

"I want to buy a gun."

"What sort?"

"What sort? Er, a handgun I guess."

Thumper looked at him intently. *Here it comes,* Zac thought. *The inquisition.*

"Twelve hundred, up front."

"Thanks. That was easy."

Zac went to his desk and started counting out more cash.

"Not quite as easy as buying gear, champion. Give me a pen and paper, will you?"

Thumper made a call. All he said was "time", waited a second then hung up.

"Pay very close attention, and don't screw it up because this crew don't muck around."

He wrote a phone number on the paper and handed it over.

"There is a cafe on the corner of Rosemont and Waterview. You will go there in the morning and at exactly 10am you will call that number. When it answers, you will ask, "Is Helen there?" They in turn will reply, "Wrong number Romeo" and hang up. You will then wait in the end booth next to the restroom."

"How long?"

"As long as it takes, sunshine. All I know is this money is now theirs. I owe them. If you're running late, fail to show, get cold feet, whatever, there won't be any refunds. Oh, and if you get caught with the gun don't even think of involving me. You found it on a bus."

BY 1AM, Zac was exhausted. He'd read all about gun safety latches, rehearsed the three-word telephone call and written a lengthy suicide letter to his parents - which really was just a paean of love to Olaf. He read through it numerous times, proud of his prose and ability to convey his long-departed emotions.

Then deleted it.

He took himself to bed to consider his decision. It had been quite a few hours since he injected heroin, so his faculties were clearer. Yes, you've made a critical life-ending decision, and that's okay. Zac was feeling a true sense of relief. He thought of the impact it might have on others, but deep down that meant nothing to him. In his morass and self pity there were no others. He needed to disdain those close to him to keep believing his own lie that nobody cared for him. And besides, within 12 hours I'll be free. Like Olaf.

Unconsciously Zac scratched at his upper arm, oblivious to it bleeding. As he thought of a future of quiet and solitude, there was no grief or sadness; he was resolute. Then the strangest of thoughts hit him. You can't be found dead in this pig sty.

He went to his computer and scrolled through the dozens of playlists he'd accumulated. He paused at a collection of high energy techno - not exactly his preference, but it had become his default soundtrack for domestic duties. Given the hour and the reception he received earlier for having left Trixie blaring all day, he scanned the lists looking for something different. He paused at one called *Frank Zacca*. This was a list of Zappa tunes Olaf had made specifically for Zac, after he'd told him he found Zappa to be puerile and undergraduate. Olaf begged to differ and collated the list to prove some point. Zac had never bothered listening to it, so now seemed as good a time as any. But please don't let there be any songs about dogs pissing on the tundra.

A slow, plodding blues began, carried along by the cheers of an eager audience. After the first 12 bars a lead guitar came in. The seventh or so note was sustained feedback, floating in and out of itself for about 10 seconds. The undulating sound mesmerized Zac, invoking a strong sense of loss. That modulating tone felt like the missing connection between him and Olaf; it was pure emotion and longing. No lyrics, just a meandering guitar solo which was a lot like his departed friend - wild; beautiful; unpredictable. And ending way too soon. He replayed it a few times, finding stirring nuances within each listening. Maybe I didn't know you as well as I thought, O.

Zac's first task was to gather all the detritus scattered throughout the apartment. Where does all this shit come from? I mean, four baseball caps? I hate the damn things. And how does a can of sardines get wedged in behind a loud speaker cover? After five full garbage bags and two trips to the basement, the apartment began to take on a modicum of order.

He put all his strewn clothing into another bag and took it down to the laundry. He loaded it into a machine and hit wash, without any intention of retrieving it.

Throughout those still hours he diligently cleaned the bathroom and kitchen, scrubbing and disinfecting tiles, toilet, shower panels and all hard surfaces. Weeks of accumulated dishes and cutlery were washed and dried, then he attended to the never-used oven. Cupboards were unpacked, wiped down and restacked, as was the fridge. He even pulled it out from its alcove and washed the floor beneath it. Despite the arctic temperature, he went out and cleaned the windows and balcony. Zac felt like he was back in rehab, only this time his labours would not be recorded anywhere as living skills.

After he vacuumed the floors and the sofa - which yielded him $8.35 in loose change - he set about getting the bookshelves in order. He took all the books out, dusted them then put them back, grouped in the colours of their spines, giving his library a rainbow-like effect. Cute as it was, it screamed OCD nutjob. By now it was 4am. He hastily rearranged the books and decided to call it a night.

Zac admired his overall handiwork. He was feeling beat, but the apartment was spotless, as though it had been prepared for sale. "Liveable again," he announced, conscious of the irony. He was covered in a sheen of sweat, partly due to his efforts but mainly because he'd started to 'hang out'. It had been eight hours since he used. He went into the kitchen and had a small bump of smack to help ward off withdrawal and allow him to kip for an hour or two. Back at the computer, he turned Mr Zappa off, created a new document and raced his fingers across the keyboard. *Today is the last day of the rest of your life.*

ZAC SAT at a bus stop a hundred metres from the cafe. He had a clear view of anyone coming and going, so decided to play a guessing game of who entering the establishment might be carrying his nemesis. He only saw two people go in, and they were there for take-away coffees. It was 9.40am and he doubted some paranoiac gangster was going to be wasting more than five seconds waiting around for a degenerate junkie.

Is Helen there?

He went through his day. Collect gun, get cab home, head to the bathroom, end all pain.

Although he'd only had a few hours sleep, Zac felt remarkably alert. When he woke he made an extra strong coffee, stood on the balcony and conducted an internal discourse around whether he would follow through with his plan to kill himself. *Why not continue using heroin for another two days then overdose yourself? For the simple reason I have such a large tolerance now I'll probably just end up collapsing onto a limb and forever losing the use of it or, worse, ending up a vegetable with wires and tubes prolonging my life.*

He recalled an article he'd read about the few people who survived jumping off the Golden Gate Bridge. On the way down, a couple of them were suddenly able to attribute their despondency solely to money troubles, but this wasn't Zac's problem. His was the whole enchilada. He was well and truly over his life, and nothing was going to thwart today's destiny.

Is Helen there?

It was 9.55am. He headed toward the cafe. He was still early as he walked past, looking in and noticing there were no customers. Slowly, he made his way back. *I know. I'll sit on that low brick wall and call from there.*

The morning was unseasonably warm, and Zac removed his coat. It was an indulgent purchase made on impulse in Washington; a Ralph Lauren sport blazer with a delicate houndstooth pattern. He admired its purple label and carefully laid it out along the bricks. *Your new owner better appreciate exquisite tailoring.*

He returned to the phone. The seven changed to an eight and the numbers glowed across his and Olaf's foreheads.

"I don't blame you my friend. But let me just say, I'll never be able to thank you enough."

He stayed fixed on the screen saver, stroking Olaf's face. Was that a tinge of remorse? His chest tightened. What was that rehab thing they asked every morning? Quick. Two emotions you're experiencing right now.

Elation.

And terror.

A battered, rusting sedan with different coloured panels and doors rolled past, squeaking and spewing a pungent, thick plume of exhaust. Zac tracked it, knowing full well it wasn't the gun dealer. Metaphor. Me, bound for the wrecking yard.

His mouth was bone dry; his teeth felt like they were shivering, and he wondered if he was actually getting any oxygen. A wall of fear strapped him into an invisible electric chair, his anxiety compounded by a massive semi-trailer thundering past, dangerously close to the kerb. It was moving at such a rate he couldn't recognise the logo emblazoned down its side. He wanted to be six again, nestled in mother's arms.

Is Helen there?

He shuddered, regained some focus then tapped the phone icon, scrolling into the directory. In the top left corner the numerals changed to 10.00.

Zac Watts paused, feeling the thumping of his heart resound in his temples. For a brief second he forgot how to breathe, then involuntarily gasped. He felt both catatonic and exhausted. He touched the blue call button, watching it vibrate in his trembling hand.

"Guten tag, In The Light rehab."

CPSIA information can be obtained
at www.ICGtesting.com
Printed in the USA
LVHW010832310322
714804LV00004B/831

9 781685 832629